From the diary of Hester Jekyll:

The inspector's eyes darted up and down my figure suspiciously. "I hunt a murderer, Miss Jekyll," he told me. "I am after Hyde."

"But Hyde is dead." I was bewildered. "I told you that he and Jekyll were one and the same—"

"You told us a wild story—something out of a fairy tale. You may not have had a hand in the beginning of this affair but you're taking part in it now. I want Jekyll and I want Hyde—both of them!"

"But they are *dead*," I cried.

"Are they now? Well, I can give you proof that Hyde still walks this earth. We opened his coffin today, you see. And, miss—*it was empty!*"

Tor books by Robert Bloch

American Gothic
Fear and Trembling
Firebug
The Kidnapper
The Jekyll Legacy (with Andre Norton)
Lori
The Night of the Ripper
Night-World
Psycho
Psycho II
Psycho House

Tor books by Andre Norton

The Crystal Gryphon
Dare to Go A-Hunting
Elvenbane (with Mercedes Lackey)
Flight ih Yiktor
Forerunner
Forerunner: The Second Venture
Grand Master's Choice (Editor)
Gryphon's Eyrie (with A. C. Crispin)
Here Abide Monsters
House of Shadows (with Phyllis Miller)
Imperial Lady (with Susan Shwartz)
The Jekyll Legacy (with Robert Bloch)
Moon Called
Moon Mirror
The Prince Commands
Ralestone Luck
*Sneeze on Sunday**
*Songsmith**
Stand and Deliver
Storms of Victory (with P. M. Griffin)
Wheel of Stars
Wizards' Worlds

*forthcoming

ROBERT BLOCH
ANDRE NORTON

THE JEKYLL LEGACY

TOR
HORROR

A TOM DOHERTY ASSOCIATES BOOK
NEW YORK

This is a work of fiction. All the characters and events portrayed in this book are fictitious, and any resemblance to real people or events is purely coincidental.

THE JEKYLL LEGACY

A Tor Book
Published by Tom Doherty Associates, Inc.
49 West 24th Street
New York, N.Y. 10010

Cover photo by Doug Fornuff

ISBN: 0-812-51583-8

Library of Congress Catalog Card Number: 90-39228

First edition: August 1990
First mass market printing: December 1991

Printed in the United States of America

0 9 8 7 6 5 4 3 2 1

*For
Ingrid
with gratitude
and admiration*

chapter

1

Hester shifted one of the grayish net curtains that veiled the single window of the room and which, from the start of its service, had been so relentlessly starched that its edge might slash an unwary finger. There was the smell of boiling cabbage in the air, battling the choking fog outside. She pulled her shawl closer about her shoulders. There was certainly no chance of lighting a fire in that cramped iron basket. Beyond the window the yellowish billows closed in more closely, rising to blot out the street and the resolutely respectable, if narrow, houses on either side.

She bit her lower lip as she let the lace weapon of the curtain clank back into place and turned a little to survey this prison for "respectable" females, which Mrs. Carruthers kept mercilessly so that it might in turn keep her—at least in toast and kippers—two new scents having now been added to the general collection controlled by the damp-exuding walls.

Skirting two unsteady chairs and a small bow-legged table, pulling her skirts as tightly against her as she could lest one of the skimpy ruffles upset all the furnishing just as a domino might bring down a whole line of its fellows, Hester seated herself upon the board-hard bed and took up her lap writing desk. Bringing out that book she had bought so hopefully two months ago, she now ruffled through its pages. Her head was turned once more to the curtained window, but what she saw in imagination were the gallant flames of maples against the less flamboyant oaks. September in Canada was a riot of color. Here in London it was the dregs of a not-too-well-washed pot.

She settled the desk carefully lest the small ink bottle drip its contents on the coverlet of the bed. Hester began to write, slowly at first, with rolling loops and the flourish of a document meant for official eyes. Then, as her fingers grew less stiff from the chill, she covered pages with greater speed. The scratch of her pen now did not produce fine penmanship but rather was ridden by the desire to keep some record of her own recent actions, reactions, hopes, and more common fear.

"Thus I left Eakand Abbey yesterday." Her pen sputtered. She needed a new one, but even so small an expense must be carefully considered now. "Her Ladyship was pleased . . ." Hester's lips tightened into a thin line and the wrinkle between her straight brows deepened—it was fast becoming a permanent feature there. She blotted one of the splatters of ink and continued. ". . . to offer me a recommendation.

"When I declined, I was treated to a major outburst of that pettish anger that Lady Ames uses to control her house and family. I no longer wondered why Major Ames had entrusted me with the care of his daughter's overseas traveling. Now I am sorry to have to leave Hazel with such a guardian. If there was only some way I could see her in better hands—but I am powerless. So I came away just before dusk with skimped pay for two months of work and an exceedingly scanty wardrobe. Thus I am to meet a London that is far different from that I have built for myself in dreams."

Unconsciously she was listening to her father's querulous voice to snap her into life, ready to take dictation.

Hester gave a slight shake of shoulder and straightened. She would never hear that voice again. This was London, not a thousand miles away and months in the past. Her hand smoothed the already too-well-worn black skirt considered suitable for a governess in mourning. Though the purchase of that, and two other very modest and most simply fitted dresses, had made a hole in her funds.

"Does my present situation really please you, Father?" Even in her own ears her voice sounded harsh and rasping. She was—was beginning to sound like him. Hester brushed her hand across her lips and refused to be silenced.

"You so often commented that I was practically useless to you—it would seem that opinion of me is nearly universal now."

Hester dropped the pen into its groove on her desk and began leafing back through the ledger. An envelope insecurely kept there fluttered to the bed. She ran her finger along its open edge to pull out its contents though she already knew them well. One was certainly her first step toward her own freedom. She had heard and wondered at the sums of money paid by the *New York Ledger* and its like— and that women writers did more than a little of that earning. She herself ventured once to send them a much copied and toiled over manuscript—though it had not sold. But she had sold elsewhere—to *The British Lady*, which was housed right here in this fog-ridden city. This note was from one of the editors approving two short articles she had dared to send. Though, of course, she did not use her own name—no lady would.

Here she was addressed as Dorothea Meadows. However, the words beneath that somewhat stiff beginning brought her

warmth even in this cold room. ". . . like your article on the
wonders of the Great Falls and your descriptions of the
primeval forests of our sister country overseas. If you should
come to London, I would like to meet with you and discuss
some matters that might be to our mutual advantage."

She folded the much-creased letter briskly—*that* must be
acted upon—and put it back in the envelope. But the other
scrap that had fallen free was different; she really did not
know why she had kept it all these months.

Father had managed to turn *all* funds toward his own comfort, buying an annuity that made no provision for her. But
he had been unable to part with the only things he had ever
enjoyed—his books. Those she had taken a kind of savage
delight in selling, doubtless for much less than they were
worth but enough then to give her a tiny refuge against becoming an utterly penniless woman. What she held now in
her hand had fallen from one of the leather-bound volumes
of poetry printed in its native Greek. It was for that reason a
good hiding place, because Hester did not know the language; she had been battered through Latin in order to better serve her father's work, but she had not been pushed to
learn Greek. The book had remained on his bedside table
during those hours he had lain like one already dead. It had
not been added to those tied up in unwieldy bundles waiting
for the bookseller to clear them away. She had even brought
it with her—why she did not know—one of the few things
to remind her of that other narrow house and the musty-
smelling rooms where fresh air never entered.

The book had borne, under its cover, a shield bearing the
arms of what she now knew was an Oxford college, hinting
at one of those parts of her father's past that he never discussed. Below the shield, in a flourish of lines and loops, a
name was penned, the ink so faded now that it had near
disappeared forever.

"L. Jekyll," a name she had never heard her father refer
to.

The clipping was not a part of the past. Just a newspaper notice she was sure her father had cut out, so meticulous was the edging.

WANTED—

Information leading to the discovery of one Leonard Jekyll, Esquire, who left England in the year 1863. If he or his descendants (if any exist) wish to hear something greatly to their advantage, let such write to Robert Guest, care of Turk's Court, The Temple, London.

"Jekyll." She spoke the name aloud now. It was a strange one and for some reason she took a dislike to the sound of it. Now she laid the clipping aside and drew from the bottom of her traveling desk, turning out paper and envelopes to secure it, the very book that had given it shelter in the past. The binding was of maroon leather, quite unlike any she had seen before. She wondered if her father or one of his acquaintances of the far past had not abstracted it willfully from its native shelf. Page by page she examined it. There were a few comments on some of the margins written in a spider-foot lettering, which she recognized as her father's before the bouts of crippling rheumatism had crooked his fingers so he was unable to write at all.

On impulse she took up the scrap of paper, smoothed it out as well as she could and laid it over the Oxford seal, closing the cover firmly. She very much doubted that the earnestly seeking Mr. Guest would consider this the sort of evidence that would be worth her paying out the price of a cab on such a day to take it to Turk's Court.

The fog seemed to have crept into the very room, gathering in the corners to build up behind the chairs and under the table and bed. She had thought that some of the rooms at Walford Castle would be good places to conceal a ghost, but this shabby, long-used chamber, in spite of its breath of too-old cabbage and kippers, might readily summon the unknown. Nonsense! She was an intelligent woman, she had run a house since she was twelve, at the death of her last downtrodden governess. Ghosts existed only on paper, and here—in this shabby room—none worthy of frightening anyone could possibly appear.

Hester turned her head to study her reflection in the dull and wavery surface of the small mirror. Her skin was olive, to be sure, but it was clear and when she was troubled or angry had a faint glow about the cheekbones. There had been rumors raised in the Sisters' School, during the two terms she had attended, that she had Indian blood. But the rumors had died when the very correct manners her father had drilled into her (and railed at Poor Mouse Fremont to do the same) met each and every covert taunt or snicker or suggestion with aloof dignity.

Her hair was not black but a dark brown, very thick and long, which sometimes in the full sunlight showed a reddish tinge. For the rest she was in want. She had a nose, neither aristocratically bold nor turned up or down—just a nose. Even all the rest was undistinguished—her mouth was over-wide, with faint lines about it that appeared to be permanently set by now. Her broad forehead was revealed to its greatest extent by braiding her hair and pinning the braids as close to the skull as firmly as she could for her governess role. There were no stylish fringes or loose locks flying. Her dark eyes, of course, did not possess any mysterious depths.

Hester chuckled, recalling the various eloquent descriptions of heroines in the books of fiction she had read during stolen moments. Fluff and trifling those novels were, but they had the art of transporting their readers into a kind of dazed shadow-life. And she did not doubt that their writers got better returns for their pains of procreation than she had been paid for the sale of travel articles that had won her grudging awards in the past. No, if one was to live by one's pen, one had to be a Mrs. Southworth and possess a powerful imagination.

She did not need to look into her purse to count her

riches—it was so flat that one worn sealskin side rubbed the other in a most familiar fashion and had done so for a long time. Hester had been trained solely to be a handmaiden to one man's selfishness and now, at twenty-three, she needed work and had no suitable skills to offer. She had not been judged a proper governess, and she had no introductions to take her past the outer door of any girls' school. Could she be a servant? She feared not. Kitty's tales of life downstairs were most discouraging, and besides, she had no written references to back her.

She began to write on a sheet of foolscap, using her best choice of word and phrase to compose a letter to the editor of *The British Lady*. When she had finished she put it aside for a second and later reading.

She tapped her penholder against her teeth and again reread the news clipping. She had never heard what had brought her father from England to the northern province of the west. All the days she had known him he had never referred to his past. Why, she had never even known his age! His narrow face, its graying skin so seldom touched by sunlight, had not seemed to add a single year as time passed.

Once more she turned to the front of her ledger and read: "Father is silent always concerning the past. He never consorts with anyone directly from England. When the new vicar came to call last year he was so chill and distant of manner that the poor man must have been speedily frozen. We have never had even a tea party."

She sniffed and hunted hurriedly for a handkerchief. Surely she was *not* going to have a cold now! That would give Mrs. Carruthers further chance to set her out on the street—or would it?

Hester, her head tilted a little to one side in thought, considered the advantages of taking to her bed and demanding comfort and nursing. Someone small and appealing—such as Hazel would probably be in another five years or so—could carry that off readily, but a big gawk of a woman such as herself—no.

Instead she gave a last sniff and returned to her reading. Even the one small essay into the wide world of these past two months had impressed deeply upon her the singularity of her own house—one could not really, she decided bleakly, have called it a home.

Of her mother she had the vaguest of memories—there had been a quick-moving lady with a wide spill of curls that persisted in seeking freedom from a net to fall to her shoulders or dangle about her cheeks. Then that presence had vanished without explanation from her narrow circle of life and all she could remember. Shades had been pulled down to turn rooms into dull and frightening caves; her father wore a dark band on his coat sleeve for a season. It was then they had moved out of Montreal to a small town near the American border. The servants she had always known left, and the wrinkled-faced woman who had been hired as a governess stayed on as housekeeper. But this arrangement had not worked and Hester, in her early teens, had taken charge of the household.

During those years she and her father had been almost totally isolated from others of their own kind. A day pupil at the Sisters' for a time, she had been strictly forbidden to take part in any unnecessary activity. Nor did she have any friends. She had turned early to her books and her own scribbling for relaxation from her father's lessons, which were hard and sharp, meant to make of her a reliable aide for his own labors. Occasionally letters arrived that she was forbidden to open, and these were subsequently burned, still unopened, in the fireplace.

Now the memory of those unread screeds somehow became joined in her mind with the cutting from the Montreal paper. The mystery surrounding that clipping was in truth her only legacy from her father. Though they had subsisted comfortably while he lived, his death meant utter poverty for his daughter.

She still thought that she had been very lucky to be introduced to Major Ames when her plight was fully realized. To escort Hazel Ames overseas, and there act as her governess for at least six months, seemed the perfect answer to her problems. For, with that natural resilience common to youth, she was sure that something fitting her talents would turn up in the future. The most common answer was, of course, marriage.

Hester frowned in a way that erased any small claim to attractiveness she might possess. The few men she had met under her father's roof had all been elderly and solemn, most of them ignoring her as if she were the statue of Truth that adorned the end of the stair rail. In addition, her father's constant disregard for any thought or desire of her own, his demand for her constant attention, had made her strongly disinclined to meet others. To allow some man complete dominance over her again was what she shrank from the most.

She reached again for the ledger and flipped over page after page, realizing that this last thought bore the ring of truth—she had looked upon her father's death as a release from a burden that was fast becoming intolerable. Hardhearted, unnatural daughter? She had in truth played a role, without realizing it, ever since she had gone through the house marking down the lists to be handed to the auctioneer. She had busied herself finding positions for the two elderly maids upon whose shoulders most of the keeping of the house had depended. It was Hester who had been left with no future but what she could carve out for herself.

She smoothed out the letter she had written earlier because she knew now she dared not overlook the slightest aid to a fruitful future. She read word by word—in the most restrained and formal way. Surely she could concoct a suitable letter for Mr. Guest.

Having taken the measure of Mrs. Carruthers, Hester had no desire to leave her two missives to await a tardy visit to the pillar-box on the part of the pinched-face maid. Fog or no fog, she could at least mail her own letters. Once more she leafed through the book—such a dull account and so drearily presented!

It was the latter pages that held her now. Though she had known very little about the care of children when she met Hazel, she had been struck by the child's shyness and began to wonder if they had not a bond in their dislike for people and situations that made them feel unhappy and miserable. Her own answer—books—came immediately to mind and she put firmly into the bottom of Hazel's "on-board" satchel some others beside the school texts. She produced the few that she had kept because, first her mother's name was within, and, secondly, she had come to feast herself upon their livelier prose years ago. Hester made Hazel aware of the works of Miss Austen and *Jane Eyre*, though she was certain that Lady Ames would not have found the misfortunes of poor Jane, the governess, suitable for Hazel's reading at all.

Her eyes found another entry in her record. "Hazel has asked me a question concerning the 'horrid' mysteries as mentioned in *Northanger Abbey*. I have never read one (what would Father have done with Mrs. Radcliffe's volumes— thrown them straightaway into the fire?), but I told Hazel that they were a kind of ghost story intended to set shivering the adult reader who professed that only in their extreme youth long ago had they known such childish tastes. I think she believed me.

"Still, it struck me odd that our entrance into this country was not unlike the general atmosphere of the 'horrids.' We came ashore on a damp, dark day of which there are so many here. A hard-faced woman clad in creased black, with a footman, met us. Hazel took one look at the woman and, straightaway, her manners became once again those of the timid and fearful child. I could not guess then to what extent this woman's influence reached. She had a voice as harsh as her face as she introduced herself as Mrs. Riggs, Lady Ames's personal maid.

"So we were ushered through the town to the house of the Ames family and informed, in one of Mrs. Riggs's clipped speeches, that the lady was suffering from an attack of nerves and would see us at teatime but not before.

"Hazel kept tight hold of a fold of my skirt drapery as we went into a suite clearly furnished for a lady of at least twice her years. She asked, in the very low, trembling voice she had lost during the time spent in my company, where I was to stay.

"Riggs sniffed and looked down a thin sliver of nose that bore a hairy nob on one side, answering that Lady Ames would decide that upon seeing me. Nor was she quite out of the room before Hazel, clinging still to me, began to cry. Between sobs she said she did not like this place and would I not please take her home again.

"'I—I know that Mama is gone,' she whimpered. 'But Papa would not make me stay where I was afraid. You know he would not, dear Hester!'

"'You are tired, cold, and hungry,' I said, trying to reassure her. Perhaps I could have made my own voice more emphatic had I not inwardly been daunted by our reception, too. Stooping, I put my arms about her.

"'Come. Come now,' snapped Riggs a half hour later when I had gotten Hazel calm and had suggested to her this was something of an adventure if she would only look upon it as such. Riggs stretched her long neck like a crow I had once seen harassing a cardinal, peering at us both as if we were succulent morsels tamely awaiting attack. "Best you get young miss here ready for tea. Her Ladyship always wants what she wants to be delivered as soon as she orders.'

"I saw an expression of obstinacy begin to stiffen Hazel's small face and I hastened to shut the door through which Riggs had disappeared. Then I turned to my charge with the best advice I could at the moment summon.

"'Come, Hazel, you must not let your grandmother think that you have in the least taken a dislike to your situation here. Remember you are the daughter of a brave soldier.

Stand up straight, and report as would one of the scouts of your father—answer fully any questions that your grandmother may ask.'

"She stood docilely enough while I combed her long, strikingly pale, silver curls, and allowed me to bring her a pair of soft slippers to change for her damp boots. The dismal color of her mourning dress threw her hair and the suncreamed hue of her skin into almost startling relief. Looking at her with approval and, yes, love, I was sure she would find a place in Lady Ames's life—and, God willing, her heart.

"Our introduction to Lady Ames was a complete failure. Me she ignored after a nod of the head that dispatched me to a stiff-backed chair at the far end of her very feminine room, where stout, hard cushions, worked in silk flowers of quite violent colors, could make even a most comfortable chair a seat of growing torment.

"She pounced upon poor Hazel with a series of questions—several of which suggested to me that she strove to discover some dispute or dislike between the child's parents! Her son had apprently married a countrywoman of mine and Lady Ames far from liked that. There was plainly an abundance of spite in her voice and no grandmother's kindness at all.

"Hazel was again on the verge of crying. I could stand it no longer and, quite forgetting my own lowly place in the eyes of this household, I came forward hastily and waited for a chance to speak.

"'My lady, Hazel is very tired and her breakfast was only milk and bread. Could you not wait until she is rested to question her about family affairs?'

"Lady Ames leaned forward. Her naturally high-colored countenance took on a quite alarming shade of red and her eyes appeared to protrude from their cushions of flesh in order to favor me with a most daunting inspection.

"'Very well.' She drawled her words, but there was a bite in her tone, which was now an octave higher than the one that had greeted us. 'Riggs!' She did not reach for the small silver bell buried in the litter of things on the table. But Martha Riggs appeared almost instantly in the doorway, as if she were indeed some eerie creature able to project her person from one room to another through the very walls.

"'You, young person,' Lady Ames continued, 'I wish to speak with you now. Hazel, you are dismissed—for the present.' Then she turned as forceful a look of judgment upon Hazel, but one of a slightly different kind.

"The little girl had already raised one real protest as Riggs propelled her toward the door. I trusted that my own gaze was as threatening to the maid as the one her mistress had directed toward me.

"'Hazel, my dear.' I hastened to soothe the rising fears of my late charge. 'I shall come to you soon.'

"'Hazel—what an odd name! What is your second name?' Lady Ames's voice had fallen into its usual screech.

"Hazel jerked free of Riggs's hold on her shoulder. She made a graceful little curtsy she must have learned in her mother's drawing room and answered with the singsong voice of one uttering a well-drilled ritual.

"'I am Hazel Renée Ames.'

"'Renée?' For the second time a wrinkle of distaste added to Lady Ames's collection of skin folds. 'That name is altogether unsuitable, child. Thus we must call you Hazel after all. Very well, go with Riggs now and she will serve you tea.'

"I forced a nod and a smile, so Hazel went off reluctantly with the stone-faced Riggs. Lady Ames was already addressing questions to me."

"'You call yourself Hester Lane—'

"'I do not "call myself" anything, Your Ladyship. Hester Lane is the name I have carried from my birth.'

"Her pudgy hands, aglitter with rings, pawed through the general mess on the table as she leaned forward among her nest of pillows, her lace-fronted morning gown actually

threatening to split in some important places. Now she came
up with a letter, the bold handwriting on the envelope easy
enough to see. It had come from Major Ames.

"'My son says'—she smoothed out the crinkled paper—
'that your father was a scholar and a distinguished historian
writing a book about those cruel Indians. Also, you have
been his amanuensis and acquitted yourself well in that situation.'

"She paused to sweep me from head to foot with a bold
stare that I was sure she would never use with one she considered her social equal. 'He also has written that you are a
lady of family.'

"'I was my father's researcher and assistant for six years—
from the time I completed my formal education.' I kept my
voice carefully neutral.

"Now she dropped the letter into her lap. 'Latin—pauhg!
Philosophy, history—all too heady and severe for any weak
female mind to comprehend. You do speak French?' she
asked sharply in that language but with an accent so twisted
that I could barely understand her.

"I replied in the same language that I could. Also, that I
could teach German if that would be required of me.

"Her pop eyes were slitted as she said then, not in a fum-
bly foreign tongue, but in English, 'Can you teach tabor
work, netting? Do you know perfectly the rules of society
and all concerning those families that are classed so? Can you
dance, play the piano, draw, teach watercolor?'

"To this list of talents I was forced to answer no, and she
gave a sigh that was one of relief as she settled back again
among her cushions. 'You are hardly an acceptable governess, Miss Lane.'

"If Lady Ames had expected some plea from me (in spite
of that touch of fear), she was disappointed.

"'You may stay the week,'" I had jotted in my ledger—
her words were not the kind that were easily forgotten.

"'The Brougher girls are to be sent to a school in

Switzerland. Luckily I foresaw something of this present situation and have approached Miss Cantry, their present governess. But, of course, I shall provide for you.'"

Hester scowled, and flipped the next three pages over together.

"The Miss Cantry of Lady Ames's choice did not appear within the week as looked for. Thus I was given respite for another week, during which I strove to prepare Hazel, as best I could, for her place in life. She was sent for several times, to accompany Lady Ames on her daily ride in the park, returning each time with either a scowl on her face or reddened eyes that were the result of an outburst of tears.

"She did not confide in me, and I did not ask any questions. Though once she inquired if it were true that 'ladies' were wrong in throwing a penny to the boy who swept the crossing outside.

"Knowing her grandmother would strongly disapprove, but not wishing to pass judgment upon her selfish snobbery, I thought it best to keep silent.

"'You cannot tell me!' Hazel crossed the room and gave a vigorous tug to the bell ribbon. Then she took her small net purse to the table and turned it upside down, allowing its contents, including several shilling pieces, to spin across the table's crimson velvet cover. Swiftly she separated them.

"The door opened for the young kitchen maid, Kitty, with my tea, unappetizing hunks of bread spread with dubious butter, and a pot already half chilled because of the long walk the bearer had had, up from the kitchen. But Kitty winked at me as she set down the tray and whisked off the cover. The chunks of bread were enriched by a delectable-looking pair of muffins. She grinned.

"'Them's prime, miss. Cook put aside a basket of them for her friend the constable. It's Old Riggs with her smarmy orders as gits you such rotten stuff! She's—'

"'Miller, what are you doing here?' Miss Riggs's voice came from the hall outside so often I had reason to believe

she listened whenever Hazel and I were together. But it was
Hazel who answered her now.

"'Kitty is going to run an errand for me, Riggs!' The beginning of hauteur touched her—a legacy from her grandmother. It made the woman stare at her somewhat bemused.
She had certainly never seen that aspect of my charge before.

"'One of the footmen,' said Riggs, who might have been
rocked for an instant but was now steady once more, 'would
be suitable for messages, Miss Hazel, and my lady would
want to know all about it.'

"Hazel snatched up the unwholesome-looking plate of
bread chunks and thrust it at Kitty. 'Give this to the little
boy—the one at the street corner. I think he must be very
hungry.'

"Kitty bobbed a curtsy. 'Yes, miss.'

"She fled the room while Riggs walked quickly to the
window. But the gathering darkness did not yet have the
street lamp to cut it.

"'Miss Hazel, 'tis my bonded duty to tell Her Ladyship of
this—' She drew such a deep breath that I was sure it
reached clear to the shoes hidden beneath her skirts.

"'Yes, Riggs.' Hazel nodded. 'The vicar spoke Sunday
about how treasure came from feeding the poor and hungry
people with bread and fishes. Only I did not have any fish.'

"Riggs was indeed shaken and only muttered something
inaudible as she went out the door. Hazel turned to me, and
there was a faint flush in her cheeks and her eyes were wide
and sparkling. 'Hester, you will do it for me, won't you?' She
shoved her shilling piece in my direction.

"I was already reaching for my waterproof cape and the
bonnet that was supposed to possess the same properties. It
was in this manner I met Freddy, a very dirty urchin in a
patched coat that Hazel had described to me. He was chew-
ing on one of the hunks of bread as if he feared it would be
snatched away from him, and a lump just above the length of

rope that held his coat together made me surmise that he was saving more than half the bounty. He looked at me with red-rimmed eyes that held the impression of sly wariness.

"'Whot yuh wants, missie?' He jerked his head to indicate the envelope into which I had inserted and sealed Hazel's charity. 'Message run? Fred's yur boy, he is.'

"He held out his hand, having crushed all the rest of the bread into his mouth, which gave him a very stuffed look. I released the envelope to the pull he gave as soon as he got his filthy fingers on it.

"'No message, Fred—just a gift from a little girl who wishes you well.'

"He clutched the envelope tightly and looked as if he had no belief that anything good might really happen to him. Then he turned and ran out into the fog, lost from sight in seconds.

"Again Miss Cantry did not appear and I was given respite for another seven days.

"My time was up yesterday—"

And now here she was, on her own.

Hester leaned back a little. Those fingers of fog that she had earlier imagined reaching for her from the corners of the room were growing longer and more menacing. It was one thing to be prepared to earn one's living and then always being assured in some fashion of the future, and another to possess four shillings and sixpence in an otherwise empty purse. What did those noble, familyless heroines do in books? Did they have jewels to pawn or something of that sort? Her rent was paid until a week from tomorrow and bread and tea could fill a stomach. What had Freddy done with all that wealth Hazel showered upon him? He'd never come back to that corner as a sweeper again.

Hester drew her shawl more tightly about her. Dragged along with its fringe across the bed were her two letters. This afternoon—yes, this very afternoon—she could send both of her answers out into the world.

But would the world reply?

chapter

2

It was a case of hate at first sight.

That, at least, was what Inspector Newcomen told himself as he perched uneasily on the edge of his chair, in Mr. Utterson's outer office.

First sight, but not first meeting. His previous dealings with Utterson had produced a somewhat disagreeable impression of the lean, unsmiling, elderly solicitor, but at the time he had seen him as an ally in a common cause.

Utterson was the friend as well as the legal counselor for Henry Jekyll, M.D., and Inspector Newcomen, the officer assigned to investigate certain events surrounding Dr. Jekyll's mysterious disappearance.

It was last March that Utterson had come forward with the story of how he and Dr. Jekyll's butler, Poole, found the body in Dr. Jekyll's cabinet—the office maintained at his home. As a matter of fact, Newcomen himself was involved from the very start. He examined the office, questioned the servants, and viewed the corpse discovered there. It was Utterson himself who corroborated statements from Jekyll's household staff and personal friends, attesting that the deceased was one Edward Hyde.

There was no doubt whatsoever that Hyde had met death by his own hands, through the ingestion of prussic acid, though the reasons for his apparent suicide were never clarified—at least not by the enigmatic Mr. Utterson, who said he had little personal contact with Dr. Jekyll's unfortunate friend. But last October, when Sir Danvers Carew was clubbed to death by a man identified as Edward Hyde, it was Utterson who conducted the inspector to Hyde's vacated lodgings, though he claimed no knowledge of the man himself. Nor did anyone else appear to know much about the dwarfed and almost apishly deformed man who had seemingly been an intimate of Dr. Jekyll's for several years.

It was then that Inspector Newcomen's reservations about the solicitor took form. Surely he must have known more about the relationship than he was willing to volunteer. After his suicide was officially established Hyde was interred in a pauper's grave. No ceremony was performed and no mourners were in attendance. It appeared that the late Edward Hyde had neither family nor friends. Except, of course, for Dr. Jekyll, who remained absent on that occasion.

Inspector Newcomen scowled and stirred impatiently in his chair. Confound Utterson for keeping him waiting like this! Months had passed since the death of Hyde and the disappearance of Jekyll, and during all that time Utterson had played a waiting game. When questioned about some of the strange apparatus and peculiar chemicals discovered in Jekyll's laboratory, Utterson protested he knew nothing of them. When confronted with the fact that Edward Hyde possessed his own key to Dr. Jekyll's private quarters and apparently came and went as he chose at all hours of the day or night, Utterson kept mum.

It was indeed a waiting game, and no mistake. But then through his years in the service of the law, Inspector Newcomen had come to despise all men of the law; barristers, solicitors, attorneys, magistrates, and judges; the whole kit and caboodle infesting Temple Bar, cluttering the courts as they pranced about in their absurd getups. Silly wigs and stupid gowns belonged at masked balls rather than in a court of law. As for the pomp and ceremony—from "Hear ye," to "All rise," to "If it please Your Honor"—Newcomen regarded it as sheer poppycock. All of it was game-playing, not to serve justice but to obstruct it.

That Utterson was obstructing justice he had no doubt; not after a passage of long months since Henry Jekyll's disappearance. And it was high time to put paid to the matter once and for all.

"Mr. Utterson will see you now."

The glorious tidings issued from the lips of the solicitor's chief clerk, one Robert Guest, who emerged from the inner sanctum to address the police officer.

Newcomen lost no time in acceding to the invitation. As he entered the private office Mr. Utterson elevated himself from behind his desk, greeting his visitor in a manner more curtly than courtly. If, indeed, "Inspector?" could be construed as a greeting. His tone carried with it the unspoken but unmistakable implication that Newcomen's very presence was a sore trial to his patience.

And trial it very well may be, the Inspector told himself. *Complete with judge, jury, and sentence, unless you come up with some proper testimony.*

"Please be seated." With a diffident gesture Utterson indicated the vacant chair placed near the corner of his desk. As Newcomen moved to occupy it the solicitor uttered a dry cough. "To what might I owe the pleasure of this visit?" he inquired.

"A matter of business," Newcomen replied. "There are questions that require immediate answers."

The solicitor seated himself behind his desk. "Please be assured that I shall do my best to provide them," he said. "Granted, of course, that such answers are known to me." Inspector Newcomen nodded. "Then I propose we come to the point," the lawyer said.

"What further news might you have of your client Dr. Jekyll?"

Utterson shrugged, his expression unchanging. "None whatsoever. I assure you, had I obtained the slightest word, you and your superiors at Scotland Yard would have immediately been informed."

Newcomen's nod brushed the reply aside. "What have you done to locate him?"

Again Utterson shrugged. "I should think that question should be best addressed to you. As an officer of the law the apprehension of missing persons falls under your jurisdiction rather than mine. You have powers and facilities not available to a private citizen such as myself. And if you cannot find him—"

"Hard words, Mr. Utterson. I grant we haven't located Dr. Jekyll as yet, but that we shall, given the proper information. Which leads me to another question."

"Yes?"

"Why did you sack Dr. Jekyll's household staff?"

"I should think the reason would be obvious," the solicitor said. "As Dr. Jekyll's counselor I see no point in maintaining unnecessary expense and have therefore closed the house pending his return."

"Why didn't you inform Scotland Yard of this decision?"

"Because I felt it to be none of their concern." Now there was the slightest hint of defiance in Utterson's voice. "Not to put too fine a point on it, it is the concern of Scotland Yard to find Dr. Jekyll and you have failed."

"Perhaps that could have been avoided if there'd been a chance to question those servants at greater length. I'm particularly interested in Jekyll's butler and the footman. If you'd supply me with their present addresses—"

"I'm afraid that is impossible," Utterson said. "At the time of their employment, all of Dr. Jekyll's household staff resided on the premises, and I did not regard it as a matter of concern as to where they might have removed themselves following their dismissal."

"I see." Newcomen nodded. "But I suggest to you that there's another explanation. If it was to someone's interest, the servants could have been paid off to disappear and avoid questions."

Utterson half rose from his chair, right hand curling to form a fist. "Are you accusing me of obstructing justice?"

"Only an observation, if you take my meaning, sir."

"Then be so good as to consider this." Utterson sank back into his seat but there was open anger in his voice now. "Both my friendship and my professional relationship with Dr. Jekyll extend to a period of over twenty years. No one is more desirous of ascertaining his present whereabouts and receiving assurance of his well-being."

"In that case, sir, you may be able to help us."

"In what way?"

"I'd be greatly obliged to see a copy of Dr. Jekyll's will."

Utterson stiffened. "But that's impossible!"

"Is it?" Newcomen spoke quietly, choosing his words with care. "I've made inquiries and have been told there are two ways to go about it. Either you permit me to glance over the document here or I get a warrant for that purpose, in which case the contents will become public knowledge."

"You leave me no choice."

Utterson rose and went to the door; drawing it open, he summoned Guest. After heeding instructions issued in a voice scarcely above the level of a whisper, the clerk departed, presently to return with the desired instrument.

Thereupon he withdrew, and Utterson, making no attempt to disguise his reluctance, extended the document to Inspector Newcomen.

"You hold in your hands," he said, "the last will and testament of Henry Jekyll, M.D., D.C.L., L.L.D., F.R.S., et cetera. Note that it is in holograph form; a comparison with other examples of Dr. Jekyll's handwriting will attest to its authenticity. Its brevity is self-apparent. As to its contents . . ."

He did not complete his sentence, for the inspector was already reading, brow furrowed in concentration. Utterson retreated behind his desk and resumed his place there, awaiting the moment when Newcomen concluded his perusal.

When the inspector glanced up again his eyes and voice conveyed open accusation. "He wrote this will without consulting you?" he said.

"Quite so," Utterson replied.

Newcomen glanced down, scanning as he spoke. "I gather that in case of his decease or disappearance or absence lasting more than three months, all of Dr. Jekyll's possessions were to pass to the hands of—what's the way he puts it?—his friend and benefactor Edward Hyde."

"That is correct."

"I notice from the date that this was drawn up over a year ago."

"That too is correct. Have you any reason to question the date of its execution?"

Newcomen shook his head. "When it was made out is a minor matter." He leaned forward, tapping the page as he spoke. "What I would like to know is when Dr. Jekyll crossed out the name of Edward Hyde as a beneficiary and substituted a new heir—John Gabriel Utterson."

The solicitor met his gaze without flinching but his voice, when he replied, lacked resolution. "I don't have that information," he said. "The change had been made before the will was placed in my possession." He gestured quickly. "Again, if you compare, there's no doubt that the change has been written in his own hand."

"Voluntarily?"

"As I told you, the substitution occurred prior to my receiving the document. You have my word on it."

"I'd take more comfort in Dr. Jekyll's word," the inspector said.

"It's true, I swear it!" Utterson exclaimed.

"Very well, sir." The police officer's tone softened; he could afford to be charitable in this instance since the answer to the next question he proposed would be of considerably greater importance. "But can you also swear that Dr. Jekyll is still alive?"

"I tell you I do not know—"

Ignoring the attempt to answer, Newcomen assailed the solicitor once again. "Have you reason to believe him dead or are you merely trying to convince the authorities so you can inherit his estate?"

Utterson shook his head. "Do you take me for a fool? If this was my intention, I would have found some excuse for not showing you the will. And now that you have seen it I refer you to the stipulation that I could take full possession of the property three months after Dr. Jekyll's disappearance, should his absence continue. As we both know, I have made no move to do so. Let me repeat, Henry Jekyll and I have been close friends for many years and I want no part of his money or possessions."

The waiting game. Inspector Newcomen nodded, more in response to his own thought than to Utterson's protestations. A cunning man of law—and wasn't this a description of the entire breed?—would do just that. He'd wait it out until all suspicions were quieted and the investigation itself was filed and forgotten. Then he could safely claim his lawful or unlawful inheritance, whichever the case might be.

"You doubt my assurance?" Utterson said. "Very well. I am prepared to offer proof."

"Of what nature, might I ask?"

"Some while ago I recalled a conversation with Poole, Dr. Jekyll's butler. In the course of our exchange he stated in passing that his master had once referred to his family connections, mentioning that he had distant relatives in Canada."

"Did he mention any names?"

"He did not. But indeed if such relatives exist, then it is my honest intention to see to it that they, rather than myself, become the inheritors of the estate. To that end I placed this advertisement in a number of Canadian newspapers." As he spoke, the lawyer opened the drawer of the desk before him and withdrew two items, which he placed on the desktop for Newcomen's inspection. One was a large sheet of foolscap on which was a list of a dozen Canadian newspapers, together with their addresses. The other was a clipping of the actual advertising notice reproduced in print.

"This is from the Toronto press, I believe," Utterson said. "I can furnish you with copies from other sources, together with correspondence dealing with their placement."

The inspector nodded but did not break his silence as he scanned the printed item. He noted how cleverly it was worded; nothing was said that could lead a reader to believe Dr. Jekyll dead, but the implication was there. A Canadian relative, however distant, might well reckon it worthwhile to respond. No doubt about it, Utterson was a clever man—clever even to the point of withholding his own involvement in the matter and soliciting that replies be dispatched to Robert Guest, his clerk.

As he finished reading, Newcomen glanced up. "Any answers?" he asked.

"Not as yet," Utterson said. "But I still have hope, and should I be in receipt of any reply, I assure you—"

"Of course." The inspector gestured quickly. There was no further need to continue badgering Mr. Utterson, at least not at this moment. For the present he was more than satisfied.

He took his departure quickly, leaving Utterson reassured. As for himself he wanted only to be alone with his thoughts. Utterson's disclosures required a bit of mulling over, and it had best be done at once.

Canadian relatives. The placing of that advertising notice opened up a whole new area of speculation.

Should such Canadian family members exist, they might have knowledge of Dr. Jekyll's wealth. If so, it was even possible that someone could have made a trip to London in secret with the purpose of doing away with him in order to gain so sizable an inheritance. In which case it might be expected that the perpetrator of such a deed would now reappear again in the guise of an heir.

No doubt about it, the advertising notice could serve as bait, and if someone answered and appeared, Inspector Newcomen would be waiting.

All that remained was to set the proper trap.

chapter

3

Did it ever do anything but rain in London? The lash of a quite severe storm struck against the grimy windowpane, washing soot down in tracks. Hester had come to believe that this sprawling city was the dirtiest she had ever had the misfortune to see. Down on the street, carts and, here and there, a genteel barouche or cab, sent liquid black mud flying, much of it at those condemned by some misfortune to plod two-footed through the gloom. She had been excited earlier by the wonder of the new electric lights that gave sparks of radiance along some streets. But now even those miracles of men's ingenuity were no longer novelties.

Dreary as the outside world seemed from her window in Mrs. Carruthers's boarding house, it was better to stay gazing into that murk than to look behind her into the barren, musty-smelling, chilly room. Her worn purse lay upon the bed and she knew just how much was in it and how far that could stretch even by most heroic efforts at semistarvation. At least in the past she had never had to scant on meals, even though the dishes served had been of the plainest kinds. What did one do when there was no more money?

Appeal to Lady Ames? She recoiled from that idea, which struck at her again and again. Surely there was some honest way of earning her living instead of groveling—there must be! Cold as it was there was a bright flush of color on Hester's cheeks.

No—she refused to let the darkness of the day dim her hopes. Not when she had this! She swept away from the window and picked up the letter that had come by second post. A letter from an editor!

She read the letter again. Miss Agatha Scrimshaw would see her at ten precisely this morning. While she had been with Lady Ames she had seen, and then got Kitty to smuggle to her, the current copy of *The British Lady*. Though that publication was considered "advanced" and sometimes very close to the line of being unacceptable in polite drawing rooms. Lady Ames dearly loved a lord, as the old saying went, and the fact that the editor, Miss Scrimshaw, was of an old family, being granddaughter to an earl, and having her own lines of information running into court circles no less, made it a publication that could be mined for some tidbits of news which never touched real scandal, of course, but allowed the reader the feeling of moving among the elect. Those articles written by Miss Scrimshaw herself, dealing with such questionable ideas as the higher education of women, the need for considering the unhappy state of females beneath the notice of anyone truly well born, could be easily skipped.

It had been those articles and not the light chitchat that had attracted Hester, and she had thought several times that in a different sort of a world, she might have been able to use her own education, acquired privately though it was, for some justifiable purpose.

She dressed carefully. Though with only the well-worn waterproof cape to abet her umbrella, she could hardly present a figure to rival the fashionable ladies portrayed in the pages of the publication whose outer gate she was about to storm.

As she pulled wet-weather boots over her feet she thought that at least she had made a good usage of her time as governess. Even Lady Ames could not scorn or consider unnecessary to the education of young ladies visits to places of historic note as recommended by the most discreet books of travel knowledge. Thus almost at once on her arrival Hester had set herself to the memorization of routes to such parts of London as she thought would be important in her own future plans.

Of course, it was true that there was much of the city into which a lady did not venture at all. Probably she should use some form of transportation, but a cab fare was too crippling to be considered now. The startling new electric omnibus did not carry passengers from this part of the city. Luckily she considered herself a good walker and she had seen quite respectable-looking females trudging under umbrellas, striving to remain clear of the showers of sludge that carriage wheels dislodged.

She gave one last lingering critical look into the dim mirror. Her hair was sternly pinned into complete obedience under the brim of the plain weather-resistant hat that had faced the storms of Canada for more than one season, and she was smoothly buttoned into the basque of her shabby black dress. The skirt had no ruffles and was almost too scant. All in all, she decided, she did not look even as smart as an upper housemaid on her afternoon off. Would the all-seeing Miss Scrimshaw think the worse of her because the package she was offering was wrapped so shabbily? High-mindedness often allied itself purposefully with dowdiness— as if there were some rule that one could not have both a useful mind and a pleasing outward appearance. She could only hope that Miss Scrimshaw was a convert to that way of thinking.

By the time she reached the street the drive of rain had ceased its first fury and settled into a steady downpour. Damp chill reached through her cumbersome weather coat and, in spite of all her efforts, there were streaks of mud about the hem of her skirt. She huddled in the doorway of the building she had sought, and made two futile attempts to erase the worst of the streaks with one of her father's large square handkerchiefs that she had kept for such usage.

There were stairs to be climbed, the drip of her umbrella pattering on each as she went. Then she was facing an open door of what was plainly an office. There was no one at the desk within so she hesitated for a moment or two before she entered. She seated herself on the hard cushionless settle on the outer side of a railing that appeared to divide the world from the inner workings of *The British Lady*.

It was not until she was seated that she became aware that the inner door beyond the rail stood ajar and she could hear voices—both of them raised in argument.

The low, almost growling voice appeared to be in command; the second was even lower in tone, as if its owner fought for a temper-keeping modulation.

". . . of the lowest sort." The lower voice was climbing higher.

"You're not being asked to live with them, gel. You will have an introduction to Captain Ellison and she will tell you to go where you can observe."

"Everyone knows they are thieves and murderers, drunkards, and—and worse! This so-called army is interested only in such. No lady would even read about them, let alone become an actual witness to report some degrading scene!"

There followed a rustling of paper and the more forceful voice sounded as if it were now engaged in reading aloud.

"'Her Grace was most charmingly dressed in a muted melody of lavender and voilet shades. The well-known splendor of the Evedor pearls shone softly, like precious dewdrops, about her throat, on the bosom of her gown, about her fragile wrists. The tiara that is the crowning piece of this famous jewel collection found a perfect setting in her sable ringlets. She was the center of a gay party from the Evedor Towers, and it is well known that this coming season will see Evedor House once more opened to the polite world when Her Grace introduces her eldest daughter, Lady Maude Evedor, into society.' Pish!"

"But Miss Scrimshaw!" There was outrage in that interruption. "The Evedors are one of the oldest families in—"

"Old? And has being longtime masters of a strip of ground ever made a family worthy of being really counted? Do you know, gel, that living on the duke's own estate are a gamekeeper and a groom whose families date back at least five generations before the time old Sir Simon Evedor diddled the first manor out of James—and in not a particularly pleasant way, either! The Evedors started marrying wealth about the same time they achieved landed status and have been noted for their luck in the matter of snaffling at least one wealthy bride in a generation. For the rest, what do they really do? The present duke sits in the House of Lords, ready with a firm no in answer to the least sign of any progressive thinking. He never opens his mouth otherwise.

"No, it is not the duke, the duchess, and their ilk that are important now. Rather it is what is going on below, a good couple of flights below their airy perch."

"But,"—the second voice had now regained some courage—"our readers want to hear about the duchesses and the gowns and the parties. There were at least twenty write-ins in response to the account of the Howe-Ainsworthys' marriage."

"Very true," conceded the other. "Oh, we'll continue to supply the pap. Mainly because we can always hope that one or two of those avid readers will turn a page and find some more forceful meat. And meat has to be hunted, Dale."

"I can't! I just can't go to one of those meetings!" What little courage that voice had held earlier was gone now. "No lady would do it. If I did, and it were known, I never could get within the gates of a decent house again!"

"But do you, Dale?" There was a braying sound that Hester could not accept as a laugh. "I think most of your 'facts' come out of the mouths of ladies' maids and sometimes at a rather stiff rate. No, it's time you got out in the real world—think about it, gel."

The door swung from its partly open position with such force that it near slammed back against the wall. A young woman darted out. Her face was deeply flushed and tears were gathering in her eyes.

She had taken two strides beyond the railing, her eyes straight ahead with no glance at Hester, and she already had a hand at the outer door when it opened so abruptly that she stumbled forward straight against the young man who had been about to enter.

Giving an exclamation that was half a hiccup, she twisted by him, the drumming of her boots sounding from the hall. The man glanced at the desk behind the railing, frowned slightly, and went toward the door of the inner office. Perhaps she had somehow become invisible, Hester thought. She was sure that neither of them had seen her. The man was already into the inner office. He had closed the door behind him. Again it did not latch but swung open far enough for Hester once more to hear.

"Well, Aunt Agatha, and what have you done now? Here is Maud Dale apparently racing from some major danger. Who put the fox into the henhouse this morning?"

He spoke lightly in a voice that Hester recognized—for it was much like her father's accent. She had only caught a glimpse of him as he passed but what she frankly observed had not particularly impressed her. This was just another young "gentleman" who did not have to depend on work to keep bread and butter on the tea table nor an unleaking roof over his head. Doubtless such mundane needs never occurred to him at all.

He was clean shaven, which was not quite the norm in a city where elaborate hirsute adornments—or disguises—were the general rule. He wore no dashing guardsman's mustache, no fluff of sideburns, nor beard. His hair was dark, so much she had seen when he tugged off an all-weather tweed hat before he entered the inner office.

For the rest, he was slender, his caped mackintosh did not hide that, and the hand with which he held his hat was well kempt. Surely he was a stray from a more lofty world and so not in her experience at all. He would have to be about forty years older, with a scholar's slightly bemused look, for her to place him properly. Young men had played no part in Miss Lane's past.

"The stupid gel." The voice that could only be Miss Scrimshaw's boomed clearly. "Working is not all silk, pearls, and what is to be offered at the buffet supper. I want that story and she only wants to dabble. But a story like this—"

"What story?"

"The one about the Salvation Army—or whatever they call themselves. I can get a gel into one of their meetings, let her write it up. By God, Albert, most of the daily papers are writing pure libel about them. If we can get them a truthful story—that Sir John of yours—get him to ask a question or two, bring things out into the open. D'you know, Albert, that it's said the police have their orders to stand by and let roughs beat up these people? Is this England—or some nasty little state in the East where no one has any freedom? I want a story, a truthful, eyewitness story—"

"Which you aren't going to get, Agatha," the man answered her coldly. "No lady has any business anywhere near one of those rebellious, unlawful meetings. It dangerously abuts on treason, you know."

There came a sound that could only have been a snort. "Don't you start talking such folderol to me, Albert. In fact, my boy, aren't you going to do a little investigating yourself? And one of the latest bits of gossip flying around is that Sir John Dermond is interested in how the other three quarters of London live. Interested enough so that he has sent you an order to skulk about to see—"

"I shall do—"

"Exactly what you are told, m'boy. Just the proper gentleman as always. Come here to the window with you!"

That order was followed by a creaking as if some bit of furniture were sturdily resisting any move. "Look down, Albert—not just at that disgusting mud which laps about the ankles of anyone who does not have a penny or so for a ride. There *are* those who are walking. What about that woman over there who has taken off her shawl to cover what's in her basket? Proper old hag you'd call her, now wouldn't you? That's Bessie Fuller. And she doesn't count as many years as you, Albert. She's got an infant to support, and a drunken horror of a husband who has battered teeth out of her jaws, given her that permanent lump over one eye—she can't see very well with that anymore. Look her up and down, Albert.

"Bessie's a decent woman, she sells her matches along this street and has for some years now. If she gets enough some days for a hot tater or a broken pastie she feels she has luck . . . She's the kind the Army looks for. In fact, she has already asked their help—so she will not even go on the poor rates, which take a penny or two out of your pocket. And there are hundreds like her."

"There are charities to which she can apply—"

Again came that disparaging snort. "Do not prate to me of charities, or workhouses, or all the other inhuman devices you and yours are so smug about. If you are going to do a bit of looking around for Sir John Dermond, do it right. Don't wade about the edge of that sea of nastiness out there. Plunge right in—if you can take it. Personally, I wonder about you, Albert—you need a good shaking up to lose your ingrained blindness, and really see the world that lies about you."

"If someone, Aunt Agatha, must go looking in this evil pit of yours it had better be a man. As I think you will agree, you can't be wholly lost to all that is right and proper."

"How I get my results is none of your pompous business. You would do better, much better, Albert, to do a little straight thinking on your own and not accept the rubbish heard at dinner parties after ladies have withdrawn and you gentlemen pass a goodly aged bottle among you."

"Aunt Agatha!" There was real outrage in his voice now. But Hester lost Miss Scrimshaw's answer because a side door to the right, which she had not previously noticed, was hurriedly opened, and another woman entered on the far side of the railing.

Apparently it was customary for females invading the business world to retain the formality of street attire, for this pinch-faced lady wore a bonnet and white gloves on about her wrists, the fingers enrolled across the backs to afford more room and freer movement for the digits enclosed within. That she was employed here was evident in her glance, which betokened a cold recognition of Hester as a stranger. This guardian of the world beyond the rail made a dramatically better appearance, in a much smarter walking suit, than Hester when she rose. A gloved hand caught up a pince-nez dangling on a black ribbon around her neck and settled it firmly on her nose.

"Well, and what can I do for you?" Her inquiry had a rude note, as if she were facing Bessie Fuller on the road below.

"I have an appointment with Miss Scrimshaw. My name is Hester Lane."

"Lane?" There was a moment of hesitation. Then the guardian went to the door. Noting it was ajar she frowned, then gripped the knob firmly with one hand as she knocked with the other. At an indistinct murmur from within, she pushed the door forward, partially opening it as she spoke. "Miss Hester Lane, Miss Scrimshaw, by appointment."

"Good—come in, gel."

The gloved guardian nodded at Hester, opening the door

wider to permit her passage. The young man who had been
standing before the desk stepped back and to one side as she
entered, but it was Miss Scrimshaw who commanded
Hester's attention at the moment.

The woman enshrined behind the large desk, whose top
was entirely covered with a thick drift of papers, might be an
earl's granddaughter, but she also might well be as much of a
sight as the match seller on the street below. The vast curves
of her body stretched a purplish serge gown almost dangerously, and she too wore a bonnet, which bore a curl of
purple feathers constantly aquiver. Her complexion was a
pallid, yellowish white, while the wide expanse of flesh held
features that seemed too small for the rest of her.

Her button eyes might be smallish when compared to the
two broad chins and the side dewlaps she attempted to control with a dog collar of reddish-purple stones, matching a
large cross resting on her shelflike bosom, but for all their
lack of size they were very keen. Hester felt she was being
examined, weighed, and measured with no little skill.

Though she was looking straight at Hester, Miss
Scrimshaw's hands were scrabbling in the drift of paper on
her desk. They retrieved a rather battered document Hester
recognized as the letter she had written to ask for this interview. Miss Scrimshaw's right hand went searching again,
while with the left she held Hester's letter almost to the full
length of her massive arm. Then she produced a lorgnette
out of the flood and held it up, bringing the letter back into
focus.

"What makes you think, gel, that you would be of service
to B.L. here?" was her opening.

Hester hoped her face remained passive and gave away
nothing of the nervousness she really felt.

"Come, come, gel! Whose servants might be made to talk
secrets with you?" She was no longer staring at Hester in
that measuring fashion but looking over the girl's shoulder,
presumedly at the young man. "That's what's expected of

us, you know. Our readers want neat little paragraphs of stories about milady's parties, the coming out of highborn misses, and all the rest of such stuff. Ladies do not fret their minds about other things—they have no brains in their heads, or so is the general opinion, ain't it, Albert?"

"Aunt Agatha!" The protest came loudly from the corner.

"Albert, you may do as you wish under your own roof—this happens to be my domain. Come out of hiding there and meet Miss—Miss Lane. She's from the colonies—Canada. Miss Lane, this is my cousin Albert Prothore."

Hester had half turned so that she could acknowledge this strange introduction. The young man's face was flushed, and she noted that his hand was gripping his hat brim with force enough to rend that article of clothing in two were he to follow the dictates of temper.

"Albert, Miss Lane, is parliamentary secretary to Sir John Dermond, and a very good one too, I have heard. He'd be even better if he shook some of the cobwebs off him.

"Now." Once more her attention fastened on Hester. The girl had murmured something in reply to that introduction, but the awkwardness of the situation embarrassed her. She had turned her head away quickly but she had heard no acknowledgment from him.

"—if you are willing—"

Hester blinked and hoped she had not colored. She had been thinking how pompous this Albert Prothore was in spite of his youth and in so doing had missed something undoubtedly important.

"You can't!" That was Prothore. "You know how unfitting, how even dangerous such action can be!"

Miss Scrimshaw's small mouth showed how far it could enlarge when necessary. And surely that expansion was meant to be a grin.

"Now, Albert, do not make decisions for others." She nodded and the tuft of feathers on her bonnet bobbed back and forth as if in a stiff breeze. "You may decide, gel. I'll

give it to you on simple terms. This can be a story that will
make your name famous—"

"Infamous!" challenged Prothore.

"Albert!" The smile became that of a frog about to close
on a fly. "This is a matter of business—but then you don't
even know what that word means." Once more she turned
back to Hester, waving a mittenlike hand, which displayed a
pair of gold rings mounted with reddish-purple stones similar
to those on her collar and cross. "We have a London out
there unknown to readers of the B.L.—a London that others
are trying to change for the better. If what I have heard is
true, they are beginning to make some headway. Have you
heard of the Salvation Army, gel?"

"No."

As Hester replied she was again conscious of Mr. Prothore's anger. For years she had been attuned to this—rage
sensed in silence. How many times had she been the butt of
that particular treatment when dealing with her father?

"Well," Miss Scrimshaw was continuing, "there is an organization working with and for the poor. They have persisted in the face of persecution and all kinds of opposition.
The time has come, it is even a little past, to tell of what the
Salvation Army has done for those we do not want to notice.
Their work should be explained simply and earnestly to people such as our readers who have no connection at all with
the depths of depravity, do not even know what exists.

"You are new to London, my gel. Therefore you would
see much that would not be clouded by prejudice. I
think"—she planted one broad elbow on the desk with her
hand supporting her layered chin—"that we need a fresh
outlook, a very fresh one. So what do you say, Miss Lane? I
shall wish perhaps a series of articles—from what I have
heard there is plenty to write about. You would be put on
staff rates, and I think that this, if done well, could be for
you a good opening into the field."

"No!" The instant protest came from Prothore. "Listen to

me, Miss Lane. You certainly do not want to become the target of gossip, to follow a course which, were it uncovered, would be unwelcome in any assembly of your sex—"

"You"—Miss Scrimshaw's pudgy forefinger pointed to the still partly open door between Hester and her cousin—"go, Albert. I would lay a wager with you—if you were in the least open-minded—that this gel shall learn more than you will ever uncover for that sensation-seeking employer of yours. Meanwhile, this is a place of business and you are disrupting my business—"

Ignoring his aunt's heated words, Prothore turned to Hester. "It is all madness, do not let yourself be drawn into her experiment." He did not name his kinswoman, only nodded slightly in Miss Scrimshaw's direction. "It is rank and utter folly, and she knows it too!"

Miss Scrimshaw ignored him. "What about it, gel? Do you think you are writer enough to give the B.L. a picture of what happens on the side streets of this town, while ladies ride snug in their barouches on the avenues?"

Hester drew a deep breath. She knew as well as this prig Prothore that her decision might be the greatest folly. Still— as Miss Scrimshaw had pointed out—it might also give her firm standing in the world she had so long desired to enter. For so many years she had yearned to escape that musty and silent web of scholarship that held nothing for her. What other post was there for a proper female?

"Yes." Though saying that made her suddenly breathless.

Mr. Prothore scowled more heavily. "All right." He spoke directly to Miss Scrimshaw. "*I* will get your story for you!"

"Miss Lane has accepted." Agatha Scrimshaw gave a vigorous nod of her head, so that the crest of feathers was flung about as it might be under a breeze. "Go your own way, Albert. But I hardly think you are one to dig deep enough— even to please Sir John."

Prothore moved toward Hester, as if he were about to shove her back through the door.

"Don't do it!" It was not said imploringly—she did not believe that this stiff young man had ever experienced the need to plead for anything—but rather as an order.

Hester moved a little to one side away from him. Thankfully she discovered she was able to meet his gaze levelly as she answered.

"I have already given my word!" Then she dared to add a dismissal.

"Good day, sir."

Miss Scrimshaw laughed. Prothore's lips were set tightly together as he passed Hester, slamming the door behind him. The girl felt a little qualm then. This was indeed taking charge of her own life and she hoped she wouldn't regret it.

chapter 4

If it were not for the grime on the windowpane and the fog beyond it, Inspector Newcomen could almost see the lion-guarded grandeur of Trafalgar Square. But even such a sight was hardly compensation for his present surroundings. The lack of central heating or even the presence of a fireplace literally sent a chill down his spine during a good eight months out of every year; warmer weather afforded little relief, for want of adequate ventilation. At this moment the dimly lit cubbyhole that served in lieu of an office, shared with two others of equal rank, was musty and dank.

Wedged behind his battered rolltop desk in the corner, Newcomen gazed glumly on his surroundings. Even though his fellow officers were absent from their own desks at the moment, he still felt a sense of vague oppression when confined here. And confinement it truly was; there were felons in Newgate Prison incarcerated more comfortably than he was here in Scotland Yard.

There was no yard area on the short and narrow thoroughfare beyond nor any hint of Scotland; long centuries ago a palace had been reared on this site to provide accommodations during the royal visits of Scottish kings. But there was nothing palatial about the present structure. Metropolitan Police Commissioner Sir Edmund Henderson promised a new Yard in a new location within a few years; meanwhile, his officers must serve their sentences in this creaking, crumbling gaol.

The flickering gaslight cast Newcomen's shadow on the wall and did nothing to disperse the shadow of melancholy overcasting his spirits.

Ever since his meeting with Utterson earlier in the day he'd been troubled by persistent unease, and now with the coming of twilight his mood intensified. From past experience Newcomen realized there was only one way to dispel such a difficulty. He must meet the problem head-on and overcome it.

A hard case. Or, as his father had been wont to say, a tough nut to crack. A question formed its kernel; was Utterson lying or not?

If the solicitor had been telling the truth, it was only in part. Too much was still unaccounted for, particularly concerning Dr. Jekyll's friendship with the shadowy Mr. Hyde.

Shadowy. Again Inspector Newcomen glanced at his silhouette wavering on the wall. Additional light would dispel that, but it would take a different sort of illumination to erase the shadow of Edward Hyde. Shade, perhaps, for Hyde was dead.

At least there was no uncertainty about that fact, or the coroner's verdict of suicide. But a new doubt had arisen to trouble the inspector since he had seen Dr. Jekyll's will.

He kept thinking about that altered clause. Dr. Jekyll's original intent had been to leave his entire estate to Edward Hyde. Was Hyde aware of this fact? Given the man's history, his knowledge of the clause might well have prompted him to murder his benefactor. Instead he killed himself, and it was Jekyll who remained alive. Or was he? If so, why hadn't he come forward? It was still possible that Hyde disposed of his longtime friend before doing away with himself. But should this be true, how and where had the deed been done and what had become of the corpus delicti?

Newcomen pursed his lips. Questions within questions. Do shadows cast shadows of their own?

In this case, yes. The shadows cast by Hyde in life had been ominous indeed. Newcomen remembered the accounts of his activities; the trampling of an innocent child in the street, the savage murder of an old man in a deserted lane. The name of the little girl who had been the object of Hyde's callous cruelty was unknown to witnesses, but the old man—Sir Danvers Carew—was easily identified. The sole witness to this particular crime had been a maidservant peering through the upstairs window of a nearby residence; according to her account killer and victim seemingly encountered one another by chance and only a few words were exchanged in the darkened lane before the man she identified as Edward Hyde struck Carew with his heavy cane. When the old man fell he was beaten senseless, then battered to death with such ferocity that the stout wood splintered and the weapon broke in two. The vision of that shattered cane and the mangled corpse beside it remained vivid in Newcomen's memory.

But Edward Hyde was still a shadow. And the visit with Utterson led nowhere. Aside from the solicitor there was probably only one person who might shed light upon the matter—Jekyll's butler, Poole. He had been present on the occasion of Hyde's death and he gave testimony at the brief inquest where suicide was established. At the time Dr. Jekyll's absence didn't enter into the formal investigation, so Poole was required to say little about it. Now Newcomen wanted to hear more.

He leaned back, frowning to himself as he recalled Utter-

son's excuse for dismissing Dr. Jekyll's household staff and
his disclaimer regarding their whereabouts. Surely the solicitor must have had a long acquaintance with the elderly
butler who had spent twenty years in service. And Poole had
known Utterson well enough to call upon him at his home in
one instance at his master's bidding.

It was possible that the solicitor was deliberately con-
cealing the knowledge of where Poole might be found. As to
motive, again Newcomen bethought himself of the bequest.
That would be reason enough for Utterson to discourage further investigation, particularly if it might lead to suspicions
regarding the circumstances under which the will had been
altered.

Inspector Newcomen rose and paced the floor. Not much
of a trudge, really; a mere half-dozen steps brought him to
the grimy windowpane, and upon turning, the ancient floor-
boards creaked only seven times before he came abreast of
the doorway at the other end of the room. The sound of his
footsteps distracted him, but there was no help for it. Bare
wood was good enough for Scotland Yard inspectors; carpets
were for kings.

The descent of darkness beyond the windowpane
prompted the inspector to consult his watch.

Donning his coat and bowler, he extinguished the gas and
stepped out into the drafty hall. As Newcomen made his way
to the stairs, he exchanged greetings with several of his fellows who were arriving on night duty. Once he reached the
lower landing the inspector sought an inconspicuous side exit
leading to the street. Here the fog was beginning to lower
and he raised his coat collar to ward chill from his cheeks.

The exit he had chosen shortened the route to Trafalgar
Square. Atop the Corinthian column Lord Nelson peered
down through swirls of fog, his one-eyed stony stare fixed on
the blaze of light below. Inspector Newcomen, his own eyes
intent on the bustle of traffic, headed for the cab stand at the
nearby curbing. As he did so, church bells chimed the hour.

Seven o'clock it was, precisely on the dot, and Jerry was waiting.

The man on the box of the cab nodded as Newcomen approached. "Evenin', Inspector," he said. "Where to?"

"Home."

"Can't say as 'aow I blame you," the cabby said, descending from his perch to close the door as Newcomen settled himself inside. "It don't look to be a proper night to prowl abaht."

"Sorry you feel that way," the inspector told him. "It so happens I had an errand for you in mind."

"Errand?" The cabby's smile expanded into a toby-jug grin. "'Appy to be of service. Yours to command an' no questions arsked."

"But that's the job—asking questions." Newcomen nodded in abrupt dismissal. "Up you go again, and get cracking. On the way home I'll tell you what's wanted."

He did so, and by the time they pulled up before Newcomen's lodgings on Bayswater Road, the cabby had been provided with information necessary for the task before him. This, plus his fare, a generous tip, and the promise of a further fee if his mission was successful, sent Jerry off into the fog with a cheery whistle.

Whether that whistle was directed at his patient horse or intended as a farewell to Newcomen himself didn't greatly matter. As the inspector made his way into the welcome warmth of the hall beyond the entrance, what mattered to him was whether or not he might have to whistle for his money. Cab fare and tip were his obligation and he preferred to pay extra rather than brave the rigors of public transport on a cold and clammy night following a long day's duties. But he could be out of pocket for the fee he'd promised Jerry; only in special instances did his superiors at the Yard repay him for extra expenditures. Pity they weren't employed by the Chancellor of the Exchequer; their stingy, mingy ways would be of more value in that branch of government.

Newcomen plodded upstairs to his bachelor quarters, changed into more comfortable attire, plodded downstairs to take dinner with the other boarders. This being eight o'clock of a Wednesday, it was mutton as usual, but he paid little heed to what he ate or to the conversation of his companions. His thoughts were far away in the fog, following Jerry to destinations unknown.

Once back in his room he settled before the fireplace, enjoying the solitary vice of a Trichinopoly, the smoke of which mingled with the gas flame flaring before him. The warmth soothed him but he could not relax completely, knowing himself to be a fool. Cab fares, cigars, fees to informants—no wonder he was fated to live out his days in a rented room rather than a proper flat of his own, complete with housekeeper and a decent cut of beef on the dinner table.

He was a fool, and it was sheer folly to fancy the Yard paying for any money he laid out in Jerry's behalf. While the question of Dr. Henry Jekyll's present whereabouts was still of interest to the authorities, it was not presently of pressing concern. What's more, Newcomen had never been officially assigned to the case, if case it was. Nothing had prompted this further and continuing inquiry except his own curiosity, and the determination to appease it.

Staring into the fire and basking in its glow, he found himself wondering once again about Jerry and what he might be finding in the fog. This was far from the first time he'd employed the cabby on such a mission; by unspoken agreement Jerry brought his hack around to the square promptly at seven every evening, and on most nights Newcomen was his fare. But on certain occasions he had undertaken special assignments, almost always carried to a successful outcome. It was the unspoken rule that the inspector never inquired as to the means Jerry employed in obtaining information. Enough to accept the fact that a London cabby was far more knowledgeable than your average constable or detective.

Enough, and yet not enough. When Newcomen prepared for bed, turning down both his covers and the gas log in the fireplace, he knew he was in for a night of troubled slumber.

This he could endure, but what he hadn't reckoned with was the morrow. Although the day dawned bright, he himself was dull, his thoughts still shrouded in fog. He was peckish at breakfast, off his feed at luncheon, and had no appetite at teatime.

But as seven o'clock approached Newcomen was positively ravenous, and it was hunger—hunger for information—that sent him out of the Yard and into the square a good five minutes before the appointed hour.

There was no fog tonight, and the lights on the encircling streets cast a garish glow, so that Newcomen had no problem in identifying Jerry's cab as it stood at the front of the long line. He'd come early, the inspector noted; that was a good sign.

As Jerry glanced down at him from his perch the cabby's gargoyle grin was reassuring, and once inside the cab, the homeward-bound Newcomen had reason to rejoice.

"Found him?" he said.

Jerry shrugged. "In a manner of speakin'. Leastwise I found 'er."

"Her? Who are you talking about?"

"The missus. Or so she says."

Newcomen frowned. "I didn't know he was married."

The cabby's voice rose above the clatter of wheels and the clop of hooves. "What say?"

Newcomen frowned. "I suggest you take a turn straightaway at the next crossing and pull up," he said. "At least we can talk without all this commotion."

"Right you are."

And it was to the right that they turned, halting beneath the street lamp just beyond the corner of a small lane terminating in a mews entrance at its far end. It was here, in solitude and silence, that a series of questions and answers began. During their course Jerry revealed for the first time just how he set about searching out information and informants.

"I reckons you 'eard of the Salvation Army," he said.

Newcomen nodded, but there was a guarded edge in his voice. "You went to them for help? Where?"

"Nightly prayer meetin'. Queen Victoria Street, one-oh-one."

"That's City, isn't it?"

"Right you are, but no matter. The boozers come from all over, an' arter the band stops playin' an' the preacher stops prayin', that's when they stand up to be counted. An' them as won't come or can't stand, it's their wives an' muvvers what gets up to testify an' pray for 'em." The cabby's hand rose to scrape the stubble of a chin that had not recently been scraped by a razor. "Staggerin', 'ow much you learns abaht, jus' by cockin' a ear."

"So that's how you found her!" Newcomen muttered.

"Found 'oo?"

"'The missus,' as you call her."

Jerry shook his head. "It was Betsy Dobbs I saw."

"I don't know the name."

"Nahrt likely you would. Sails on 'er bottom down Tower way, gettin' street trade from the barracks. Come to pray for 'er dear ol' dad, she did, 'im as turned 'er out to earn keep for them both. 'E drinks up the rent money fast as she brings it in, so she stopped by the meetin' to pray for 'is salvation. While she was at it she thought to put in a word to the Lord for 'er friend 'oose 'usband suffers from the same complaint. That's when she made mention of 'is name—Edgar Poole."

"It was that easy?" Newcomen shook his head. "I can't believe it!"

The cabby shrugged. "Bit o' luck. Most I 'oped for when I went there was bumpin' inter some bloke I knew 'oo might steer me onto anovver. You keeps on going 'an somewheres down the line you 'it the target." Jerry's gap-toothed grin returned. "But 'oo am I to tell you, Inspector? That's yer line of business."

"Get on with it, man. Tell me what you learned."

"Per'aps I'd best tell you on the way there."

"Where do you propose to go?"

"To Poole and his missus. I 'ad a chat wiv friend Betsy arter the meetin' broke up. She give me their number over on Newgate Street. Seein' as 'ow you was so keen on the matter, I took the liberty of askin' Betsy to speak to Mrs. Poole and noterfy 'er y'd pay a call on the 'appy couple tonight."

"Why didn't you tell me this before we started? Now I daresay we've come a good quarter of a mile in the wrong direction?"

"No 'arm done," Jerry assured him. "We'd 'ave ter clear round the square in any case, an' if I doubles back at the next crossin' we can 'ead into 'Igh 'Olborn by way of Shaftesbury."

During the journey the inspector pressed for more information on Poole's background. He discovered that Dr. Jekyll's longtime butler had entered matrimony only a few months ago, after being discharged from his position by Utterson. That in itself was hardly unusual; it was not customary for house servants to marry without the specific permission of their employers, because experience had shown it tended to disrupt them in the performance of domestic duties. What surprised him was that Poole's bride was Nell Curtis, who had been Jekyll's housemaid.

Even more surprising was the fact that between the two of them they had apparently saved a sufficiency to rent decent living quarters. Instead of settling in an East End tenement they now occupied a rear three-room flat on the ground floor of a comparatively respectable dwelling. Quite possibly they had it on the cheap, for Aldergate was hardly a fashionable address, at least not in the shadow of Newgate Prison.

Once past St. Paul's there was little traffic to be encountered on the darkened side streets, and when Jerry's cab rounded the corner Inspector Newcomen anticipated a similar situation ahead.

But there was light aplenty surrounding the address they sought: a bobbing of bull's-eye lanterns darting to and fro before the entryway to the four-story dwelling.

Apparently it had been emptied of its occupants, for most members of the clamoring crowd on the walkway were in shirtsleeves or house aprons, with no protection against the evening's chill. Rays of lantern light slivered the sides of box-shaped vehicles stationed along the curbing; the form of these conveyances left no doubt as to their function, nor did the uniforms worn by the lantern bearers.

"Pull up!" Newcomen commanded. Even before the cab halted completely he was out the door and headed toward the nearest light source. The constable was wielding his lantern as a warning signal, waving it in the face of the crowd and shouting at them to stay clear of the walkway.

Preoccupied with the enthusiastic performance of his duties, it took a full moment and a hard nudge in the ribs before he acknowledged the inspector's presence. He turned with a glare matching that of his lantern.

"'Ere now, whacher fink yer doin'?"

"Inspector Newcomen, Metropolitan Police." The reply was accompanied by a proper display of identification, but had scant effect on the constable's glowering. And no wonder; there was little love lost between the Metropolitan and the City police. But rank has its privileges, and the City constable forced himself to be civil to a superior.

"Sorry, sir." A perfunctory pinch of his helmet served as the modern substitute for a tug at the forelock or a full military salute. "I diden' reckernize—"

"No matter," Newcomen said. "Just tell me what's happening here."

The constable's lips moved in a reply that could not be heard, for as he spoke the voices from both sides of the walkway rose to a deafening level. Newcomen glanced toward the dwelling as, preceded by a lantern carrier, four uniformed members of the City constabulary emerged bearing a stretcher. The coarse departmental-issue blanket completely covered its occupant, as they moved in the direction of an ambulance at the curb.

No need now to inquire what had occurred; there was only one question and Newcomen asked it.

"Who?"

"Can't rightly say, sir. But we come 'ere on report uv a murder. Some chap as lived in the flat at the rear."

chapter 5

Edgar Poole had been beaten to death.

There was no question about that; Inspector Newcomen obtained the name of the victim from one of the City detectives on the night of the murder.

But little else was forthcoming and no further information had been volunteered. It was made plain to him—not in so many words, but rather by their absence—that the City Police were definitely in charge of the case and wanted no interference from their Metropolitan rivals.

Naturally, he had no opportunity to speak with Poole's widow at the time. She had been taken immediately to headquarters on Old Jewry Street for further questioning, and Newcomen had to content himself with the cursory accounts of the crime published in the papers on the following day.

As determined by these reports, Poole had absented himself from home during the afternoon before he became the object of foul play. Where he had spent his time, and quite possibly a shilling or so, was still a matter of conjecture, but there was no doubt regarding what he'd spent it for. When he reeled home shortly after six o'clock in the evening, Poole immediately took to his bed, ignoring both the reproaches and the tears of his spouse.

According to Mrs. Poole he had been despondent ever since the loss of his former position and made no effort to find further employment. It was she who had been contributing to their support by doing piecework, "sewing hats and such," at home. Indeed, it was the necessity of delivering the results of her day's labor to a millinery establishment in nearby City Road that required her to leave their lodgings while her husband, fully clothed, lay in deep slumber on the bed.

"Drunken stupor, more likely," Newcomen had muttered to himself when he read the newspaper story. But his uncharitable comment was the product of professional frustration rather than moral judgment. What Poole did was his own business; what was done *to* him was Newcomen's.

Just exactly what had been done to him during the hour's interval between his wife's departure and her return remained unclear. None of the other occupants of the dwelling who'd rushed outside to view the spectacle after the police arrived had since stepped forward in the role of an eye- or even an ear-witness to the crime.

"Same old story—hear no evil, see no evil, speak no evil," Newcomen muttered to himself. "Fine lot of monkeys they are, too."

As for Mrs. Poole herself, she'd come back from her errand with some hope of a cold supper but little expectation of sharing it with a cold-sober husband.

What she was not prepared for was the discovery of his battered corpse sprawled just beyond the doorway of their bedroom.

Bones had been broken and facial features disfigured by the force of the blows inflicted upon the victim; even if he'd made no outcry, surely the impact of his fall should have attracted some attention from other residents. But no one admitted as much and it was only Mrs. Poole's own screams that summoned the neighbor woman from down the hall and sent her out into the street in search of a constable.

There had been no further notices in the public press, a circumstance that did not greatly concern the inspector, for he placed little credence upon the probity of the penny papers. His immediate thought was to seek out another opportunity to interview Poole's widow, but the plan was scotched; upon presenting himself at the Aldergate address following her return there, he was informed by a neighbor—coincidentally, the one who had first summoned the police—that Mrs. Poole was in a state of prostration and had taken to her bed.

It occurred to Newcomen that the bed in question was the one occupied by her late husband at the time he met his death; as such, hardly the place in which to seek comfort and consolation. Still, he supposed one had to make the best of it, and Mrs. Poole could hardly be expected to sleep on the floor. Somehow, despite its tragedies, life goes on.

And so did the neighbor lady who informed him of these circumstances. Or would have gone on and on if the inspector hadn't cut her short, thanked her, and made his departure. He had no time to waste on gossip and hearsay; tomorrow morning there'd be a coroner's inquest from which the facts might be forthcoming.

Autopsy reports, official findings of police officers at the scene of the crime, answers to questions addressed to Mrs. Poole under oath—this was the stuff clues were made of. Despite the ongoing petty rivalries between Metropolitan and City police, formal inquest proceedings were open to the public and Newcomen intended to be present even if only in the role of a private citizen.

It was not meant to be. Unfortunately, in his role as inspector he spent the morning of the inquest in the apprehension and detention of one Archibald Hix, who had been discovered jimmying open the rear door of a haberdashery just off Regent Street. The arrest itself was a simple matter; not so, however, the tedious paperwork required thereafter. And by the time Newcomen was free to extract the watch from his vest pocket, the inquest was long over.

Allowing for the equally tedious task of transcribing its findings at City Police Headquarters, Newcomen realized he must somehow contain himself for yet another day until he could hope to secure a copy.

This he somehow managed to do, and on the afternoon of the day following, paid a call to Old Jewry Street, identified himself, and received a transcript grudgingly given.

The findings of one Dr. Angus Blystone were, as might have been anticipated, of little help. The deceased had suffered a fractured skull—Newcomen made no effort to set down the sawbones' medical Latin—contusions on and about the face and neck, plus broken bones in both arms, the fingers of his right hand, and the rib cage. The immediate cause of death was a massive cerebral hemorrhage at the point where the skull had been crushed by a blow or blows from an unspecified blunt object or instrument.

Meaning they didn't know a bloody thing about what had happened, or how. Newcomen scowled to himself as he read the familiar phrases woven to form a threadbare but convenient cloak for ignorance.

Only two brief bits of testimony from the City detectives offered some slight enlightenment. The first reported the presence of bloodstains on the upper surface of the shabby sheet that did double duty as a bedspread. The second involved the absence of anything that might have served as the murder weapon.

Presence—the murderer had surprised Poole and probably

struck the first blows even as he awakened; then, staggering upright, he was battered to the floor.

Absence—the murderer came armed, or else had found something in the room for use as a weapon and subsequently carried it away upon departure.

But when asked, Mrs. Poole had been unable to specify that anything was missing that might have served a deadly purpose. For that matter, when asked, Mrs. Poole was not too specific about anything.

Newcomen's frown deepened as he went over her answers given at the inquest, which did little to augment what the newspapers had already reported. No, she could not account for her late husband's depressed state nor his recent overindulgence in drink except that both seemed the result of losing his position. No, they hadn't quarreled. No, Edgar didn't have an enemy in the world.

And no, Newcomen told himself, it couldn't be that much of a mystification. There had to be more to it than that, and she had to know more than that. Or at least suspect.

Death at the hand of person or persons unknown. The expected verdict that didn't explain the unexpected, the answer that resolved no questions. Thus the law simply washed its hands of the matter without removing the bloodstains.

Again Newcomen stared down at his hastily scrawled notes. Something about them jarred his memory. Of course—it was almost like the Carew case. Sir Danvers Carew had been murdered on a public thoroughfare, Edgar Poole in a private residence; one victim was a member of the aristocracy and the other a discharged manservant. But the similarities were there. A sudden surprise attack without apparent reason. Death from a blunt instrument—in Carew's case, a cane that had been broken and left at the spot where the onslaught occurred. But in the assault on Poole a similar weapon could well have been used without breaking, whereupon the murderer merely carried it away with him.

There was, of course, an important difference between the two affairs. In the first, testimony from an actual witness identified the perpetrator of the crime as Edward Hyde. But Edward Hyde was dead. Other later witnesses had identified his corpse. He could not have risen to kill again.

That left only one more link, and a slim one. Both Carew and Poole had a common enemy in the late Mr. Hyde. And both had a connection, personal or professional, with Hyde's former friend Dr. Henry Jekyll. Dr. Jekyll, who might be described as the *late* or the *former* himself, for all Newcomen might know.

All he might know indeed, but not all he *wanted* to know, which was precisely the point—there must be something else, *had* to be.

It was in his office that the inspector's ruminations were interrupted by the arrival of a uniformed runner from downstairs who presented him with a missive received in the last delivery of the day's post. The envelope addressed to him contained only a brief note bearing the signature of Robert Guest, writing at the behest of his employer, Utterson, but its message erased Newcomen's frown.

Utterson was inquiring if it might be possible for the inspector to wait upon him tomorrow afternoon at three? If so, he would have the opportunity of meeting Miss Hester Lane, a relative of Henry Jekyll's who had recently arrived from Canada.

Recently arrived? Now there was something to chew on. Had she been here when Poole died? Did she know the whereabouts of Dr. Jekyll? In any event he was grateful for Utterson's invitation. Barring the unforeseen, he intended to have a bit of a chat with this recent arrival.

But that would be tomorrow's business. Right now his watch was ticking closer to the hour and a glance through the begrimed windowpane confirmed the imminence of seven o'clock.

Seven o'clock and all was well; Jerry was waiting, nodding

down at him as he approached the curb. One minute later, and all was confusion.

"She wants to see me?" Newcomen said. "Tonight?"

"That's wot she said to tell you. I popped around there on the orf-chance abaht an 'our ago when I dropped a fare at Liverpool Station. Says she's sorry she wasn't up to seein' you earlier, but better late than never."

"What's that supposed to mean?"

Jerry shrugged. "She diden' say right out. I reckern there might be somefink she 'eld back at the inquest an' naow she's 'aving second thorghts."

The inspector wasted no further time in reckoning for himself. Once he was in the cab they circumnavigated the square to Lord Nelson's stony satisfaction and headed toward the Strand. Newcomen's mounting anticipation made the journey seem to last forever; he urged Jerry, who in turn urged the horse, and the cab rolled through the roiling traffic of Fleet Street.

When at last they arrived, Newcomen found the quiet he had expected to encounter earlier in the week. "Wait here," he told the cabby, then hurried inside.

Three minutes later he was seated in the parlor with Poole's widow. The former Nell Curtis was a mousy little woman whose straight brown hair was streaked with gray. She was wearing mourning, and its bleak blackness accentuated the pallor of her haggard face. But her welcome seemed sincere and Newcomen thought he could detect relief in her eyes and voice as their conversation began.

"Yer the one 'oo come 'ere to see my 'usband the night 'e was buckled?" she said.

Newcomen nodded.

"Nart in any trouble, was 'e?"

"None that I know about. All I wanted was a chat. Jerry can tell you that."

"So 'e did." As she spoke, the widow's eyes narrowed in calculating scrutiny. "But 'e ain't telling wot you'd be chatting abaout."

"That's because he doesn't know." The inspector leaned forward. "Anything that passed between your late husband and myself was to be strictly a private matter."

There was a moment of silence as the diminutive woman weighed the big man's words. When she spoke again her stare was less intent, but there was still an edge of suspicion in her voice. "'Aow do I know I can trust a rozzer?"

Newcomen shrugged. "For what it's worth, you have my word."

"Meaning this weren't go no further?" she said.

"No further than me. The City police are in charge here. That's why I wasn't allowed to see you at their headquarters. And that's why I won't be running to them with what you tell me tonight."

"Wot if I was to tell you somefink I din't let on at the inkques'?" Again she hesitated. "Mind you, I ain't sayin' as 'aow I will—"

"No need." Newcomen permitted himself a smile that was both solicitous and self-congratulatory. "That's why you were disposed to see me."

"Been 'eavy on me mind ever since it 'appened." The widow shook her head. "City police—they treat you like dirt, comin' at you wiv questions day 'an night. Good thing I 'ad witnesses, or like as not they'd 'ave me take the drop for pore Edgar's murder. Fine lot o' ruddy blaggards if you ask me, 'an them as 'eld the inkques' was the worst." She gripped the arms of her chair, knuckles whitening.

Inspector Newcomen spoke softly. "So you got angry and rattled and didn't tell them all you knew," he said. "Now it's a case of second thoughts, because you want to find your husband's murderer."

"Can you?"

"I can't promise anything until I hear what you have to say." Newcomen gestured. "Before we get to that I'm minded to ask a question or two first. And I'll want the truth."

"Do me best."

"I understand your husband had been feeling poorly these past months. Started when he lost his position, eh?"

"Oh no, sir!" Mrs. Poole shook her head. "Edgar weren't 'isself for a longish time afore that."

"When did you notice anything was wrong?"

The widow frowned thoughtfully. "'Ard to say. 'E seemed right as rain up 'til Dr. Jekyll got too friendly-like with that 'Yde bloke."

"Edward Hyde." The chair creaked beneath him as the big man leaned still farther forward. "Did you know the man?"

"Never set eyes on 'im. Used 'is own key for Dr. Jekyll's private quarters, so's to come an' go as 'e pleased."

"But your husband knew him. Did he ever say anything about Mr. Hyde to you?"

"Only that 'e was an ugly customer, one as Dr. Jekyll would best be rid of."

"And did he?"

"Did 'e wot?"

"Did Dr. Jekyll murder Mr. Hyde?" Newcomen's eyes were intent upon her face. "Straight out now. Did he?"

"'Ow can you say such a thing? Dr. Jekyll was a proper gentleman, allus kindly disposed, Gawd rest 'is soul—"

"God rest his soul." The inspector's voice boomed its echo. "Do you think he's dead?"

"Edgar did." The widow nodded quickly. "'E reckoned 'Yde made away with the doctor an' then finished 'isself orf." She grimaced. "Narsty piece o' work that was. Edgar saw the body. 'E really took it 'ard, even afore we was sacked. I 'ad the feelin' Edgar was chuffed to get away from that 'ouse. But arter that it was all downhill, wot wiv the nightmares an' the drink—"

"Pity." Newcomen spoke softly. "A great pity, as I well know." He paused. "What I don't know are the things you didn't tell them about at the inquest."

Mrs. Poole sighed. "Per'aps it's best left at that."

"Not if you want to bring justice to whoever killed your husband." Studying her reaction as he spoke, the inspector modulated his voice to a confidential whisper. "Now that the inquest is over you can't expect much more from the City police. They've got other fish to fry. Which means this business is strictly between the two of us."

Mrs. Poole hesitated. "But you scarce knew Edgar! Wot's yer concern?"

Now it was Newcomen's turn to hesitate as he pondered his reply. Telling her his real reason would be a gamble, but as the saying has it, in for a penny, in for a pound. "Truth is, I've a notion the murderer of your husband might be connected with the death or disappearance of Dr. Jekyll. And with your help, I intend to find out."

Mrs. Poole nodded, then leaned forward, speaking in low tones. "The glass," she said. "I din't tell them that part."

The inspector frowned. "I read your statement at the inquest. You said the window had been broken."

"But I left out abaout 'earing it. I give the front door a right proper slam when I come in. No one else paid 'eed so I figger as 'aow they'd not 'ear what I 'eard on me way down the 'all."

"The sound of the window-glass being smashed in your bedroom?"

"More of a tinkle, you might say. Winder weren't locked—I reckon the glass broke when it was forced up too 'igh. Cracked and fell on the floor in smallish pieces, bits and slivers all over the place—"

"Stow your gab, woman!" Newcomen's voice boomed out before he could control it, nor did he attempt to. "You're telling me your husband's murderer was still present when you arrived?"

Mrs. Poole shook her head. "Give me a miss by seconds, must 'ave popped aout the winder when I opened the front door."

The inspector sat back, and when he spoke the sharp

edge of his voice was dulled by disappointment. "Then you didn't see him."

Again the widow shook her head. "Not in the room. Seein' pore Edgar give me a fair turn, it did, but one look and I knowed 'e done for. Then I 'ears noises from outside the winder—like someone runnin' up the alleyway. That's when I stuck me 'ead aout to take a look. No light in the passage, mind you, and all I 'ad was the one glimpse afore the thing went 'round the far corner. Then I let out a scream—"

"Get on with it!" The inspector's voice was sharp again. "What did he look like?"

"Pore Edgar use to say it give 'im the 'orrors to see Dr. Jekyll's friend."

"Edward Hyde?"

"One and the same." She nodded. "But what puts it to mind is 'ow 'e spoke of Mr. 'Yde. Didn't once say ''e'—only 'it.' Like 'Yde weren't even 'uman." Her eyes flickered into an awareness and a hint of apprehension crept into her voice. "I never took 'is meaning until I saw that thing in the alley, running all twisted and hunched over—"

The inspector nodded quickly. "Some kind of cripple?"

"It moved too fast for that." She gazed directly at Newcomen, pouring forth the fear in her eyes. "I 'ope and pray you can find the murderer. But don't look for a man, Inspector—look for a creature."

chapter

6

Hester read over the much-creased list again and then surveyed the clothing she had hunted out to try to conform with
instructions. It was both exciting and a bit troubling to think
that her first essay into the writing world would come from
acting a part. The more the day wore on the uneasier she felt.
Or maybe part of it was sheer hunger. She had a bun and tea—
what Mrs. Carruthers considered a suitable breakfast for a lady
boarder. It had been brought to her by Dorry, the weak-
chinned, slack-mouthed maid-of-all-work—and work she did,
all of it, under the eye of Cook. Cooks, Hester had learned at
the Ames household, were exalted personages with an unend-
ing series of privileges, some of which even the housekeeper,
or that supreme being the butler, could not challenge.

Anyway there had been a bun (two days old at least) with
a miserable scrape of butter, and tea (weak and tepid) for
her. As an added aggravation the entrancing smell of bacon

seeped up the back stairway, with just a suggestion of well-toasted bread. Mrs. Carruthers's two male boarders were, respectively, her son and her nephew, and of course everyone understood that a gentleman needed sustenance in plenty to prepare him for the labors of the day.

A bun and tea for breakfast and nothing for lunch, since she had not kept the proper hours and Cook did—the table was bare by the time Hester returned. She wished she had courage enough to stop at one of the noisy street stalls to buy a mug of what was called coffee and a potato bursting out of its skin, needing only salt and butter to make it a feast. However, it seemed that the stalls were also refreshment centers for the male sex, and, independent though she had always deemed herself to be, Hester had not had the audacity to eat and drink right on the street with perhaps a goodly portion of London watching her.

What Hester would like from Dorry now was not food but clothes. Miss Scrimshaw had been very clear on the point that she should dress down for this assignment, for though Hester would be there under the guidance of Miss Scrimshaw's acquaintance, she could not mingle properly unless she was shabby—more shabby than ordinary. She knew by the time Miss Scrimshaw had finished with orders, advice, and the list Hester now held, that she was indeed about to enter a new world.

Dorry's street clothes, if that poor thing ever had an afternoon or evening off (which Hester doubted), might be a dress suitable for the darker side of London. Unfortunately, there was no possible way of obtaining the use of such. The very asking would create a storm as wild as one of the wintry blasts back home.

She was startled out of imagining just what Mrs. Carruthers would say if she heard of such a request when there was a tap at the door.

Her landlady stood outside, holding a square envelope, decorated by a blob of red sealing wax, between two pudgy fingers.

"Message for you, Miss Lane, sent around by hand—must be important."

"Thank you, Mrs. Carruthers." Hester accepted the envelope. Apparently Mrs. Carruthers's curiosity was one of her prominent character traits, for she was making no move to retire. There was no outer subscription except Hester's name—how tantalizing it must be. Hester's hand closed firmly on the doorknob. "Thank you, Mrs. Carruthers," she repeated in a slightly louder tone. With an offended sniff the landlady turned toward the stairs.

Hester, having been trained how to properly open an envelope, looked around in vain for a letter knife, then had to substitute a hairpin.

> Dear Miss Lane:
>
> If it is at all possible, can you wait upon me at the chambers of Utterson and Williams as soon as possible? Your information concerning Mr. Jekyll is of the utmost importance, or I would not make this request in so abrupt a manner.
>
> *Robert Guest*

Abrupt indeed, very near the border of open rudeness. Yes, Hester considered, there was a feeling of some disaster, that time itself was a matter of high importance. Who *was* Mr. Jekyll?

She turned up the one extravagance she had known her father to indulge in—the silver watch fastened to a twisted bowknot of the same metal that he had presented to her in a quite offhand manner some four years back, so that she might time the mail and make sure always that his pile of letters was ready to be collected at the village post office. It was slightly after two o'clock—she must be back here by four if she were to eat and then get dressed for her adventure of the evening. It depended upon just how far away these "chambers" were. In the Temple, of course, she had the address given in the advertisement to direct her.

Another tap at the door, or rather a hammering of knuckles

that was certainly not Mrs. Carruthers, even if that lady was as provoked as Hester believed her to be. She picked up the book inscribed with the name L. Jekyll, which she was bringing with her to show the solicitor, and caught up her damp coat again.

At another knock she opened to find Dorry.

"Please, mizz, she says there be a cab a-waitin' an' yah should know—" That was the longest sentence she had ever heard Dorry say, and the girl was already edging backward, ready to scuttle down the back stairs.

"Thank you—" But Dorry was gone, her badly cobbled boots pounding in her haste.

A cab sent—Hester hoped that meant sent and paid for. She had certainly received no funds in advance from Miss Scrimshaw.

As they rattled away through the growing fog, she shivered, drawing her coat closer about her in spite of its dampness. The inside of the cab smelt of horse, and also of what she thought must be a cigar. On her empty stomach the combination did not sit easily.

The journey seemed endless but of course it wasn't. They drew up before a door and a man in the decent blacks of a clerk handed her out, making some neutral comment on the weather. Londoners, and rightly, could always discuss the weather, there was so much of it—mostly unpleasant, Hester thought. But her greeter was paying the cab driver, so that small worry was assuaged.

She was ushered through a room with several desks, three of which were occupied by younger men dressed much as her escort, as far as she could tell by the light of candles. It would seem that even at this late date Utterson and Williams had made no change in their lighting.

Just before she reached the door at the other end it was opened, and the man standing within eyed her with a keenness that somehow fitted his sharp nose and his very correct tall cravat, which also hinted of earlier years.

"Mr. Guest?" she asked hesitatingly.

His thin-lipped mouth quivered a fraction, perhaps that was the best he could do for a welcoming smile.

"Ah, no, Miss Lane. I am Utterson. May I make you known to Inspector Newcomen?" He indicated a second man, also half hidden by the lack of proper lighting, though there was a lamp in Utterson's office.

If the man of law was as dried and blanched as his own parchments, this burly, wide-shouldered stranger, whose manners at their introduction moved him to no more than a nod of the head, suggested strength and a kind of obstinacy, with his square chin, weathered skin, and small eyes that never seemed still. They darted up and down her own figure now, Hester thought, like a pair of those black beetles that ran from the light at night if one had reason to go into the nether regions of a house.

Her own chin went up and she did not acknowledge that introduction at all, but spoke to Utterson with some of the strong reserve her father's daughter could use upon occasion.

"I was asked to meet with Mr. Robert Guest. He is not here?"

Utterson indicated the man who had escorted her in. "This is Mr. Guest. There was a very good reason for all our obtuseness, Miss Lane, as we are ready to explain. But pray, do sit down, and you must have some tea."

Somehow she found herself seated in a chair, a steaming cup at her hand, and beside it on the desk an ebony and silver biscuit box that seemed well filled. But she was certainly not to be so easily won as that! She looked straightly at Utterson, who had gone to the chair behind the desk and was now seated there, his fingertips together pushing in and out a little as he spoke.

"You surely understand, Miss Lane, that when an advertisement such as you made answer to is published in the paper, there are a great many people who will guess that it may mean something of value to the answerer. It is thought better therefore that another name be used to weed out such answers. Guest is partly involved in this matter and he suggested that his be the one."

Neither Guest nor the big man had seated themselves. Newcomen had edged along the wall a little, until he was almost beside the door, while the clerk had come to stand by his employer. She could understand Utterson's argument, of course. But there was something wrong—she thought that most of it stemmed from the big man, and she resolutely decided it better to ignore him entirely.

From under her coat she took the book she had wrapped in paper and then spoke to Mr. Utterson.

"As you know, my name is Hester Lane, I am from the province of Quebec in Canada. My father was Harrison Lane. He was not Canadian by birth, he was from England. But he never discussed the past with me. Being a scholar of independent means he spent most of his time in study, and he had me educated privately so that I could serve as his amanuensis. My mother died when I was a very small child."

She paused. Her throat felt dry and the tea scent tempted her. At that same moment Guest poured a like cup for his employer, who raised it and took a sip. The clerk did not serve the man by the door. Hester was overtempted, she drank thirstily and the warmth within her allayed some of her wariness.

"Also, his employment among his books precluded his having many acquaintances. We entertained no relatives. He never spoke of any and most of his correspondence concerned his research—"

"Which was on what subject, Miss Lane?"

"The nature of good and evil," she answered simply. "He was trying to prove that neither absolute good nor complete evil could exist."

Utterson had raised his cup again. But without drinking this time, he set it down abruptly so that china clinked alarmingly against china. "Good and evil . . ." he repeated.

"He had many discussions—with clergymen, with those

connected with the courts and the like." Hester continued. "Then he became ill and was confined to his bed for some months. After his death I found this on his bedside table. He was somehow very attached to this volume. I saw him hold it in his hands many times, but he would never let anyone else touch it. When I opened it I found this—" She slid the cover open to show the bookplate and the signature across it. "Placed in between the pages was the advertisement I answered."

Utterson held the book closer to the light. "Is this your father's signature?"

"It might once have been."

"How is it"—Newcomen took a forceful step forward—"that a daughter don't know her own father's handwriting, miss?"

Utterson's hand had gone up almost in protest but Hester answered quietly.

"My father did not have full use of his hands—that is why he had me trained to help him. He had had, when I was quite young, a very serious attack of rheumatism and suffered thereafter very much. His fingers were drawn up and he could not straighten them out enough to use a pen."

The solicitor had been leafing through the book, but when he reached the section near the back he gave an exclamation, held the volume very close to the lamp, and then picked up a letter opener. To Hester's surprise he worked the point of the opener between two of the pages, proving that they had been pasted down. There was a tear but at last he got it open and brought out a double-folded sheet of paper, which he spread open with care, displaying a second and smaller one inside. From these he returned to study the book itself and then spoke to Hester with a new, crisp note in his voice.

"You did not know of the presence of these, Miss—Miss Lane?" He stumbled in an odd fashion over her name and something about him made Hester suddenly even more wary.

"That book was my father's favorite, sir. It was in his

hands often, always by his side within reach, even when he was so ill. I do not read Greek—you will note that it is written in that tongue—and what my father wanted me to read to him he selected himself."

"Here now, what's all this?" Newcomen came away from his place at the door and made as if to grasp the two papers, but Utterson had planted one hand very firmly on them.

"This," he said, indicating the larger of the two, "is a marriage certificate signed by a Judge William Grafton. It states that he was present at the marriage of one Amy Durrant to Leonard Jekyll in the city of Montreal in the year 1865. It is also countersigned by a Forrest Wyman, vicar of St. Robert's Church of that same city.

"This"—he turned up the second piece of paper as if it were a card upon which rested a considerable wager—"is the baptismal certificate of Hester Durrant Jekyll, dated November twentieth of the year 1867—"

"My birthday!" said Hester before she thought.

"So." The big man swung halfway around so that he could see her the plainer in the subdued light. "Maybe you ain't Miss Lane—Jekyll is a name we have an interest in hereabouts. When did the doctor decide to send you here, miss? Nice neat plan—goes into hiding when his friend dies, waits a goodish spell till he thinks it's all forgot, and then makes a play-acting business of it! Where did you really come from, Miss Whateveryernamebe?"

Hester looked from that big rough face to that of the solicitor and back again. She had no idea what was going on—her head felt light. "Sir, I have never used any name save that of Lane. To my knowledge that was my father's and the one I had a right to. It is true that my mother was Amy Durrant. She died very young and I have no true memory of her. My father, as I have said, lived a very retired life, something he also asked of me.

"Upon his death I discovered that we had lived entirely on the payments of an annuity that he had purchased the year my mother died. He left nothing but the house and his library, which I was forced to sell in order to pay a few remaining debts—"

"What about the doctor? No money from him, eh? Left his blood kin to go hungry? That's not the way I've heard that he did things. When did he meet you—and where? Went to Canada, eh? So that's why we couldn't find him to have a few words. And you knew it!" He almost roared that at Utterson. "Set it all up—advertisement in the paper . . . and young lady, poor orphan, come to get her rights and—"

Utterson pushed back a little from the desk, though he still kept his hand on the papers. "You forget yourself, Inspector," he said in an icy voice. "I am by profession an officer of the court, or did you not know that? There is nothing illegal about this matter. As for Miss Lane—Miss Jekyll here—I knew nothing of her existence until this afternoon."

"Ha!" The man Utterson addressed as "Inspector" made that one exclamation forceful enough to deny everything he had heard. "Where's the doctor?"

"I don't know any doctor," she said, fighting to keep her voice steady. "I came to England three months ago with Major Jeffrey Ames's daughter. She is only twelve and her mother died last year. The major could not arrange leave to bring her to her grandmother's—she is Lady Ames—so he hired me as her governess."

"And you are with Miss Ames now?" That was Utterson.

"I was there until last week, sir. But Lady Ames desired a governess with more experience of London life. She was able to find one and—"

"Turned you off clip and clean then, eh?" Newcomen nodded. "And the doctor, he had nothing to do with all this coming and going?"

"Sir, I do not know any doctor. As for my living, I have this very day been able to find a very pleasing and promising position with the magazine *The British Lady*. You may inquire of Miss Scrimshaw, the editor. I had written some things in

Canada and she was pleased to publish them a year or so
ago. Now, I must go." Somehow Hester found she was able
to stand up and put out her hand for the mistreated book and
the documents it had concealed. "Miss Scrimshaw has already given me an assignment to work on."

"My dear young lady." There was more warmth in Utterson's voice than she had heard previously. "There is good
reason to believe that you may be related to Dr. Jekyll," he
said, still holding the papers. "Unfortunately, the doctor disappeared some months ago under circumstances that are difficult to explain. Should our future discoveries prove to be of
an unpleasant kind"—he hesitated a moment—"Doctor
Jekyll would have wanted his estate to go to his kin."

"Was that blackguard Hyde kin then, too?" snorted the
other.

"Hyde!" Utterson's voice was cold. "Hyde was kin to the
devil. He certainly imposed on Jekyll shamefully. At least
the doctor was rid of him at last."

"Rid o' him? Mr. Utterson, none of us will be rid of that
one, dead or alive, until we get answers to a good peck of
questions." The inspector shook his head, but Utterson was
already speaking to Hester.

"Guest will get you a cab, Miss Jekyll. And you will hear
from us as to any progress in this sorry affair."

Her hand shook involuntarily as if to raise it in denial of
that strange name. One could not just be reborn—as it
were—so easily. But it could well be that Mr. Utterson was
wrong—even as much as he gave the impression of being
indeed a master of legality.

"My papers, if you please, sir."

He seemed almost reluctant to gather the notes into the
book, wrap the paper loosely around it, and hand it back to
her.

"Be very careful of those," he said.

"I will," she promised.

From now on, Hester told herself, she must be very careful indeed—perhaps of more than papers.

7

Once Hester was back in the cab, which luckily Guest had paid for, she fingered the paper-wrapped book, trying to remember everything that had been said in that lamplighted room.

The presence of the big man had come as a surprise; she had not expected to be talking to a police officer, and Inspector Newcomen's manner and questions were rude and impertinent. But it was Mr. Utterson who most deeply disturbed her.

What troubled Hester most was his revelation regarding her father's name. Could it possibly be true? If so, then at some point her father and this mysterious Dr. Jekyll had colluded in a conspiracy of silence.

Most disturbing of all, of course, was the question of her own identity. Nor did the problem end there. If Hester Lane was indeed Hester Jekyll, she had inherited far more than a mere change of name this afternoon. There might be a legacy involved; unfortunately, however, there were other involvements as well. The most puzzling, and possibly perilous, was the question of where she stood with the police. Did they actually consider her an accomplice of Dr. Jekyll's in a scheme to plunder his own estate? Had that estate already been squandered away, and was Mr. Utterson anxious to establish her as a relative so that she might become responsible for its debts? Or worse still, an accessory to his disappearance, mayhap his death?

But she must not allow herself such thoughts. It was this sort of reasoning, this propensity for imagining the worst, that led to the secretiveness of her father, the bitter austerity of Mr. Utterson, the omnipresent hostility and suspicion of Inspector Newcomen. As for herself, whether Lane or Jekyll she was still Hester, and Hester she would remain. *This above all, to thine own self be true—*

Outside the fog was thick; passersby disappeared into its depths and vehicles vanished. Clutching the wrapped book and papers, Hester was tempted to hurl her parcel into the murk in hopes it too might be swallowed up without a trace.

But that would solve nothing in the end; the problems that had been posed would still remain, and right now it was time for other considerations. The events of the afternoon had definitely dashed hopes of a possible immediate inheritance. Under the circumstances it was much more practical for her to take heed of Miss Scrimshaw's instructions for the evening listed in the note she'd sent round. Pleasing an editor would provide a present source of income; heeding the summons of a solicitor had only resulted in a gratis cab ride.

Hester sat back. Somewhat to her surprise, she found that she was shivering. Tonight's plans would definitely call for warmer apparel. And had she not promised herself to execute Miss Scrimshaw's orders she would thankfully content herself with the cold comfort of her room.

Luckily she did return in time for high tea, which was

offered on the massive dining room table. Since this was a meal her landlady shared, there was no skimping. Even the tea itself was of better quality than the one Dorry fetched in the morning. Hester's main difficulty was avoiding direct answers to Mrs. Carruthers's indirect questions regarding where she had been this afternoon.

Hester finally escaped that inquisition but she was well aware she had left Mrs. Carruthers dissatisfied, and there might come a time, not too far in the future, when it would be necessary for her to find other quarters. The problem she faced now was not getting out of the house, for Mrs. Carruthers's nephew had not yet returned. But the landlady would surely have the door locked after he did, and to awaken the house later would provide the last touch to making sure she would be out of a room.

She hurriedly changed into her oldest and shabbiest dress. The macintosh and hat must be discarded for a shawl. She unpinned her watch regretfully and refastened it within the folds of the shawl, determined to have a means of keeping an eye on the time.

Luck was not with her. She had heard no step in the hall but when she eased open her bedroom door there was Mrs. Carruthers, lamp in hand. The stout woman paused, her eyes narrowed as she looked at Hester in her improvised disguise.

"Miss Lane! Where in the world can you be off to at this hour? And in those clothes?" Her expression was that of one who has discovered the worst at last.

Hester's imagination awoke quickly. "I am going to a special meeting at St. Robert's, Mrs. Carruthers. Mrs. Arthur, the vicar's sister, wishes the two of us to call upon a distressed gentlewoman who is in very unhappy circumstances. She suggested we adapt clothing that might not be marked in that neighborhood."

"What can Mrs. Arthur be thinking of? Surely any such visit must be made at least in daylight!"

"The lady in question is employed during the day and cannot receive us," Hester returned glibly. "I was asked because the lady has lived in Canada and it was thought I might know of some help she could receive from there."

I should be writing novels, she thought. At least Mrs. Carruthers was drawing aside. *Dare I ask her for a key? No, that might be going too far.* She hurried down the flight of stairs and let herself out.

The fog that had earlier blanketed the street was still there. It seemed to muffle all noise. Hester hesitated. She had the address pinned in her shawl and had memorized the directions Miss Scrimshaw had given her, but now that she was alone and the shrouded night was around her, she felt a very strong inclination to return to the safety of the house.

She cried out as something a great deal thicker than a shadow materialized at her side.

"Miss Lane? It's me—Fred."

Fred? Who was Fred? Then she remembered the crossing sweeper to whom Hazel had sent the small gift. She was unable to see his face clearly because a broken-brimmed hat, much too large for his head, was pulled down to perch precariously on his ears. For the rest he seemed to be a bundle of clothing rolled and tied and yet walking.

"Th' cap'n says as 'ow yuh wants ter come see 'er—"

"Captain Ellison, of the Salvation Army?"

"That's wot I said, warn't it?" Fred's hat brim slid back and forth against his forehead as he nodded.

Hester stared at him, puzzled. "I thought you were a sweeper. What would you have to do with the captain?"

"Errands an' odd jobs mostly, to earn me keep. Some nights I doss at a Army shelter."

"But how did Captain Ellison know where to find me?"

"Some 'un name o' Scrimshaw sent round the address. Says to come fetch yer." Feet shifted beneath the base of the bundle. "Dassent to ring, an' fair froze waitin', so let's get on wiv it, eh, miss?"

A portion of the bundle detached itself to become an arm, and a hand closed firmly on the edge of Hester's shawl, urging her away from what little light existed about the lamp on the street and leading her into the opening of a side alley.

"Beggin' yer pardon, miss," said the urchin. "But I knows alleys best. Shorter way to go, an' safer, too."

Hester was always to remember that journey, through a London she had been warned existed but had not quite believed in, as a descent into darkness and horror. Streetlights were visible only momentarily when they emerged from an alley and crossed a thoroughfare to enter another. Yet Fred wove his way through the maze without pause, gripping a corner of her shawl to guide her forward.

Only occasionally did she glimpse a dim flicker of candlelight from a window in one of the buildings bulking blackly on both sides of an alleyway. The smells were gagging and the pavement underfoot slippery from sources she did not wish to know. And at no point along this route did they encounter a vehicle, or a passerby on foot, except when moving across a street that intersected their way.

At length they deserted a final narrow passageway, turning to the right on the street beyond. It was slightly wider than an alley, a trifle less odiferous; lanterns hung over several doors and there were people moving about. But what Hester saw and heard brought budding fear.

Her first impression was of beery brutes and frowsy women staggering in groups or stumbling singly past other figures crouched or huddled against doorways. Raucous voices shouted out words she did not understand as two of the women suddenly sprang at each other, fingers crooked, tearing for hair and face. Screeching and clawing, they were swiftly surrounded by a crowd urging them on.

Animals, Hester thought to herself, they're like wild beasts. But then, glancing at them apprehensively as Fred tugged at her shawl, initial impressions gave way to further reflection.

Animals do not wrap themselves in rags, nor do wild beasts willingly choose to dwell in mean and confined quarters. A closer glimpse of the crowd encircling the combatants disclosed more than faces rendered bestial with excitement. Some were scarred, savaged by disease or pitted with pox, some seamed with the wrinkles of premature aging; all were either unnaturally ruddy and flushed with the effects of drink or else sallow with the pallor of poverty.

For the first time Hester truly understood Miss Scrimshaw's sentiments concerning the London poor and the squalor in which they dwelt. She had been correct in her description, but this alone was no substitute for the sights and sounds—and smells—that one encountered here. To properly retranslate the actuality into words again would be an impossibility, but worth the try. And it was only this resolution that sustained her against the impulse to turn and flee from tumult and terrors.

Releasing his grasp on her shawl, Fred sidled along a building that seemed to be exuding a thick slime from several points on its wall. Hester followed, keeping close to his heels. Luckily they had reached an area beyond the clamor of the fight when Fred turned and rapped on a door so much a part of the wall that Hester had hardly noticed it.

The door opened promptly and Hester was thankful for the light of several candles beyond as she stepped inside to confront the figure standing in the shadow of the doorway.

"Got 'er," Fred said, pointing a grimed hand in her direction. Then he was gone through another door before Hester could move.

The woman facing her was tall, broad shouldered, with the alert posture of a person who got things done and was brisk about it. She wore a plain dark dress with no hint of flounce or bustle, and her gray-streaked hair was mostly covered by a bonnet that had something of the same authority of a nurse's cap. Her eyes seemed tired but there was no droop to her wide mouth as she spoke.

"Miss Lane, I am Captain Ellison of the Salvation Army. And we are most glad to see you."

Hester glanced down self-consciously at her shabby garments. "Please excuse my appearance—"

"There is no necessity to apologize. It was I who suggested Miss Scrimshaw instruct you to dress so as to be inconspicuous during your journey here. And she has earned our gratitude for nding you. To tell our side of the story will be a novelty."

Her voice was cultivated, though there was no affectation in tone or manner and her openness of expression appealed to Hester strongly. She had not expected such ladylike demeanor from those in the ranks of the Salvation Army.

"Tell me, Miss Lane, how much do you know of our work here?"

"Very little, I must admit. I hoped you might be able to provide me with some information regarding the Salvation Army's history and purpose."

Captain Ellison nodded. "And so I shall." Turning, she moved to a hall table on which rested a bundle with the border dimensions of a folded newspaper, although considerably thicker. The parcel, wrapped in brown paper secured by string, was also much heavier than it appeared, as Hester discovered when the captain handed it to her.

"Here is some literature that should help," she said. "There is more available at headquarters, but I made do with what could be gathered at such short notice. At least it may supply you with a basic account of the Army's history.

"As to our purposes, they are twofold. While General Booth's primary aim was ministering to spiritual welfare, physical welfare is of equal concern. Total salvation embraces both body and soul." Captain Ellison paused momentarily, her wide mouth curving into the crescent of a self-conscious smile. "Forgive me, Miss Lane. I fear I've been preaching at you."

"Not at all. I find what you say most interesting."

"What I say is of little consequence. It's what you see that's important. Or, rather, what you *will* be seeing."

Hester shifted the paper-wrapped package to the crook of her left arm. "Miss Scrimshaw's note mentioned a meeting."

The captain shook her head. "Nothing quite so pretentious—merely one of our regular street gatherings. There will be a formal assembly at headquarters before week's end, but it seemed best to introduce you to our activities by way of a simpler example." As she spoke Captain Ellison glanced down at Hester's footwear. "You have come quite a way, I know. Could I impose upon you to accompany me a short distance further?"

"By all means."

"Then let us be off."

Taking a shawl from a rack in the corner between the wall and the threshold, the captain drew it over her shoulders, then opened the door.

Prepared as she was by her previous experience, Hester steeled herself against the onrush of sights, sounds, and smells surrounding her upon emerging again onto the street.

A quick glance to her left indicated that the battling viragoes had vanished and their impromptu audience was dispersed, but her companion did not lead her in that direction. Instead, after turning her door key and removing it from the latch, she beckoned to Hester and moved off to the right.

Here lighted doorways were less frequently in view. Captain Ellison's eyes may have indicated fatigue when exposed to lamplight, but in the darkness she possessed the visual acuity of a cat. At least so it seemed to Hester as her guide nimbly dodged around reeking piles of refuse heaped against the walls or littered to block their way along the pavement.

But the moldering mounds of rubbish and offal were not the only obstacles in their paths. Earlier this evening Hester had noted sleeping figures curled in doorways and slumped in recesses along the walls. Here amidst the deeper darkness similar figures sprawled at random on the street itself. The garbage of humanity? Or merely the fallen in an outcast army?

Those who walked, reeled, or lurched past them paid no heed; they addressed one another, or the empty air, with slurred sallies, muttered oaths, coarse laughter, and snatches of drunken song. Men stumbled after women, women stumbled after men, men and women stumbled together.

Shadows scattered along the walls on either side of the street or darted low between recumbent and upright figures alike—shadows of children, shrieking and chanting in shrill echo of their elders.

Now Hester realized what Captain Ellison had meant about the importance of seeing instead of saying. As if in confirmation of the unspoken thought, her companion nodded.

"Allow me to explain the lack of a conveyance, Miss Lane. While a cab would be more comfortable I am persuaded that what you are observing at close hand speaks far more eloquently than any sermon."

Hester nodded. "There is so much for me to learn."

"You'll find facts and figures aplenty in the material I assembled for you. Hard facts and hard figures, appropriate to the conditions they represent. But life here is a hardening experience. One learns to endure the sight of human suffering."

"And yet Fred told me that you allow him to take shelter in your home."

Was it a trick of light and shadow or did Captain Ellison's cheeks betray a blush of embarrassment? "I acknowledge young Fred represents a chink in my armor," she said. "Still, he makes himself useful."

As they approached an intersection ahead, the way grew brighter, and from the crossing came sounds of the passing traffic's clop and clatter, the buzz of voices raised in excitement. Then, drowning out all else, the booming beat of a bass drum.

"Just in time," the captain murmured.

She rounded the corner and Hester followed, blinking involuntarily amidst the sudden blaze of light framing the gaudy façade of the public house just to the right. A row of carriages had halted to line the curb and a crowd massed and milled on the walk at both sides of the garrishly lit entrance to the grogshop.

Within the circle cleared before it Hester heard the boom of the drum and then, as if in celebration of their arrival, trumpets blared, cornets chorused, a trombone sounded in unison with the wheezing of a concertina.

"The band is here!" Captain Ellison's voice rose exultantly over the drumbeat and its accompaniment, but her announcement was unnecessary.

Hester's eyes searched the circle. So *this* was what the Salvation Army looked like! The bandsmen in their military jackets of red twill, their bespectacled leader holding a violin under his left arm and conducting the music with a bow held in his right. And, grouped behind them, men wearing military caps and uniforms of blue guernsey; women clad in blue jerseys, their black straw bonnets trimmed with black silk.

Once again Hester's companion seemed to read her mind. "I am not assigned to duty this evening," the captain said. "Hence no uniform. Although I could not forgo the bonnet." She smiled, nodding toward the musicians. "I trust you understand what is taking place here."

"You told me there would be a gathering," Hester said, hoping she was making her voice heard above the boom and blare. "But I didn't expect a brass band."

"The band was General Booth's idea. Music attracts the crowd, many will stay to hear the hymns, and it is to be hoped that a goodly share will remain for the preaching that follows. Each night a score or more of street gatherings are held throughout the city—skirmishes, you might say, in an unceasing battle against the evils of drink."

If she intended to say more, the possibility was precluded

by the voices rising to augment instrumental accompaniment. Hester thought she recognized the hymn as "Who'll Be the First to Follow Jesus?" but she could not be sure. At this distance words not drowned out by music were lost in the tinkling and tapping of timbrels carried by most of the chorus.

Timbrels? From some recess of memory, perhaps a newspaper account of an American minstrel show, Hester recalled that timbrels were now generally referred to as "tambourines." She turned to ask her companion, but it was then that the shrill shout rose.

"Cap'n! Cap'n! Come quick!"

Even above the stridency of sound Fred's voice was clearly recognizable, as was the face beneath the broken brim of his hat.

Captain Ellison stared down at the panting urchin. "Do restrain yourself, Fred! What is this all about?"

"Sallie Morton. The one as was knocked about so terrible by 'er dad."

The captain nodded. "I sent her to stay with Mrs. Kirby this afternoon. You know that, Fred."

"So does 'er father. Passed 'im wiv 'is mates down the street, proper boozed up, all of 'em. Figgered to find you 'ere at the meetin' so I come runnin' quick as I 'eard."

"What did you hear?"

"'E's on 'is way to fetch Sallie from there right now. Says she's worth ten quid if 'e sells 'er to the slavers!"

chapter

8

They set off quickly, and soon the music and voices faded, the boom of the drum lost amidst the thudding of their feet upon the pavement.

Twice they turned, Fred in the lead, Captain Ellison lifting her skirt as she strove to keep pace with him, Hester clutching the paper-wrapped parcel tightly against her bosom. Except for the sound of their footsteps, they moved in silence; Hester had no breath to spare for questions, nor Captain Ellison for answers. Clamping hat to head, Fred darted forward swiftly and gave Hester scant opportunity to note the details of their surroundings.

From what she did observe, however, these streets were dissimilar to the ones earlier traversed. Here the hovering hulk of tenements was replaced by rows of cottages and small well-lit houses; she noted little odor and a scarcity of litter. Save for themselves there were no other figures, either upright or recumbent, visible along their way. A respectable neighborhood, Hester told herself.

But their progress was hasty and so was her conclusion. As they turned a final corner respectability vanished, driven from the scene by the sound of oaths, imprecations, and a banging that echoed as loudly as the booming of the Army drum.

Weaving back and forth on the stoop before the front entrance to a house directly ahead, a mountain of a man, his face ruddy with rage, pounded on the door with percussive fists. Behind him on the walk below two companions shouted and gesticulated, urging him on.

"'Ave at it!" cried the mustached man wearing a leather apron.

"Teach 'er to mind 'er manners," the other man advised. "Bash it down!"

Fred halted abruptly, his words emerging in gasps as he jabbed a stubby finger in the direction of the trio. "Like I told yer—Sid Morton an' 'is mates."

Captain Ellison nodded, then turned to address Hester. "Wait here," she said.

"What are you going to do?"

"Stop them, of course."

"But you can't," Hester murmured. "They're too far gone in drink—they won't listen to you."

"Then they must listen to the Lord."

Hester took a step forward. "I'll come with you."

"That would be most inadvisable." The captain nodded toward Fred. "Please see to it that Miss Lane remains here. I charge you with her safety."

"Done." As the older woman moved away, the youngster captured the lower left portion of Hester's shawl in a grimy grip. "'Ave a care," he called.

If Captain Ellison heard she did not heed. Crossing the pavement to the opposite side, she marched directly to the two men reeling on the walk. Both the one wearing the apron and his coster-clad companion turned at her approach.

"What cheer?" mumbled the costermonger. Striding past, the captain ignored him, but the man with the mustache lumbered forward to bar her way.

"Where yuh fink yer goin'?" His bleary blink fixed on her headgear, then widened into a stare of sudden recognition. "Hallelujah bonnet!" he muttered. "Yer from the bloody Army!"

Now his mutter mounted into a shout as he called out to the man pounding on the front door. "Company comin', Sid!"

Fists ceased to hammer as the big man turned, staring down from the stoop. When his red-rimmed eyes focused on the woman below, his stare became a glare.

"'Oo the 'ell are you?"

"Captain Ellison of the Salvation Army." She peered up at the burly figure. "Are you Mr. Morton?"

"Jus' plain 'Sid' will do me. Naht to say it's any o' yer bloody business."

Beside her his mates greeted Morton's response with alcoholic appreciation, but the captain didn't share their laughter. "I fear it is my business," she replied. "You are committing a public disturbance on private property. I happen to know that this is the residence of Mrs. Gertrude Kirby."

"Is it, now?" The big man put his hands on his hips. "An' I 'appens ter know Mrs.-bloody-Kirby 'as me daughrter Sallie 'id away someplace inside."

"I assure you Sallie will come to no harm in her care." The captain's voice was level. "Indeed, she was taken into custody to ensure her safety."

"Never you mind 'er safety!" The big man's hands left his hips and balled into fists. "I'm 'er father. I 'ave me rights."

"The right to abuse her body? The right to sell her in white slavery?"

"Yer a bloody liar!" Now the glaring eyes were directed at the figures of Sid Morton's companions. "'Oo's been blabbin'?"

Both of his mates shook their heads in vigorous denial.

As Hester watched she was conscious that other heads were present, silhouetted against the light as they peered from the windows and doorways of dwellings surrounding the Kirby home. But while others watched, none ventured to move. It was only Captain Ellison who started forward.

"For the last time," she said, "I demand that you desist."

"Demand, is it?" As the bonneted woman started to mount the stoop, the big man's fists rose. "Stand clear 'o me, yah bleedin' cow!"

For a moment it seemed to Hester that time stood still and that what she perceived was a picture fixed forever within its frame. Now she noted particulars that had escaped previous attention; although drapes had been drawn, those covering the first-story windows above were slightly parted, so as to reveal the presence of watchers within. Hester had a fleeting impression of eyes widened in terror, half-opened mouths ovaled in anxiety. At the same instant she was conscious of color; the play of light and shadow against the burly man's contorted countenance, the raw redness of his knuckled fist upraised to strike.

Then, as suddenly as it had come, the moment passed, and the fist started to descend. Now everything was happening at once as though time moved at a gallop in compensation for its momentary standstill.

The fist swung down, Captain Ellison swerved to dodge the blow, Hester tore free of Fred's restraining grasp. The big man bawled a curse, Captain Ellison stood her ground, and ignoring Fred's frantic cry of warning, Hester ran forward across the pavement.

Again the captain moved, but not in time to avoid the glancing impact of the fist, which sent her reeling back, bonnet askew. A growl emerged from deep within Sid Morton's throat, the growl of a beast aroused by the sight of blood. He

started down the steps, right arm rising to swing and strike
again.

Captain Ellison neither fled nor flinched, but her lips
moved in a murmur. "May the Lord have mercy—"

Whatever the Lord's intentions may have been, Hester
felt no mercy in her heart. But there was strength in her
stride as she came abreast of the captain, strength in her own
arm as she raised it, gripping the wrapped parcel to strike the
big man across the side of his face.

His grimace and outcry were more the product of astonishment than of pain. "Scuzzy slut!" He started forward again,
both fists balled. "I'll learn yeh—"

But his words were scarcely audible amidst the sudden
surge of sound from opposite ends of the street beyond;
hooves from the right, running footsteps from the left. The
latter was by far the louder, and now the big man's mates
sought and saw its source.

"Run fer it, Sid!" the coster shouted. "'Ere come the
rozzers!"

Turning to the right, he set a good example that his
leather-aproned companion lost no time in following. Sid
Morton hesitated, head cocked left. The thud of feet grew
louder as a half-dozen uniformed City constables appeared,
helmets bobbing as they ran.

Sid Morton too invoked the Lord. "Jesus!" he muttered.
Without so much as a further glance at the two women, he
darted after his chums.

Hester moved to Captain Ellison's side, peering at her so-
licitously. "Has he hurt you?"

"No harm done." The captain adjusted her bonnet. Her
lips moved but Hester heard no sound.

Then a hand closed about her left arm.

Surprised at the touch, Hester was even more startled as
she glanced up into the face of Albert Prothore.

His lips too were moving, and now she heard as he tipped
his hat to Captain Ellison and addressed her.

"I am taking Miss Lane to her lodgings," he said. "If you wish to be escorted elsewhere—"

The captain shook her head. "No, thank you. I shall be quite all right." She turned, light fanning her from the doorway, which was opening above and behind her. "You see? We'll be admitted to the house now that the bullies are gone." She started forward. "Perhaps you'd join me—"

Hester's lips parted, but before she could reply, her unexpected companion spoke for her. "I'm sorry. The cab is waiting."

Albert Prothore's grip was surprisingly strong; it tightened as he swung Hester around and guided her toward the hansom at the curb.

Now she understood why she had heard hoofbeats; what she did not understand was the reason for young Mr. Prothore's timely appearance.

There was no opportunity to reflect upon it at the moment. Prothore bustled her quickly into the cab, shouted to the cabby, then climbed in and closed the door as they started off. Hester had only time for a hasty glance as they pulled away, assuring herself that Captain Ellison had entered the house, its door closing behind her.

Down the street they overtook and passed the flying squad of constabulary, but Prothore paid them no heed. His attention was directed toward her, and when the sound of pounding feet diminished in the distance he was the first to speak.

"Allow me to apologize, Miss Lane. My arrival was delayed by the necessity of circling back from the far corner where the gathering took place, and then determining which of the various routes of departure you and your companions might have chosen."

Then he knew she had been at the street meeting! But what was *he* doing there?

It was a question she dearly wished to broach; instead she

chose another. "You gave the cabby the address of my lodgings. May I ask where you obtained it?"

Even as she spoke the answer was apparent, and now, adjusting the somewhat battered bulk of the brown paper parcel on her lap, she voiced it. "Miss Scrimshaw, I suppose?"

"Your supposition is correct."

"Did she volunteer the information or did you ask?" She strove to make the query seem casual, but his reply would explain much.

"That is a matter of little moment," Prothore answered. "Enough to say I am relieved you left the meeting when you did. Had you remained, the consequences might have been highly unpleasant."

"What do you mean?"

"That squad of City constables you saw. Have you given thought to account for their appearance?"

Hester nodded. "I imagine some nearby resident summoned them to apprehend the miscreants attacking Mrs. Kirby's home."

"In that, I fear, you are quite mistaken. They were summoned, no doubt, but not by a neighbor. It would be the owner of that public house who sent round for them, and they were on their way to disperse the forces of Holy Willie."

"Who?"

"A popular nickname for William Booth, self-styled general of the Salvation Army."

It was the first time, Hester realized, that she had seen Albert Prothore smile. And she didn't care for the thought she sensed behind it. *I warned you to keep out of this*, his smile was saying. *I told you so.*

If she divined his thought correctly, there would be reason enough for the ebb of her sense of gratitude and its replacement by a rising tide of resentment.

Now the smile vanished, to be replaced by an equally unwelcome look of stern sobriety as he spoke in the tones of a lecturer. *Father's look. But he's not my father!*

Hester strove to keep her composure but the effort cost her distraction; only an occasional word registered clearly, though the import of the whole was unmistakable. He was pointing out to her in his supercilious way the folly in which she had been engaged—and that he required her solemn word she would abandon this "nonsense."

To make him cease his badgering she nodded at intervals. Perhaps he was right, inasmuch as she would not venture into any of those darkened ways at night again. But she would not forfeit her resolve to gather knowledge, to write such an article as would reveal what horrors lay waiting in the tangled, twisting lanes of a city esteemed the best in the civilized world.

If half of its dwellers were as blind and self-assured as this cold and conceited young man who finally handed her down at the door of her lodging house, she did not wonder that such horrors continued to exist.

And invade her dreams.

chapter

9

Hester awoke twice during the night and sat up in the icy cold of her room, looking to the door and half expecting that some of those ruffians like Morton would emerge from her dreams and burst their way in. It was still only faintly gray out when she settled herself tightly in the covers on her lumpy bed and tried to think in the sensible pattern on which she had always prided herself.

She accepted the fact that she could not write about the riot—and she had seen only a fraction of that. But there was another subject, one that any womanly hearted reader would understand.

Surely the story of Mrs. Kirby and Sallie would serve to demonstrate the message she determined to convey concerning the importance of the Army. Rescuing young girls from such brutes as Morton and his friends, teaching them a better way of life, finding them homes and work away from filth and danger—all could be told, must be told.

The only difficulty was that she didn't know enough. She would have to go back, find Captain Ellison, and obtain, through her, a proper introduction to Mrs. Kirby.

But how to traverse those hidden lanes and noisome streets, even in daylight, was the problem to be faced. She had had no way of learning the route there in last night's dark, and certainly she could not discover the address through Mr. Prothore—as if there were even any addresses in such kennels!

Suddenly Hester remembered the packet of material the captain had given her for reading. She had thrown it at Morton as a weapon, but she had a memory of—

Hester got out of bed and padded through the cold room to where the clothes she had worn during her adventure lay in a most unseemly huddle on the floor. For she had not hung away or smoothed anything as she got to bed the night before—her main anxiety at that time being not to attract the attention of Mrs. Carruthers.

Yes, she was right, there was a bundle of muddied papers thrust into the pocket of her skirt—where she had pushed them even as Prothore had whirled her up and away. The outer sheets were soggy and she peeled them free, throwing them into the fireplace where Dorry had not yet lit the scant fire.

There were two at the core that were still clean enough to be legible and those she eagerly spread out. Fortune certainly smiled upon her, as one dealt with the work for women and children. Hurriedly Hester ran a finger down one column of smudged print to the next. And, there it was: The Haven—Mrs. Kirby.

Hester hurried to the better light of the window, not stopping to light either candle or lamp, and read.

A haven, indeed. Girls from ten to fourteen—and sometimes younger—taken from homeless street wandering, protected from abusive parents, or orphans given shelter and a chance for the future. They were fed, clothed and housed, taught housekeeping, the use of the needle, simple cooking, and then placed as serving maids in safe and respectable houses. Not many could be so rescued, of course. Hester surmised that Mrs. Kirby could hardly have managed more than the scooping of a single drop from the sea of misery. But that it was being done at all surely was a beginning.

She found words coming into her head, the enthusiasm for writing a truly moving appeal combined with the explanation of what was being done. For such a goodly cause there must be backing to be found and backing could be raised by just such accounts as she was going to write. So, Mr. Prothore, we shall see, we shall certainly see!

Of course all she had to write could not be learned sec-ondhand from the leaflet. She must go back to that house, brave again what might lie in wait along those dreadful streets, meet with Mrs. Kirby, talk with the girls. Hester clapped the top closed on her inkwell, fitted her pen into the box, and sat for a moment considering ways and means of doing just that. Without Fred's guidance she would never find the way by herself. And to find Fred—he must have run at the appearance of the police—would be almost as impossi-ble.

The police . . . Hester considered them. But her meeting with Inspector Newcomen had sorely shaken her belief in the police, and Prothore's statement concerning their hostile connection with the Army was an added warning. No, she dared not ask aid from the police. There remained only the Army and she was still concerning over Captain Ellison.

Once more she went down the list of services that ap-peared on the crumpled leaflet, and there she discovered an address that seemed possible—that of a workroom set up where women could earn something of a living doing coarse sewing.

There was also a note mentioning that the workroom ac-cepted castoff clothing—anything that could be used to help provide for the completely indigent. She could appear there, perhaps as a lady's maid or housemaid, inquiring for her mistress's benefit just what donations were most needed . . . Hester nodded to herself. She drew her map of London from her shabby writing case and began to study it carefully, starting with the portion that she knew a little and striving to trace a way toward the address given in the leaflet.

She could take one of the horse buses; she would just have to use some of her sadly dwindling store of money for that purpose.

Money—she had faced the lack of it all her life. The household in Canada had been run sparsely and tightly on very small sums. But at least she had not had to worry about a home or enough plain food to keep her. What she had left was so very little! For one moment the memory of Mr. Utterson crossed her mind.

She could not think of herself as Miss Jekyll. Nor dare she weave any daydreams about a possible fortune, though she would settle right now for a very meager competence, perhaps to be reckoned only in shillings.

Miss Scrimshaw had not made any offers of payment in advance and Hester felt that the editor would look very much askance at any suggestion of such. No, she would have to gamble again on her own skill with the pen. Sighing, she separated a couple of small coins and forced herself to think that these would only be temporarily away from her purse.

What she had planned she determined to carry through. And so after what seemed to her a very lengthy journey she arrived at the decrepit old building that had been appropriated by the Army. The woman in the outer room wore the blue jersey and the black bonnet of the corps, but manifestly was of a far different type than the captain. Her speech was coarse in tone, far from Mrs. Ellison's cultured voice, but she smiled when Hester voiced her concern for the attack of the night before. After she asked about the captain the woman became very cordial.

"Yes, ma'am. She's right 'ere now. Come in." She switched open a panel of the counter behind which she had been standing and ushered Hester, past baskets and boxes heaped with tangles of what looked to be dirty and stained clothing, into an inner room.

Two long tables ran the length of the room. Benches on either side provided seating for a number of women, before each of whom was placed a mug and a chipped plate on which rested a bun. Their work had been laid to one side and the conversation was now rising louder by the moment.

Captain Ellison sat at the end of one table overseeing a pair of very large jugs from which arose steam and the smell of strong tea. She glanced up as Hester came in. There was a pad of bandage on the captain's left temple and she did not wear her bonnet. However, when she saw the girl she smiled and arose hurriedly to cross the room.

"My dear Miss Lane!" Both of her hands reached out to seize Hester's. "Then we did not lose your interest after all. That was a most discouraging introduction to our work—"

Hester interrupted to ask about her hurt and was assured that it was really very well cared for. Then in a rush—for she had longed so all day to speak with someone about her plan she could no longer control herself—Hester explained what had brought her there.

Captain Ellison led her to the top of the table, and one of the seamstresses moved a little aside to give her room on the bench, another swiftly supplied a mug of the steaming tea.

To Hester's surprise the captain did not seem happily excited at her promise to write about Mrs. Kirby's establishment. Instead she hesitated for a long moment while Hester sipped the rapidly cooling tea, putting the mug down hurriedly, its bitterness very distasteful to her.

"My dear Miss Lane, what you propose has merit, but it must be handled carefully. Many of the stories of the girls Gertrude Kirby shelters would be unbelievable to the gently reared ladies who read *The British Lady*. I think you would be well advised to write generally and not attempt to use any real stories. On the other hand, Gertrude's shelter, while not officially connected with the Army, has done very much good and has already attracted support from some who would perhaps not have given it directly to us. We are not," she said, smiling a little lopsidedly because of the bandage, "greatly liked or even recognized for good in many quarters, you know. For example"—her smile was gone and instead there was a frown of righteous anger on her face—"the police—those who themselves do not or will not venture into sections where we go—are firmly against much we do—"

"Why?" demanded Hester.

"One of the worst curses for these people, one that sends a man and his family into the deepest degradation and poverty, is that of drink. Many of our Army are those who have managed to tear themselves free from that blackness and now fight to save others. There are on the other hand many in positions of authority, even high authority, in this country whose personal fortunes are founded on the selling of strong drink. They have no reason to wish that their incomes be lessened. We continue to fight, they continue to oppose us—first by inflaming those poor wretches who are already lost to drink. And, because they can wield influence in many places, also by the very force of the law, which is intended for the protection of all. Major Wenthly is even now showing the secretary of a member of Parliament just how we are in battle. Unfortunately, the whole of our difficulties cannot be made plain during one short visit and those who come are sometimes already prejudiced against us. It is the thinking of such visitors that is reflected often in the public print. And even a suggestion of some of the other problems we face are never spoken about in the world the readers of *The British Lady* inhabit."

"But surely the work with the girls . . ." Hester was completely amazed at such a warning.

"Yes, that is of great value. And if you handle your story well, Miss Lane, you might even attract some patrons for Mrs. Kirby's work. But do not associate your account too strongly with the Army. Now, you wish to visit with Mrs. Kirby and meet her girls. That can be arranged. Mattie—"

She raised her voice and one of the seamstresses at the end of the table arose and bobbed her capped head in answer.

"This lady is to meet with Mrs. Kirby. Will you go with her and show the way?"

Then she spoke in a lower voice. "Do not be dismayed at what you see. Poor Mattie was very badly injured when she came to us and she was with Mrs. Kirby several months recovering from her wounds. She is a little simple because of what has been done to her but teachable in some ways, and she is very timid except when she knows you well. We try to aid her by giving her work here and trusting her in small errands. Come, Mattie!" She raised her voice again to call to the girl, who was lingering, her head down. One of her neighbors at the table reached out and patted her arm, then grasped it firmly and turned the girl toward the head of the table, which she approached as one who dreaded what she would face there.

Even having been warned, Hester was barely able to suppress a gasp as she saw the scarred face beneath the edging of the cap that had been pulled forward as far as possible in a vain attempt to hide the battered features.

Without a word Mattie pulled a shawl from one of those hanging on pegs driven into the wall and stood waiting by the door, her face averted, for Hester to join her. Uncomfortable, fearing that maybe her horror had shown, Hester forced a smile as they went out together.

"It is very kind of you, Mattie, to take me to Mrs. Kirby's—"

The capped head did not turn and there was only a very faint murmur from the girl. But Hester refused to be so rebuffed.

"I have heard many good things of Mrs. Kirby . . ." Perhaps she could even add something to her knowledge by learning from one of the girls who had benefited from this help earlier.

This time there was an understandable answer. "She is a saint—one o' them angels as them back there"—she twitched her shoulder to indicate the building from which they had come—"says as there is. Nursed me her ownself so she did, miss. Not many as would'a even looked at me, so nasty-lookin' as I were. I'd do anythin' for her—so I would." She even raised her bowed head to look Hester straight in the face.

"Me—I'se a proper one, now ain't I? Carved me up good, Jed did, jus' as 'e swore 'e would if I didn't go wi' that there devil. But I couldna, 'deed I couldna, miss. 'E were bad—we's all bad in someway or t'other. But 'e was black bad an' I couldna let 'im take me. 'Eard tell as 'ow someone did for 'im good not long ago—that was a proper end, so it was!" Her voice was raised as she spoke and she ended with a flare of anger.

Mattie turned her head sharply away and there was something now that kept Hester from trying to get her to talk further. As it happened their walk was not a long one. But despite the weak sun, which reached these streets as if it grudged the need for touching into such shadows, the dilapidated buildings and the lounging men, the wan-faced children who played listlessly about gutters full of foulness, were daunting, and Hester had to fight the tendrils of fear that reached for her. If Mr. Prothore could see her . . . Hester's chin went up. She identified him with the investigator Captain Ellison had mentioned; both were on the side of that aloof authority able to brutalize people below their own lofty stations.

When they reached the drab street that she was familiar with from the other evening, the house to which Mattie led the way stood out sharply from its neighbors. The roof showed fresh patching, the windows were clean, and behind them hung fresh curtains. The sills and the door had been

painted not too long ago and the scrap of yard before it,
though mainly beaten earth, also gave rootage to some small
scrubs, which dared to display green, if soot-spotted, leaves.

Even the knocker on the door must have been freshly polished, for the sunlight glinted on it brightly as Hester raised
a hand to use it. But she needed not complete that gesture
for the door was opened quickly and a girl in a trim dress of
blue, warm chestnut hair braided and coiled around her
head, stood smiling.

"Come in, miss— Oh, Mattie—you, too. We'se got bun
tea in the kitchen and there's aplenty. Come on with you!"

She stepped aside into the hall and motioned to Hester.
"Mrs. Kirby, she's in the parlor, miss. Jus' step this way,
please."

The girl could not have been much older than Major
Ames's daughter but she had an assurance that was in no way
impertinent, merely that of one who knew her duties and
found satisfaction in them. Then the parlor door closed between them and Hester found herself facing the mistress of
the establishment.

Mrs. Kirby, staid as her dress and unusual as her chosen
work, was unmistakably a lady. Her parlor could not be compared with the splendid setting that Lady Ames used to her
advantage, but there was no doubt they were of the same
class, as different otherwise as they might be.

She was slightly taller than Hester and her figure was ma-
tronly. Though she made no pretense of anything approaching the realm of fashionable dress, her black basque was
relieved with a narrow ruffled collar of fine old lace fastened
by a jet brooch. She wore a small apron over her skirt, the
drapery of which hung in no-nonsense folds, having nothing
but a very narrow ruching of the same material as trimming.
But it was not the apron of one who had just put aside some
demanding task, rather it too was of fine muslin edged with
lace.

Her hair was dark and dressed very simply, though on her

temples and across her forehead small wisps suggested that it was naturally curly. Her face was plump and she was smiling, dark eyes regarding Hester with what the girl recognized was a shrewd and weighing gaze.

Now she held out her hand and said: "My dear, Emily sent me a note to tell me about you—but I feared we would not see you after the terrible events of last night! That you have come assures me you are indeed interested in what we strive to do. And, my dear Miss Lane, any help is so welcome. Come now, sit here with me and then . . . you will ask questions, will you not? I know so little of what your task involves. Be assured that I shall answer them to the very best of my ability."

Hester found herself in a plumply upholstered chair before the fire, her hostess half facing her. There was a knock at the door and the girl who had met her at the door entered with a tray. She walked very carefully, and Hester noted the tip of her small tongue just showed on her lower lip as if she were engaged in some task she was not quite sure of but wished to accomplish with success.

As she placed her burden on the small table by Mrs. Kirby's side Hester was certain she heard a sigh of relief. However, her hostess was inspecting the tray with what seemed an oddly critical glance and then she nodded.

"Excellent, Sallie—very well done."

Sallie beamed and bobbed a small curtsy and then left the room. As the door closed firmly behind her Mrs. Kirby spoke.

"Sallie will be one of our great successes. She is very bright and quick to learn and has amply repaid all the instructions we provide. There will be no trouble in finding her a good place in a month or two. In fact, I have one already in mind. But you would not believe, Miss Lane, that this could be the same girl who was brought to me two months ago. She had been badly beaten"—Mrs. Kirby's eyes flashed—"and they had given her gin until she was sodden drunk. It is unbelievable how some of these wretches use their own children!"

"Captain Ellison told me about Mattie . . ." Hester ventured.

A shadow fell across Mrs. Kirby's face. "Yes, yes, that poor child. She has been so abused that she is hardly more than half-witted. I could find no place for her. But she is fairly good at plain sewing and she feels safe in the company of Captain Ellison and those who run that small industry. She has food, and clothing, a safe place to stay, and work for her hands. In that much we have changed her lot for the better. But her case was one of the worst I have seen . . . Tea, Miss Lane?"

Her hands had been busy with pot and cup and saucer—it was perhaps not the fine china one would find under Lady Ames's roof but it had a flower-sprigged daintiness that would not be out of place in any respectable household. Mrs. Kirby must have been very acute to catch the glance Hester gave to the tray, the plate of nicely sliced bread and butter, the offering of small cakes.

"This is all part of the training for our girls," she explained. "They must get used to things of a standard different from any they have seen or thought existed. You see how Sallie has set up the tray? She did it on her own with no supervision this time. And it has been very well done. Josie, who is training for a kitchen maid, cut this bread and baked the cakes this morning. She too is going to be one of our successes, though she is not as bright and quick as Sallie. And there is Violet, who looks after the younger girls—she will turn out to be an excellent nursery maid. We can well be proud of them."

"And they are all . . . from the streets?" Hester found it hard to connect Mrs. Kirby's girls with those she had seen outside.

"Every one of them! Josie now—" Mrs. Kirby launched into a story that to Hester sounded impossible, as if she were spinning some nightmarish tale meant as a dire warning, as a nurse might do for a naughty child.

Hester had groped for the small notebook and pencil she had thoughtfully brought along in her reticule, but she discovered that the facts as they fell from Mrs. Kirby's lips were so dark that she had trouble setting them down. The woman must have noted her distress for she interrupted herself.

"I speak frankly, Miss Lane, perhaps too frankly. You are young and not of London, I have heard. Perhaps in your homeland there is not such want, such evil to be known. But I have so long worked with these poor girls that my indignation, no, my anger, sometimes leads me into speaking more plainly than I should."

Hester remembered the warning Captain Ellison had given her earlier—that perhaps some facts would be too strong for her readers. Now it seemed that Mrs. Kirby had come to the same point of view.

"The stories I have to tell, Miss Lane, are perhaps not for the eyes of the readers of *The British Lady*. It is best to show a brighter side, present our needs in a softer and more acceptable fashion. I am sorry that I became so carried away as to show you the darkest side of the lives of these girls. Let us turn to more cheerful matters—the first being what happens to girls such as Sallie and the rest after they have had a chance to better themselves and move into a sunlit world." And she talked of the teaching practiced in her establishment, of this graduate (as one might term them) or that who had gone forth to very acceptable positions. These young girls found that they could make their way as respectable workers able to hold up their heads with pride.

After Mrs. Kirby finished her stories, she showed Hester through the establishment. There were eight girls there now, and each showed a happy face as Mrs. Kirby complimented one after another on the work they readily showed to the visitor.

"If we could but attract some patrons," Mrs. Kirby said

with a little sigh when they had returned to the parlor. "There is a probability we could buy the house next door, give more girls a chance. Oh, we have some very kind and charitable people who remember us from time to time, but only three assist us regularly. Now that you have seen our life, Miss Lane, do you think you can show it to others by the aid of your pen?"

"Oh, yes!" Hester's eagerness had grown with every new project Mrs. Kirby had revealed. She could write such a story as would bring the patrons Mrs. Kirby needed—certainly she could.

And back in her boarding house, write she did. Perhaps this was far too long, she thought, troubled, as the sheets covered by the careful penmanship her father had demanded piled up. But also perhaps Miss Scrimshaw would find it of such importance that she would make two rather than one article of it.

Her lamp had to be trimmed when she finished and there were ink stains on her fingers, even one on her cheek where she had brushed aside a wandering wisp of hair. She looked at her watch—it was a quarter to twelve! Now she realized that her back ached and her fingers had so stiffened around her pen that she had to rub them. But the story was finished—all of it. And inside herself she was certain that it was the best thing she had ever written.

She was still certain of that the following morning when she gathered all her sheets of paper and folded them into an improvised envelope she tied carefully together. And she hardly waited to choke down her meager breakfast before she was off to the office of *The British Lady*.

Her manuscript was accepted with a gesture not far from disdain by the ruler of the outer office and she was waved to the bench while it was carried within. She waited, leaning forward in the hard seat. The first flare of the enthusiasm that had been with her ebbed as time passed. Then there was the sharp ping of the bell from the inner room. The woman at the outer desk answered it and reappeared to motion to Hester. She was smiling sourly as she watched the girl pass into Miss Scrimshaw's private sanctuary.

"So . . ." The editor of *The British Lady* had leaned back in her chair to stare at Hester as if the girl were as strange and unpleasant a sight as some Hester herself had seen on her ventures into that other London. The sheets she had brought in were no longer in a neat pile—several had been crumpled as with a very angry hand and at least two had been torn across. "What do you mean by bringing this—and expecting a respectable publication to even consider it?"

There was flaming anger in Miss Scrimshaw's voice. Her broad countenance was fast turning a dusky red and her eyes bored into Hester as though she were something as dirty as the street.

"Muck! Miss Scrimshaw's beringed hand turned into a fist and she brought it down with punishing vigor on the remains of the manuscript. "Filth!"

chapter 10

As Miss Scrimshaw's fist came down, Hester felt her temper rise.

Somehow she managed to control the level of her voice, but not the words that came unbidden from her tongue. "You call this muck? All I have set down is simple truth. If what I wrote is filth, it's because what I saw was filthy. I think it high time your readers' eyes were opened—"

Again Agatha Scrimshaw's fist slammed down on the desktop; this time as interruption rather than indictment.

"That's enough, gel!" Apparently her anger had ebbed as Hester's flowed, and she spoke firmly but without ill-temper. "D'ye take me for an utter fool? I'm far from blind to reality, and far more willing to face it than most. But it's my readers whose opinions I echo. One look at this rubbish and they'll call for their smelling salts; a second look and they'll cancel their subscriptions."

Hester leaned forward. "But at least they would be given the opportunity to see."

"And so might you, gel. An opportunity to see the inside of a British gaol."

"Surely you're not serious?"

"This is." Miss Scrimshaw tapped the tattered sheets on the desk before her. "The implication that Mr. Morton intended to sell his own daughter is highly distasteful. Worse still, since you possess and present no proof of this allegation, it could lead to a suit for libel."

"But gaol . . . ?"

"My apologies, Miss Lane. Since you speak our language, I tend to forget your foreign origin. But it would seem to me that even in the wilds of Canada the exploits of W. T. Stead would not be altogether unknown."

Hester shook her head. "I have never heard that name. Was he someone like Sallie Morton's father?"

For a moment there actually seemed to be a gleam of mirth in Agatha Scrimshaw's eyes; if so, it was quickly suppressed. "Quite the opposite. Mr. Stead was interested in buying, not selling."

"I understand. You are speaking of what they call a procurer."

"Stead was called far worse before they finished with him." Again the glint of mirth in Miss Scrimshaw's eyes, but there was no hint of it in her voice. "Actually, Stead was a member of my profession, the editor of the *Pall Mall Gazette*, no less. A highly successful journal, which, aided by proper puffery, he hoped might soar even higher. To this end he sought to prove his contention that a young girl, *virgo intacto*, could be purchased here in London for as little as five guineas.

"I shall spare you the sordid details; suffice to say that he made good on his word but only ill came from it in the end. Even the Booth family—yes, I speak of the Salvation Army leadership—became involved in the lawsuit that followed.

But it was Stead himself who was convicted and imprisoned two years ago. Granted, the sentence was short and served in comparative comfort, but I have no desire to follow his example. I much prefer remaining here in my private dungeon, with my own dragon to guard it."

Hester spoke quickly. "I had no idea—"

"I fear quite the opposite," Agatha Scrimshaw said. "You have far too many ideas, and all of 'em wrong." Her sigh was sonorous. "That nephew of mine is an insufferable prig, and a bore to boot, but for once in his life Albert was right. I had no business entrusting you with a mission you were incapable of performing."

"But I can perform it," Hester told her, "now that I understand your requirements."

Once again choler was coloring Miss Scrimshaw's cheeks. "You understand nothing," she replied. "And my only requirement is that you remove yourself and your—your offensive material from these premises." Pudgy hands scrabbled with the torn and crumpled litter of sheets on the desktop before her.

Before it could be gathered and proffered, Hester rose, shaking her head. "Please do not trouble yourself. I have no further need of these pages, thank you." She turned on her heel to avert the likelihood that her expression might reveal what her words strove to conceal. "Good day, Miss Scrimshaw. I appreciate your consideration."

Then she was over the threshold, forestalling the possibility of a reply. Ignoring the baleful glance of the dragon guarding the editorial dungeon, she hastened her footsteps; only upon reaching the street did the energy of her anger ebb.

The chill that numbed her came not from autumnal air but from within. Indeed, there was more than a hint of sunlight shafting its way through the scattering of clouds above. But now that same sunshine offered no solace. Not from the chill within, nor from the muck and filth of the streets surrounding her.

Muck and filth. That's what Miss Scrimshaw thought of the work in which she had taken such pride. Verbal rejection was enough of a burden to bear without the added indignity of physical attack upon the manuscript itself. What gave that woman—that ogress—the right to destroy another's property, and with it, another's dignity as well?

The question echoed as Hester elbowed her way through crowded streets, together with the recollection of Miss Scrimshaw's answer. The facts were clear enough; publishing an article such as hers entailed the risk of litigation and, if one were judged guilty, of fine and imprisonment. What Hester found unclear was the intensity of Miss Scrimshaw's anger and vituperation. Unless, of course, the childish outburst masked a fear of endangering herself and the prestige of her position.

Muck and filth. Was her work really that bad?

But she hadn't said that. All of her temper tantrum, all of her name-calling, had been directed at the content of the article, the subject matter rather than the style.

Now she reexamined the elements of Miss Scrimshaw's anger in a new light. As an editor she had requested Hester to attend and report upon a meeting of the Salvation Army. It had been Hester's own decision to ignore that request in favor of writing something entirely different, something that might offend its readers and carry with it the additional risk of an action for libel. Given her temperament, Agatha Scrimshaw's actions and reactions seemed less extreme in this context. Face up to it, Hester told herself, it was your own lack of judgment that brought you to this pass.

Could she better that judgment now to redeem herself?

By the time she reached her room the question seemed academic. Given her present plight, it was worth the attempt, for she had nothing to lose.

Pen sharpened and resolve steeled, Hester busied herself with setting down notes and observations pertinent to the street meeting she and Captain Ellison had attended the other evening before their hasty departure. If only she had remained to witness the arrival of the police! Then indeed she would have a story to tell, an account of an actual event with which Miss Scrimshaw could find no grounds for complaint.

Hester sighed and put down her pen. The irony of the other night's decision was not lost upon her. Yet she admitted that even if she had possessed foreknowledge of the consequences, her choice would have remained the same. Saving that unfortunate child was of far greater importance than losing a journalistic assignment. And if Agatha Scrimshaw and the readers of her periodical couldn't see as much, then their lorgnettes were sadly in need of polishing.

Hester sniffed, both in acknowledgment of the cold enveloping the room and in reproof of her own self-righteousness. A holier-than-thou attitude was not going to help her compose the article she had in mind, nor would the skimpy notes she'd set down here. Descriptions of band instruments and uniforms were all very well, but scarcely enough to warrant notice in the pages of *The British Lady*.

Hester recalled what Captain Ellison said about the large Army indoor meetings at various halls located in and around London. She had mentioned that prayer meetings were held daily at noon in the headquarters of the Salvation Army itself. Recently, evening meetings had been added as well, featuring appearances by high-ranking members of the Army or the more prominent amongst their supporters. As a matter of fact, it was precisely that sort Hester had anticipated attending, until Captain Ellison led her down the garden path with her talk of first becoming familiar with street gatherings.

Now there was no reason to be put off from her purpose. She could still attend such a meeting tomorrow noon, or for that matter, this very evening. Yes, tonight would be by far the better choice, given the likelihood of larger crowds and more important speakers. Hester rose and crossed to the window, peering at the prospect beyond. Sunlight had been usurped by shadow, but there seemed no indication of oncoming fog at the moment; the same shabby attire she had donned the other evening would probably suffice to protect her, both against cold and unwelcome attention.

Unfortunately, her problems stretched far beyond the mere matter of dress; they extended all the way to 101 Queen Victoria Street.

Knowing the address of the Salvation Army's headquarters was one thing, but reaching it was quite another. By now Hester had managed to ascertain the cab rates here within the city—the cost of traveling by hansom was a shilling for the first three miles and sixpence for each mile thereafter. Omnibus fares might entail up to sixpence each way; Hester was not certain of the exact amount. But she didn't feel up to making another lengthy journey on foot.

Once again Hester had recourse to her map of London. How many times had she consulted it before? And how many times had she failed to notice what she now observed? There, plain as day even in this dimming twilight, were the tiny scattered black squares marking the individual sites of Underground stations.

Bringing light to her aid, Hester managed to locate a station only a few squares distant from Mrs. Carruthers's establishment. And yes, there was a Mansion House station close to Queen Victoria Street itself.

Hester waited patiently for high tea—she vowed not to be cheated out of what little additional nourishment it offered—then found an opportunity to have a word with Dorry. And it was the maid who furnished her with the information she required; the welcome word that travel by Underground cost only tuppence.

Fortune favored her further in that Mrs. Carruthers was presently absent from the premises, having presumably elected to spend the night with a married daughter in the distant wilds of Richmond. Her landlady's absence obviated the necessity of Hester inventing an excuse for her own excursion or the clothing she intended to wear for both comfort and protective coloration.

The only obstacle that remained to be surmounted was the one to which she descended—the Underground itself. Hester had never given thought to nor set eyes upon this marvelous yet menacing miracle of modern engineering. But she gave quite a bit of thought to it once she set foot in the tunnel beneath the teeming streets. Thanks to her shabby outfit no one paid particular heed, but she observed others closely in order to emulate their progress from stairwell to platform to train.

It was there, and amidst the rush and roar of the journey that followed, that Hester again reminded herself that what she had longed for had come to pass; she really was in London. Not only in, but under, hurtling through howling darkness along with the company of clerks, costers, students, soldiers en route to the Tower, shopkeepers wearing bowlers. There were only a few females, most of them boasting less shabby outfits than her own. Apparently, as was the case with the omnibuses, a silent covenant conferred immunity from unwelcome masculine attentions while traveling via Underground. Had these same women ventured to traverse the streets above as lone pedestrians, they would easily have risked being accosted.

Certainly, despite the startlement resulting from sound and motion, this mode of transport was infinitely more preferable. Of course, members of the gentry would eschew the sooty, odorous Underground completely; glancing around, Hester decided there were no subscribers to *The British Lady* aboard. Ladies did not travel unaccompanied at night, even by private carriage here in London.

Here in London. What would Father have to say about that? Hester mused. He, who had so shielded her from the present-day pitfalls of the world, had himself been imprisoned in the past. What his personal past may have consisted of still remained a mystery; but whether he began life in London as

Lane or Jekyll, he had left it long ago. He would never have ridden the Underground, for at the time of his departure it did not exist, nor for that matter was there a Salvation Army.

But there was now, and after a noisy and jolting arrival at Mansion House Station, Hester emerged upon the street and consulted her mental map before starting off toward the organization's headquarters.

Lights were brighter and vehicular traffic more abundant here; passersby better dressed and more mannerly. Were they not, Hester was confident that her present appearance would still be such as to put off mashers. As it was, she gave only a portion of her attention to her surroundings, for a portion of her mind still busied itself with thoughts of Father. What would he think of his dutiful—and deliberately downtrodden—daughter if he could have seen her clad in this unseemly fashion as she ran her risky errand the other evening? What would he say to her repeating the masquerade tonight? How might he respond to the gibes of Miss Agatha Scrimshaw?

The mere notion brought a smile to Hester's face. Then, as she rounded the corner into Queen Victoria Street, there was no opportunity for further fancy. Her destination rose before her.

Hester had scarcely expected the headquarters to be quite that impressive. Located across from the British and Foreign Bible Society, the building at 101 Queen Victoria Street had formerly been the property of a billiard club. Since its acquisition by the Salvation Army, an adjoining unit had been given over to a Uniform and Book Department, but the larger five-story structure housed a ground-floor meeting hall and a variety of offices above.

If the sight of the headquarters' exterior was a surprise, its interior held others yet to come. The first proved to be the paucity of attendees straggling alone or in pairs as Hester entered the edifice. There was nothing remarkable about those she observed; in the main they represented much the same types as had her fellow travelers on the Underground. It was just that somehow she had anticipated being part of a larger turnout. Her second surprise came upon glancing upward at the large wall clock in the outer corridor just before the stairway which rose to the floor above. The time was scarce past seven-thirty. She had not reckoned with the swiftness of her passage here. But her unexpectedly early arrival did account for why there were as yet so few others moving along toward the entrance to the meeting hall beyond.

Thus, minor surprises easily gave way to simple explanations. But now as Hester set off down the corridor she was startled by the sound of a voice from above.

"Miss Lane—!"

The sudden greeting echoed from above and its source, now descending the stairway, was another surprise; this one explicable only as coincidence. Hester recognized Captain Ellison and returned her smile as she approached.

Tonight the lady was in full uniform and, as Hester was pleased to observe, looked little the worse for wear despite the telltale evidence of recent contusion that remained. "What a pleasure to welcome you here," the captain said. "But why did you not inform me of your coming?"

"It was a last-minute decision," Hester told her.

Captain Ellison nodded. "I'm delighted to see you. Miss Kirby has already told me of your visit. She was most pleased by your interest."

"Will she be attending tonight?"

"I think not. You must remember she serves as a volunteer rather than an enlistee in our ranks. And as I'm sure you noted, there is overmuch to command her energies." Captain Ellison had consulted the wall clock while speaking. "It is customary to convene our meetings at ten past the hour, to ensure sufficient time for latecomers to be seated. If you're willing to undertake the stairs, I would afford you at least a fleeting glimpse of our premises."

Hester was willing, the stairs were undertaken, and the resultant glimpses—though fleeting, indeed—proved rewarding. Hester had not been prepared for the degree to which the Salvation Army was organized, or the broad scope of its activities. Even at this hour many of the offices on the upper floors were still occupied; she remarked upon the fact that work was apparently continued around the clock.

"And around the world," said Captain Ellison. "We are establishing a foothold internationally as quickly as funds permit and our training centers increase the ranks. But it is from here most activities are directed, including publication of prayer books and song sheets."

Standing now in a large office on the top story, Hester glanced at the half-dozen uniformed figures huddled over individual desks. "These people seem truly dedicated," she said.

The captain smiled. "It takes a great deal of dedication to write material for our newspaper, *The War Cry*, and then run back and forth with it between here and our printing presses in the basement."

These last words were uttered against a musical counterpoint emanating from below. She paused, then nodded quickly. "The program is starting. We'd best be on our way."

Their descent terminated, they made their progress along the ground-floor corridor to the large meeting hall beyond the entranceway. Here another surprise awaited Hester; the place had now been filled almost to capacity. Captain Ellison spied and escorted her to an unoccupied seat at the end of the very last row.

"I trust you will be comfortable here," she said.

"Yes, thank you. But I was hoping you'd join me."

"Perhaps later, once my duties upstairs permit."

The captain moved away, leaving Hester to survey her surroundings. The auditorium's stage was broad, its illumination bright, its orchestra pit commodious. The as-

semblage of musicians occupying this area more than tripled
the number she'd seen—and heard—on the street the other
evening. They were, in addition, better uniformed and far
more accomplished performers. Hester did not recognize the
melody they were playing, but the militant overtones issuing
from the brass section identified the selection as a Salvation
Army hymn.

Transferring her gaze to the audience, Hester beheld an
unusual sight. The early arrivals she had noted were pre-
dominantly female and almost entirely members of the working class. But during the interval she had spent upstairs,
their ranks had been swelled by a sizable number of more
prosperous citizens. None, she fancied, would necessarily be
numbered amongst Lady Ames's acquaintances, but dress
and decorum indicated a status far superior to their surroundings. And it was indeed curious to see gentility seated cheek
by jowl with those who could easily pass as their household
servants.

For a moment Hester felt a twinge of regret over her own
choice of garments; no need to play the slattern here. Then
her pang passed as she reminded herself that the majority of
the well-dressed women in this audience must have come by
cab or carriage, accompanied by male escorts. No, she had
good reason to wear what she did, and in the end it was a
matter of little consequence. What really mattered was her
reason for being here.

". . . And now, without further ado, our chief of staff,
William Bramwell Booth."

Hester blinked. Absorbed in her own thoughts, she had
observed nothing of what had been going on once the music
ceased. The jaunty little woman wearing her regulation uniform and bonnet stood center-stage, already concluding an
introduction. Now, as she glanced to her right, an imposing
figure advanced toward her to the accompaniment of ap-
plause from the audience.

So this was Bramwell Booth! Hester had not expected the

son of the Army's founder to be so imposing a figure. But the bearded man had the flashing eyes and imperious presence of one born to command.

Now it was his voice that commanded. His subject was the plight of the homeless, and as he spoke Hester matched his words with her own recollections of what she had seen the other evening.

"When I journey afield in the service of the Army, residents of small communities often greet me with questions concerning our problems here in London.

"'Is it true,' they ask, 'that people actually live there in the street?'

"'Some live,' I tell them, 'and some die.'"

Bramwell Booth nodded. "We are told that the East End alone harbors a population of close to a million. A hundred thousand or more have no fixed abode. Is it then surprising that many of them perish?

"As some of you doubtless know, there are lodging houses offering shelter to both men and women, provided they can pay. Some have a common kitchen to which food can be brought and prepared, though few can afford such luxury. The usual price of a bed for a night is eightpence for double, fourpence for single, tuppence for the rope."

Scattered murmurs rose from the audience, and Booth nodded quickly. "There may be fifty or more beds situated in one large room. For those who cannot afford to rent one, a rope is stretched across the end of the room to lean upon and sleep in a standing position. Provided the unfortunate can sustain the expense of such a privilege."

Again the murmur, which, Hester now observed, came from the more fashionably attired members of the audience. Local residents seemed already well acquainted with the hard facts of hard lives, facts that Bramwell Booth was offering now.

". . . All life is hard here. Merely to exist in these surroundings is something of a miracle. More than half of the

children born in the East End are dead before they reach
five years of age. If you could but see the filth and foulness
within the walls of those tottering tenements—where often a
dozen or more poor souls of both sexes and all ages are
penned together, living in the same single room."

Booth paused, nodding. "I am well aware that some of
you have seen such sights, and if so, there is no necessity for
me to discourse further upon examples of misery and distress. But those who have come here this evening for a first
visit—whether stirred by charitable inclination or mere idle
curiosity—I say to you, the time is upon us. The time to
march forward, to march swiftly, to march victoriously
against the foe. Hunger, illness, the ignorance of youth and
the infirmities of age, these are mortal adversaries, aided by
their tireless allies whose names are Avarice and Corruption.
But the greatest enemy of all is Indifference."

And it was indifference to which Bramwell Booth now addressed himself—the indifference of the powerful and
wealthy who refused to relinquish either a whit of their
wealth or a portion of their power on behalf of the impoverished and oppressed.

Yes, it was true that the homeless and the orphaned could
seek refuge in the workhouse, but here again the conditions
he described were virtually beyond belief. Hester listened,
horrified at what she heard, simply because her own limited
experiences vouched for the truth of his words.

It was the intention of the Army, said the chief of staff, to
provide for the homeless, and to enlist both public and private financing to that end. At present, reliance was still
largely placed upon the assistance of volunteers who opened
their homes and hearts to give shelter to those who might
otherwise fall prey to the perils of the street. Yes, he was in
hopes that those assembled here this evening might heed his
plea for funds. But everyone, rich or poor, young and old
alike, could heed a greater and even more urgent plea.

To those physically capable he issued a call for volunteer

services for assistance in the many tasks that the Army alone could perform. And it fell to the lot of all to join him in the fight against public indifference, to aid by word if not in deed.

Oratory was succeeded by ovation, ovation in turn by donation as uniformed Army enlistees moved down the aisles and extended tambourines to be passed along each row of spectators until, weighted with contributions, they reached the hands of another Army member at the far end.

Hester was in no position to give anything but silent thanks for the fact that she was occupying the rear row, where her dereliction from donation could not be widely observed. In her present circumstances a contribution was out of the question, and once she had passed the upended tambourine along to her neighbor, she rose hastily and moved toward the exit.

Others from rows below her own were already beginning to crowd the aisle behind her and it was from their ranks that the call echoed.

"Miss Lane!"

Startled, Hester turned to see a familiar figure moving toward her through the crush of the crowd behind. Even in this initial moment of surprise she noted how he progressed without rudely elbowing others aside; it was as though they recognized an authority in his bearing that caused them to make way. *Moses parting the Red Sea,* she told herself. *Or had it been God?*

No matter—Albert Prothore was neither.

The smartly dressed young man reached her side just as she emerged into the corridor beyond the auditorium. Taking her arm, he led her to the far wall beneath the stairwell, which afforded shelter from the movement of the crowd.

Plucked from anonymity and subjected to Prothore's scrutiny, Hester was suddenly sharply aware of her drab appearance. Was she forever fated to meet him when clad in so unbecoming a fashion?

Not that it made any difference, she hastily reminded herself. She was suitably and sensibly dressed for this particular occasion. God and Moses would understand; as for Albert Prothore, it was none of his business.

Apparently he thought otherwise. "I must own this is a most unexpected meeting," he was saying. "After your experiences the other evening, I did not presume you would be rash enough to repeat the indiscretion. You gave me your word—"

"I did no such thing!" Hester, conscious of temper on the rise, paused for an instant, then continued in more modulated tones. "And my presence at a public meeting can hardly be termed an indiscretion."

"Then might I be so bold as to inquire why you are here?" Prothore said.

"I should think the reason is obvious enough. I am writing an article about this meeting for *The British Lady*."

"But that's impossible." Albert Prothore shook his head. "Aunt Agatha gave me that assignment this afternoon. She said there would be no further need for your services."

Stunned, for a moment Hester's only response was a speechless stare to meet and match his own.

Neither of them observed another's stare embracing both. Watching them unobtrusively from the nearby doorway was Inspector Newcomen.

"Surely the vagaries of Fate are beyond comprehension." Despite the twilight chill of her room that numbed Hester's fingers, her pen moved swiftly across the paper.

"This morning I was so distressed that I could not bring myself to write of the misfortunes that had befallen me." Hester paused momentarily to grant another transfusion of ink to her pen. "Suffice to say that my account of Mrs. Kirby's shelter for homeless children was summarily rejected. And last night my attempts to gather material for another article proved fruitless when I discovered Mr. Prothore had been given that assignment."

Once more Hester dipped her pen. As she did so she mentally reviewed her encounter with Sir John Dermond's parliamentary secretary. It developed that Prothore was not attending the meeting merely to accommodate Miss Scrimshaw; his actual employer, Sir John, was pressing him to investigate the problems of the slums.

This disclosure had not been forthcoming until she was already in the cab, homeward bound, again at Prothore's insistence. During the journey he expressed himself regarding the meeting, his views differing widely from her own.

Disgusting. Bilge. Sheer twaddle. Tommyrot. Although lacking his aunt Agatha's talent for invective, he managed to convey distaste with equal ease. Bramwell Booth was dismissed as a sanctimonious hypocrite or else a pious nincompoop, as were all who presumed to meddle in such matters. The problems of poverty were meant for the consideration of economists, not amateur theologians. For that matter he didn't approve of political intervention; his own employer was keen to learn about conditions solely to exploit such information and further the Liberal cause in Parliament. As for his disapproval of Hester's activity—

Hester put her pen aside. The gesture was abrupt but decisive.

Had she been able to confide in her journal earlier today, she would probably have set down everything in detail, but now there was no longer any need to do so. In fact, there was no question of need at all, thanks to those selfsame vagaries of Fate to which she had previously alluded.

Why write of yesterday when it was today that really mattered? This noon, to be exact; high noon, coinciding with the height of her own anxieties. The fix she was in had her literally pacing the floor when Dorry arrived with the notice summoning her to Mr. Utterson's office, at her earliest convenience.

The message had been delivered by a cabby who was still waiting, either for a reply or for her accommodation as a passenger on the return journey to Turk's Court. Hester gave Dorry instructions; the cabman was to continue waiting and she would join him presently.

"Presently" proved to be a matter of some few minutes, during which Hester hurriedly donned the one properly becoming outfit she had not worn on her previous meeting with the solicitor. Whether the prospect of this coming visit boded well or ill, she would at least confront it while wearing her Sunday best. Perhaps a change for the better in her appearance augured a change for the better in her fortunes. Then again, she vaguely recalled reading a volume from her father's library that described the care Marie Antoinette lavished upon her dress just before she was escorted to the guillotine.

No matter, she was on her way. The early afternoon sunshine danced and dazzled over the dome of St. Paul's, and pigeons soared above the battlements of the Tower. Hester made a mental resolve to visit both of these London landmarks at, as Mr. Utterson would put it, her earliest convenience.

But what if there was no convenience in her future? As of this moment her worldly possessions consisted of an inadequate wardrobe, a meager assortment of personal effects—all worthless, save for her watch—and barely four shillings in cash. Perhaps Mr. Utterson's invitation indicated an intention to improve her resources. Or was it actually a summons to wait upon Inspector Newcomen?

Recollection of the big man's suspicions and the authority with which he could implement them dimmed the sunshine's dazzlement, and for a moment the thought of poor Marie Antoinette crossed her mind again.

Hester dismissed the conceit with a shrug. She was hardly a tragic figure, let alone a queen, and this conveyance was certainly not a tumbril.

Once more Hester contemplated the vagaries of Fate. *Like father, like daughter*, she told herself. Was it not the very mystery that Father unknowingly sought to solve by his earnest examination of Good and Evil? All those letters to learned professors and philosophers in faraway places, all those personal consultations with clergymen, and with what result? His verdict was that pure goodness, like pure evil, could not be proven to exist in any manifest form.

Which meant, when carried to its logical conclusion, that there was neither a God nor a Devil to rule or motivate mankind. They were personifications of forces that in reality were not separated but intermingled. And the true and only name for such forces was Fate.

Hester shook her head. Strange thoughts for a sunny afternoon. And she was by no means certain of her conclusions. Surely the learned professors and philosophers would disapprove, and the clergy cringe, at such blasphemy. What Father himself might say she would never know. But then there were so many things that Father had left unsaid. It was for those very reasons that she now found herself in her present circumstances, on her way to a meeting that might well determine the course of her future. Such indeed were the vagaries of Fate.

Her actual arrival at Mr. Utterson's office was scarcely the stuff of high drama. Again it was the ubiquitous clerk, Mr. Guest, who greeted her and paid the cabby, then guided her to the inner sanctum of his employer.

To Hester's considerable relief, the lawyer awaited her alone; there was no sign of Inspector Newcomen's presence unless, of course, he had chosen to conceal himself in the closet.

But that was nonsense. And it was obvious from Mr. Utterson's greeting and expression that this was meant to be a serious occasion. Or was it merely that her own somewhat more ladylike appearance elicited a more respectful response?

For a moment Hester flattered herself that this might indeed be the case, but if so, the solicitor abruptly corrected the notion.

Now, some several hours later, she could not recall his exact words; only the clarity of their meaning remained. Mr. Utterson had, he said, taken immediate steps to check out her claims—even to the point of contacting Major Ames by cable—and was satisfied that they were valid. His next statement she remembered verbatim.

"You are now the heir," he told her, "the sole and only heir, to Henry Jekyll's fortune."

Startled, it took several seconds before she could muster and murmur her reply. "But how do you know Dr. Jekyll is dead?"

Mr. Utterson regarded her somberly. "Because I was present when he died."

Hester leaned forward. "I thought you witnessed the death of Mr. Hyde."

"So I did." Mr. Utterson nodded. "Dr. Jekyll *was* Mr. Hyde."

If his previous announcement had been startling, this present statement stunned Hester to a point where she was incapable of a reply. She sat in shocked silence and it remained for the solicitor to break it with a heavy sigh.

"What I am about to tell you is a matter of strictest confidence," he said. "And before I do so it will be necessary for each of us to take an oath. Mine, which I now solemnly swear, is that I tell the truth. And in return I want your word that you never reveal what I disclose."

Hester hesitated. "You suggest we enter into a conspiracy of silence—"

"Not suggesting," Utterson said. "I am insisting upon it. As for conspiracy, I tend to find that too harsh a term. Let us instead regard it as a matter of mutual agreement."

"Can you not speak plainly?" Hester asked. "I need an assurance that there is nothing of a criminal nature involved."

The solicitor frowned. "I fear no such assurance can be granted you. Criminal acts must be spoken of—indeed, the very heart of the matter is a crime against Nature itself."

Hester sat irresolute. Why men of the law insisted upon talking in riddles was a conundrum for which she had no answer. But the riddle that Utterson presented was tantalizing, and the answer must be important.

Curiosity overcame reluctance. "You have my promise to remain silent," she said.

And silent she remained as Mr. Utterson spoke.

What he had told her loomed vivid in her memory, though his precise phrasing was clouded, very much like the sky presently visible beyond the window of her room.

Shabby as her surroundings might be, Hester was grateful for the sense of security they afforded. There had been no feeling of security in Utterson's office once he revealed the particulars of Dr. Henry Jekyll's experiments.

"Experiments." That was the term the solicitor used, but it scarcely began to describe the activities of his late client and longtime friend—activities that Utterson had never suspected.

Henry Jekyll inherited his wealth but earned his reputation, as a practicing physician and through private research into medical science. It was not until his middle years that such research resulted in a conclusion both philosophical and psychological. There was, he reasoned, a duality in man, two separate and distinct aspects of being, imprisoned in one body. Call them moral and immoral or civilized and primitive; the terms merely described polar twins perpetually warring for the control of a single bodily vestment.

The battles were continuous, the victories merely temporary and far too costly. If intellect prevailed, then instinct suffered; when flesh triumphed, spirit agonized. In either case the single mind and body that housed both forces was the ultimate victim.

Ideally, each force should inhabit a body of its own. Such was Jekyll's psychological solution to the problem. But what if there was a physiological solution as well?

As best Hester could now recall, Utterson had not described the details of the "experiments" conducted by Dr. Jekyll in his laboratory, or just when he attained final and physical proof of his theory. Whatever the occasion, the solicitor was unaware of it at the time; his only information came after Jekyll's death.

But it was principally of Mr. Hyde he spoke this afternoon; Edward Hyde, as Dr. Jekyll had christened his alter ego. The combination of chemicals ingested by the doctor did not result in the creation of a second body; instead they physically altered his own to form a more fitting receptacle for the unbridled urges of his other self. Dr. Jekyll was long familiar with the effects of various drugs upon the mind and body, but never had he dreamed of so potent a potion and so remarkable a result.

A single draught altered outward appearance: there was no recognizable resemblance between his usual self and the hirsute, dwarfish figure of Edward Hyde.

Now he was free to go his own way, as the respected and self-respecting physician, untroubled by baser thought or deed. And when upon occasion he resorted to the use of his discovery, the drug was a veritable elixir of life to Mr. Hyde, allowing him to give full rein to any impulse.

That Hyde was a being of impulse, Dr. Jekyll did not deny. Nor could he delude himself for long that Hyde was truly a creature in the lowest sense of the term, a creature devoid of conscience or compassion.

Hyde led a separate existence of his own whenever Jekyll prepared and drank the agent of transformation. But when Hyde returned, satiated, to swallow the antidote that restored Jekyll to his rightful self, the physical change did not erase memories of Hyde's deeds.

Thus Dr. Jekyll, when in his proper form, remained a prisoner of his own conscience. The freedom he had sought to achieve for beneficent usage was conferred only upon Mr. Hyde, whose purposes and practices were malign.

But the drug was powerful, and despite his knowledge of its effects, the craving for it persisted. Each time his resolution weakened, Hyde's hold on him grew stronger. In the end came a horrifying turn of events; Henry Jekyll found himself transformed into Edward Hyde without the use of the potion and without conscious volition. Increasingly he resorted to use of the antidote, which alone was capable of temporarily restoring him to the form he had once so eagerly abandoned and which now he so desperately desired to maintain.

And then the supply of antidote started to run out.

"He realized his danger once it was depleted," Mr. Utterson told Hester. "But despite the most frantic efforts, he was unable to replace the necessary ingredients. Now Jekyll stood doubly condemned; both as a prisoner of conscience and as a physical inmate of Hyde's body."

It was at this point in Utterson's recital that Hester broke her vow of silence. "And no one knew?" she asked.

"Such was the case," the solicitor said. "But suspicion was growing and discovery inevitable. The first to learn the truth was Jekyll's personal friend and physician, Dr. Hastie Lanyon. He confided his narrative to paper and sent it to Jekyll, warning him that he would soon place a copy in my hands.

"The rest, I believe, is known to you. Dr. Jekyll, held captive in the dwarfish form of Hyde, hid away in his chambers. It was there that the butler Poole and I found him, only moments after he had taken his own life.

"Apparently he expected my arrival, for he left certain papers behind, together with a note drawing them to my attention. The first was his will; the second, a copy of Dr. Lanyon's narrative. The third document was Jekyll's full and final confession."

Hester's shock gave way to relief. "Then you do have proof," she said.

Mr. Utterson shook his head. "I did have, but only for a brief interval. Much to my present shame I acted upon impulse and burned all of the papers that might serve as evidence, retaining only the will."

Hester's question was inevitable. "Why didn't you go to the police?"

For the first time during their conversation the solicitor replied without meeting her gaze. "I mentioned acting on impulse, but did not identify its nature. Poor Harry Jekyll's confession at first horrified, then moved me to pity for his misfortune. There seemed little point in making such disclosures; the cause of justice could not be served by so doing because the criminal, Edward Hyde, was already dead and so was his chief victim, my old friend Jekyll, whose good name would be forever tarnished by this testimony." Utterson sighed again. "It is a decision that has weighed heavily upon my conscience, and one that I now deeply regret."

"What of the other witnesses?"

"Alas, none remain. Dr. Lanyon is dead and so is the butler, Edgar Poole. Lacking their testimony or other verification, if I were to come forward now with this account, it might be regarded as the ravings of a madman. My reputation, as well as my late friend's, could be ruined. Call it cowardice or caution, I see great harm but no gain in pursuing such a course."

Reflecting upon his sentiments now, Hester found herself in agreement as she thought of what someone like Inspector Newcomen might make of Utterson's story. She herself believed the solicitor was telling the truth, which only served to shock her the more.

Hester's reaction had not gone unnoticed. "Bless me," Mr. Utterson exclaimed, "I trust you realize that I have made these disclosures only because it was necessary to do so. But as Dr. Jekyll's heir—or, rather, heiress—"

Hester interrupted him with a swift gesture. "But you are named in the will. What is your true reason for renouncing a claim upon the estate?"

"It is a question of principle," Utterson said. "Perhaps I delude myself that this decision is not prompted solely by the prickings of conscience, but the facts of the matter speak for themselves. You are Harry's kin and I am not. You are young and I am old. You are, bluntly speaking, presently impoverished, while my possessions are more than ample for my needs."

Hester had listened without comment, and it was Utterson who again took up the thread of discourse. "Under the circumstances, it will be some time before Dr. Jekyll can be declared legally dead, but I intend to take action to hasten proceedings. And when the affair is settled you will come into an estate of roughly"—here the lawyer hesitated long enough for a dry cough—"fifty thousand pounds."

It took a moment before Hester could catch her breath, but Utterson's voice still echoed in her ears. *Fifty thousand pounds.* The amount was staggering.

Again it proved difficult for her to recall exactly what Mr. Utterson said next. He was doing his diplomatic best to inform her there was no longer any need to live in near poverty. As Dr. Jekyll's attorney and executor-to-be, he was empowered to disperse funds as he deemed fit. He intended to place her immediately on an allowance of two hundred pounds a month, payable in bank drafts drawn upon an account to be set up for that purpose.

"I think this to be sufficient for you to live according to your station and properly maintain your establishment," he said.

"Establishment?"

"You may not find it necessary to employ a butler," Utterson said, "but if you wish a personal maid, I can furnish you with the name of a reliable agency. Poole's widow refuses to serve, which is understandable after her loss, but she did inform me as to the whereabouts of Bradshaw, the footman, and the cook, Mrs. Dorset. They are willing to enter your service and await your word. Meanwhile, here are the keys."

"Keys?"

"To Dr. Jekyll's house."

And here they were now, right beside Hester upon the desk. The keys that would open the home of a man who, like Fate itself, was the embodiment of both Good and Evil.

chapter

12

Though the weighty keys had been in Hester's hand during their ride, Utterson, who had accompanied her, did not make any motion for her to use them as he assisted her from the cab to face the imposing house he had declared was now hers. It was a handsome building of an earlier time, facing a square and effectively shouldered on either side by others of its kin—except the others bore signs of having come down in the world, being shabby-genteel as it were. The one she faced had been well kept up, the steps to the door scrubbed, the brass knocker on its surface well polished.

Utterson did not have time to raise a hand to the knocker before the door was flung open and a tall man, in a dark coat that had no touch of livery about it, but which nonetheless gave the impression of a spruce and competent servant, bowed deeply at the sight of the solicitor. The man ushered them into the large, low-ceilinged hall warmed by a bright fire and furnished more as a drawing room than an entrance. There were chairs that suggested perfect ease for the sitter, as well as a number of cabinets along the walls. Hester caught glimpses inside of what must certainly be costly curios evidently collected by someone with a love for the old and the beautiful. Regularly spaced between the cabinets, burnished frames held appealing pictures. In all, the look of this entrance into her new domain was that of a place of wealth and taste, and she felt more than a little daunted, though she had determined on the way here that she would give no sign that what she found was either more or less than she expected.

However, her attention was centered not so much on the hall itself now, but on the small group of people gathered there, all facing her with looks of avid curiosity. There was a middle-aged woman from under whose ruffled cap strayed a lock or so of grizzled gray hair. Her face was round and the rest of her decidedly plump. Hester did not need Bradshaw's rather affected words of introduction to guess that this was Mrs. Dorset, the cook, and, in the absence of a house-keeper, the most important female member of the staff. She was flanked by the thin, youngish Hannah in the decent black dress, ruffled apron, and cap of a housemaid's after-noon formal wear. In her shadow stood the much smaller, shrinking figure of Patty in blue cambric, twisting her apron with large, raw, work-swollen hands; her frame was that of an immature child and it was apparent that she was com-pletely overawed by both her surroundings and situation. Not so the rather undersized boy in a buttoned-up jacket. Though he kept a wary eye on Bradshaw, he was very inter-ested in all else within sight.

Thus Hester met the staff of her new home, indeed a modest one for a gentleman's abode, especially one as well in the pocket, according to the saying, as Dr. Jekyll had been. With Poole dead, Bradshaw now stepped into his boots, for Mrs. Poole refused to return as housekeeper. Utterson had informed Hester of this, but it did not trouble her. Accustomed to running her father's household, she anticipated no problems. There would be no need for great entertainments, and to live quietly was all she desired.

When she had spoken pleasantly to the gathered servants, she suggested tea be served to Utterson and herself before the fire. While it was being prepared the solicitor informed her he had taken the liberty of sending his clerk Pope around to settle accounts with Mrs. Carruthers and fetch Hester's trunk. Indeed, it arrived before their tea was ready, and Bradshaw deposited it, together with a bundle of garments gathered from the closet and bureau at the lodging, on the landing before the stairs.

When at last they took their tea, Utterson fell into setjawed silence, staring into the flames. It seemed to Hester that his thoughts were occupied with the dark and horrorfilled story he had felt forced to share with her.

If ever a house deserved to be haunted, perhaps it was this one. She gave herself a little shake, as if to dislodge the notion.

"The staff . . ." Utterson spoke suddenly. "I trust it will be adequate. If you need others—though Jekyll found these most satisfactory—you have the right to hire such."

Hester thought suddenly of Mrs. Kirby's Sallie. The girl's bright face, willingness to learn, and that intelligence her mentor had commented on, would make her an excellent addition to any household. Yes, she might well offer Sallie a place here. Even though Utterson had already advised her during their ride hither that she could not present Mrs. Kirby at once with funds enough to acquire the second dwelling wanted to shelter more girls, she could assist in modest ways—this being one of them.

Hester planned a visit to the Kirby establishment as soon as possible, perhaps the very next day. In the meantime the house itself afforded her matter for conversation.

At her questioning Utterson arose further out of whatever

dark study had held him for a while and informed her that the doctor had been a noted collector in several fields.

They finished their tea, Hester noting with satisfaction that the bread and butter had been of the proper thinness, the cakes fresh and lightly made, and that Bradshaw was deft in his service. She ate hungrily but Utterson did not. And it was only too soon that he arose to go.

As Bradshaw showed him out Hester stiffened her back. The hall room that had seemed so welcoming at first now overshadowed her. She longed for more light though there were candles aflame in two candelabra on a table nearby and several lamps aglow. The afternoon seemed to have faded far too fast into twilight.

Hester faced up to what she felt to be her first duty when Bradshaw returned. "I would like to see the house."

He at once picked up one of the smaller lamps. "Of course, miss."

She was introduced into a library where the cold of the unlit fireplace seemed to reach out into the whole of the chamber. There was the large desk of a man of business and more cabinets of curios, as well as two long walls lined with books, their covers a uniform dull mud color, which looked as if they had never been read and no one would ever desire to take one from its proper shelf. Yet there was the smell of polish in the room, and she had a feeling that no dust had been allowed to settle there.

The dining room was a much more cheerful place and apparently had been in continued use. A second fire blazed there, and over the mantel hung an almost life-sized portrait to which Bradshaw gestured.

"That was the master—when he was younger. Mr. Poole said it was very like him."

He held the lamp higher so that she could see better. This man pictured here, how could he have been the protagonist of that evil and haunting tale Utterson had told her? He was handsome in an open way that pleased the eye, his mouth curved in a gentle smile. Looking at him she felt an odd warmth and fleeting desire to have known him. That he could have been led into such darkness—that hardly seemed possible.

"He looks as though he were very kind." She spoke the thought aloud.

"That he was, miss. A proper gentleman, and yet with a thought for them as weren't so high in the world. Many a time he gave aid to them as were ailing and could not pay. A good man, miss."

Bradshaw sounded sincere, but then he did not know his master's secret. Perhaps it was for the best.

Hester decided to postpone inspection of the offices, kitchen, and pantry. That would be reserved for the morning when she must interview Mrs. Dorset and make plain the intention to run her own house.

Instead she instructed Bradshaw to conduct her upstairs. He did so, carrying the trunk and the parcel of clothing without further orders, then setting them down in the upper hallway while she confronted the task of choosing a bedchamber.

The first room to which Bradshaw now ushered her most certainly would not do. The bed was huge, with curtains of a figured green stuff to match the carpet of a similar shade. It was, Hester realized, a room in which she would never feel comfortable.

Bradshaw verified her unspoken guess. "This was the master's room."

"Yes. But it will not do for me . . ."

"No, miss," he agreed at once. "Hannah has turned out the old mistress's room for your approval."

"Dr. Jekyll's mother?"

"Oh, no, miss. Dr. Jekyll bought this residence from Dr. Donner's heirs. T'was Mrs. Donner as had this room."

He had brought her to a second door and now flung that open. She did not need the lamp he carried to see what

was here, for a fire was lit and candles in four branched
sticks stood on the mantel, as well as two lamps and lit candles in the holders on either side of the dressing mirror.
The room itself brought a gasp of delight from her. It was a
place of fancy such as one might find in one of the fairy
tales she had read surreptitiously as a child. The walls were
covered with painted fabric decorated with birds and but-
terflies. This bed also was curtained but the draperies were
roped back, while the head and foot so displayed were
black inlaid with mother-of-pearl, silver and gold touches.
In the bed Hester recognized the papier-mâché so esteemed by an earlier age. Slender-legged chairs held dark-
colored cushions decorated with faded but beautiful em-
broideries, which also adorned the draperies now pulled
over two wide windows.

Near the well-lighted dressing table, only half showing
around the edge of an oriental screen, was a washing stand.
The tall standing wardrobe was patterned in fanciful designs
like the screen's.

"This is . . . very suitable." She disciplined her voice
firmly. "And the other rooms?"

Of a sudden she wanted to get this inspection trip behind
her, return alone to luxuriate in this fairy-tale room.

"The master had few guests, miss. Nothing has been allowed to go, but much is kept in wraps."

His words were verified as she glanced quickly into four
other rooms, where the furniture was shrouded; all of them
cold with a suspicion of damp. It might be well to have fires
in them now and then, too.

Bradshaw brought trunk and belongings to the chamber
she'd selected, then departed, and at last she was alone in
her own room. Her own room!

Hester reached out to run her hand down the side of the
wardrobe, as if to confirm its tangible reality. In all her life
she had never aspired to such a turn of fortune. Though
what it was founded on summoned a chill the fire could not
dispel.

What would her father have made of these circumstances? Had he known, or perhaps suspected, his cousin's propensity for the morbid, if not the secret itself? Had that been the reason for their alienation, for the changing of his name?

Nonsense, she must not let herself dwell on the past. It was the future that mattered now. Hester hunted out the key to her trunk and frowned when she inspected its contents. The frown deepened as she faced the long mirror on one of the wardrobe doors. If Father saw her now, he'd say that shabbily dressed stick of a girl had no place here. She must have the proper clothes and very soon. Surely the servants had already marked her drab appearance. A governess, a servant little higher than themselves, that was what she looked like.

But how did one go about finding clothing in London?

She needed advice. Now if Mr. Utterson had only possessed a wife. But there was no way of appealing to any other acquaintances, or any that pride would allow her. Miss Scrimshaw? Lady Ames? Captain Ellison? Oh—Mrs. Kirby! The latter's elegance—or what had seemed so to her at their meeting—was quiet, very much that of a lady, and suggested that she had good taste and would have access to such aids as Hester needed, say, the address of a seamstress. Not one of high fashion perhaps, but able to understand the needs of a lady—or rather of an heiress who had no mind to shine in any society, but needed garments befitting her new station.

Hester was still sorting through her clothing, putting most of it in a discard pile to be passed along to Captain Ellison's charities, when the sound of a gong summoned her to dinner.

She dined alone in state at the head of the long dinner table, amazed at the variety of dishes offered her, unable to do much more than nibble at a few of that wide array. Mrs. Dorset was undoubtedly set upon impressing her new mistress with her prowess. However, the girl determined that she would not be so burdened with formality again.

There was a tall can of hot water awaiting her in her room. Hester settled into drowsy content by the fire, a tablet and pencil in her hand, to make lists of what she must do in this new life, as far as she could guess. However, she should go slowly, feel her way, as one walking down an ill-lighted path. This all seemed very much of a dream.

It was not until the following afternoon that she had Bradshaw call her a cab, and she had some trouble in maintaining her independence then, since the ex-footman took it as a matter of course that she would command his company. But she held to the firmness she had assumed that morning when she had confronted Mrs. Dorset, taken over the tradesmen's books (to the manifest displeasure of the ruler of the kitchen), and inspected for herself not only that domain and the stores' cupboard, but gone over the linen supplies with Hannah and agreed to the employment of a day woman for the "rough."

Hester had noted that the service quarters gave upon a neglected back garden and a grim-looking courtyard. Across the courtyard stood the building of ill repute that had been the center of Utterson's story. The small building had another entrance on the bystreet, but Utterson had assured her it was kept well locked, and Bradshaw bore him out, saying it was not only securely locked but had been boarded up and there was no way into the old laboratory save by way of the courtyard. Even so, she was glad there was a sturdy manservant under the roof.

Hester looked forward to the coming of Sallie. If she was to have a new wardrobe, she would need someone good with her needle. Also, though most of the household washing was sent out, there must be a maid to wash and iron the finer things. Hannah had stolidly said that such a duty was not her place. And truly Hester did not want the severe-looking woman about her. Hannah doubtless was a worthy female and a good worker, but in a house that already seemed to have too many shadows, she was not a cheerful asset.

Hester had sent a note ahead to Mrs. Kirby via the boy. Thinking of that now she frowned. Though she knew very little of Ratsby, the boy, she had sensed something strange about him on his return with Mrs. Kirby's reply. He had stared quite openly at her when he thought she was not looking. Or was that only part of her unease with these servants with whom she had so little contact?

Under Lady Ames's roof she had been neither fish nor fowl, as the old saying went, perched as a governess most precariously and unhappily between two states of being, that of a gentlewoman and that of a servant. She was very much aware that all servants' quarters were hotbeds of gossip, and they must certainly have much to say and speculate concerning her right now. She would need all the allies she could assemble and she was determined that Sallie must be one of them.

Once she was seated in Mrs. Kirby's cozy sitting room and held a cup of freshly brewed and most acceptable tea in her hand, she told of her inheritance. While she could not play lady bountiful to the full of her desires, she was determined to aid all she could in the work her hostess was carrying through. In proof of the matter she had handed Mrs. Kirby an envelope containing five pounds, impulsively counted out of her first month's allowance. The sum was exclaimed over with much thanks and the assurance that it would go far to provide shelter for at least one more girl.

Still, when Hester outlined her own situation and expressed her desire to hire Sallie, Mrs. Kirby's bright smile faded and she looked quite distressed.

"I know that Sallie would be very happy with you, my dear Miss—Jekyll." She stumbled a little over the name as if still finding it difficult to believe in this sudden change. "However, she has already been hired by the Donaldsons. It is only because they are presently out of town that she is not right now under their roof. We work on the apprentice principle with our girls—their term of service is laid down be-

forehand and cannot be changed except for some grievous
fault on their part, or some reasonable alteration of plan on
the part of their employer. I would most gladly have seen
her go to you. Dr. Jekyll was one of our patrons, as I may
have told you. He was most generous . . ." Hester thought
that she saw the luminosity of tears in the other's eyes.
"Your own interest and generosity is of such benefit that I
am very unhappy that I cannot send you Sallie."

Hester's disappointment was acute. From the first she had
taken a strong liking to the girl, and since she felt some apprehension about a staff she did not altogether trust, she had
looked forward to having Sallie with her. But plainly Mrs.
Kirby intended to abide by her rules.

It was wise to change the subject. Hester spoke frankly of
her need to assemble a new wardrobe. At once Mrs. Kirby's
smile returned. She lifted both hands from her lap as if to
applaud, a gesture Hester would have thought too effusive
from this very controlled woman.

"Now we have the very answer to your problem, Miss
Jekyll. When you visited us before, Bertha was not here. She
came to me two months ago but has been assisting Captain
Ellison at the workroom. She is sixteen, older than most of
our girls, steady and reliable. When she was eleven she was
apprenticed to a dressmaker. I regret to say that this was a
shop with a reputation for fashion among those who do not
care what goes on in the back rooms of such an establishment. Bertha showed talent for the needle and was quick to
learn. Because her work was outstanding she was given more
and more to do. During the 'season' it was not unusual for
her to work until midnight and rise at five the next morning
to begin again. She and her companions were poorly fed and
allowed little rest.

"In addition"—now Mrs. Kirby's voice fell a little and she
looked away from Hester, as if what she had to say was very
unpleasant, almost unmentionable in company—"the establishment had another and most evil side. Females, sup-

posedly of standing in the world, used it as cover for meeting— But Miss Jekyll, need I go further? All of us know that in this day there is much that is morbid and even filthy hiding under covers seemingly above suspicion.

"Unfortunately Bertha was brought into the shop one day to do some fitting and caught the eye of a so-called gentleman who was waiting for his wife." Mrs. Kirby's lips tightened and her eyes flashed. "After this man had left, Bertha's mistress reported to her that she was to be 'nice' to the gentleman on his next visit.

"When Bertha utterly refused, she was made a prisoner, even beaten, finally turned into the street, where she was found totally destitute by one of the Army followers who took her to Captain Ellison, and so she came to me.

"She is quick and willing, neat about her person, able to help with the work of the house, and most accomplished as a needlewoman. She would, I believe, be most eager to come to you."

Thus it was that Hester left, not with Sallie to whom she bade a regretful good-bye but to share the waiting cab with a slender girl in a neat dress and an attractive bonnet, who seemed almost tearfully willing to come on trial as a member of the house staff.

Though Bertha appeared at first very subdued, inching back into one corner of the cab as they jolted away from Mrs. Kirby's, she changed greatly as Hester spoke frankly of her need for an entire new wardrobe, and as quickly as possible.

Bertha Tompkins came to life. The pallor of her face showed the faint beginnings of a flush when Hester, smiling, said: "Now, Bertha, as I am new to London you must tell me just where we are to begin. Mrs. Kirby has been kind enough to give me the names of several shops, and if these are not too out of our way, perhaps we might begin at this hour to lay in what we may need."

"Oh, miss . . ." Bertha breathed, her eyes shining. "Oh, miss . . . yes! I know about patterns, and the places where

Madam Emilée bought things—they have the best. I know the names of those who are in charge—and the proper prices, too!" She nodded vigorously. "They needn't try any of their tricks. They have sometimes two prices, Miss Jekyll, one for them as is mindful of what they spend, and another for them as never looks at the bills carefullike."

So followed a breathless couple of hours. Hester, never in her life having been able to be unmindful of what she spent, was dazzled by lengths of materials, spools of ribbons, festoons of lace, baskets of flowers meant to bloom forever on dresses or hats. But she trusted that she kept her countenance and did not show her ignorance, and she was more than impressed by how deftly Bertha could manage to point out the best selections.

To her surprise, their last stop—at a hat shop—was in the street directly behind her new home, the old houses there having been remodeled into a number of modish, small shops, their bowed windows displaying fripperies enough to catch and hold any feminine eyes. When their cab rounded the corner at last and they disembarked at the Jekyll house, it required the services of both Bradshaw and Ratsby to unload the mound of boxes. Hester introduced her companion, and suggested that Bertha go with Ratsby who carried her own small battered box, to the other side of the baize-covered servant's door. Hannah had been summoned to help with the packages, but when Hester started to follow her up the stairs she was detained by Bradshaw.

"There is someone to see you, miss. He is waiting in the consulting room." And the tone of the servant's voice speedily reduced Hester from the euphoria of shopping to a state of apprehension.

The consulting room was a small and very darkish rear den off the hall that had not been used since Dr. Jekyll had given up his active practice some years ago. The only light came from a window where Bradshaw had drawn aside the drapery, and that opening looked out upon the grimness of the courtyard shared by the laboratory. Standing foursquare at that window was the broad-shouldered, beefy man whom she had last seen and instantly disliked in Utterson's office. He was alone, and at the sound of the closing of the door behind her, he swung around to face her fully. The set of his mouth and jaw, the boring stare of his small eyes, brought her to a quick stop. She could conceive of no reason why she must entertain a visit from Inspector Newcomen.

"You wished to see me?" Hester put all the chill she could summon into her question.

"Miss Jekyll . . ." He seemed to drawl out the name and to her mind his tone was either a sneer or mockery. "You've settled yourself well in, I see. Heard from the doctor? Seems as if you'd be in mourning, miss, if what Mr. Utterson says is truth, now ain't that a fact? There's been them in the past as has tried games—what they thought of as very clever games, Miss Jekyll—and yet there is always something what brings them down in the end."

There was, Hester thought, menace in his voice. Anger began to rise in her, a hearty antidote to the fear this man could cause her.

"Inspector Newcomen"—she was glad to hear that her voice was still cold and steady—"I am totally at a loss as to the purpose of your visit here."

He took two steps away from the window so that they now faced each other across a small table.

"What brought me here? Why, a need to know brought me here." He turned around a little to wave at the pane behind him. "Look out that window there. You see that building? A man died there, and not too long ago. They said he drank poison—which was perhaps better than a rope about his neck—because he was a murderer. He was also a friend of Dr. Jekyll's, so good a friend as Dr. Jekyll gave him the run of this house, paid good money once to keep him out of trouble, told his servants to obey him as if he were master here.

"And that man poisoned himself in the doctor's own room and maybe, just maybe, with something the doctor himself gave him. That Hyde—there are questions yet to be answered about him."

He was leaning forward across the table now, his heavy face not far from hers, so that Hester pulled away. The inspector smiled a far from pleasant smile.

"Jumpy, ain't you, Miss Jekyll?"

For the first time she felt an acute dislike for that name. Unlike Mr. Utterson, the inspector seemed to use it as an accusation.

"Well as you might be, well as you might be," he was continuing. "I was hunting Hyde, but he slipped through my fingers because he was hiding here, and you cannot make me believe that Dr. Jekyll did not know that! Interfering with the law the doctor was, aiding a murderer! Then he goes away clip and clean—and what happens next? Why, you come out of Canada and Mr. Utterson says as how you are the doctor's kin and that he's dead and you're the heir. 'Tis a web you've been spinning. I want to know when the doctor died, and where, and how—that's what I want to know, and I'm going to learn that, so I warn you."

He had stepped around the table now and was advancing toward her again. For all her desire to stand up to the man, Hester could not quite make it. Instead she turned and opened the door wide.

"Inspector Newcomen," she said, her voice still steady, "you take altogether too much upon yourself. If you have any questions, ask them of Mr. Utterson! I do not think that your superiors would take kindly to a report that you have spoken this way to a lady."

The mockery was back in his voice. "Yes, ma'am, perhaps I was a bit sharp now, but this is a sharpish case and we shall get to the bottom of it, never fear." He nodded. "I'd best have another word with your solicitor presently. He'll not put me off any longer."

"Bradshaw?" Hester raised her voice, hoping that the servant had remained in the hall. "Inspector Newcomen is leaving, will you please show him out?"

Bradshaw *was* there and he had the outer door already open as the inspector crammed on his hat and strode down the hall toward the gathering dusk of the evening outside. Hester watched the door close firmly behind him and then turned to the staircase. But before she had put her foot on the first step Bradshaw spoke.

"Miss Jekyll."

"Yes?" She was impatient to get back to her room, to be able there perhaps to collect herself and put this interview from her mind.

"I wish to tender my notice. Ratsby has asked me to speak for the same for him."

"Your notice?" Hester was astounded. "What leads you to this, Bradshaw? Mr. Utterson told me that you were very willing to come here as a butler. You know the house and the routine well. And is it not true that this advance in position is very favorable for you?"

"A man cannot be easy in any position, miss, when the police come to the door, when he is asked questions by them he cannot answer. I ask for my notice to be taken, miss. It is my right." His face was flushed and he looked down, refusing to meet her eyes.

Why did Bradshaw fear the police? she wondered. And then rumors of the gossip in Lady Ames's establishment came to her mind. An ambitious servant disliked being in a house threatened by scandal that might wipe away respectability. Had this suddenly become that sort of an establishment? She and Utterson were the only ones who knew the true story—which, indeed, was beyond the bonds of all respectability. There had been a most unpleasant death here—if not under this roof, then only across that slip of courtyard. And the last days of Jekyll-Hyde must have caused many tongues to wag in the servants' hall.

"And Ratsby?" There was a note of sarcasm in her voice as she asked that. There could be no one lower on the general scale of the house hierarchy than he who was known generally as "the boy," unless it was a scullery maid.

Now Bradshaw truly colored, and his eyes shifted from side to side. "He did not—" he began and then apparently could not give her an outright lie. She thought of the errand she had sent the boy on that day, the message to Mrs. Kirby. And she nodded to herself. Of course, a lady should have no dealings at all in that part of town. Not only the history of the house but her own actions had brought this about.

"And the others?" she forced herself to ask quietly. Was she to be abandoned in this huge house that was growing darker and more menacing by the moment?

"I don't know, I am sure, miss. We chooses for ourselves."

She accepted that but she did have one weapon left, and from her acquaintance with it on her own behalf she knew it to be a powerful one.

"You will give me the month, Bradshaw. Otherwise, having had your services so short a time, I cannot honestly write you any recommendation."

Having left him that to think about, she turned and went up the stairs.

She now had much to think about herself.

chapter 13

"Will that be all, sir?"

"Yes, Pope." From without, the winds that funneled down Gaunt Street carried the echo of distant church chimes. There was no need to note their number; the time was eight o'clock. Pope had seen to it that his master's postprandial libation was served to him in the library several minutes before the hour as long-established nightly ritual decreed.

"You may go now," Utterson said. That too was part of the ritual.

"Thank you, sir." A slight inclination of the head, a deft turn, followed by inconspicuous withdrawal from the room and the closure of the door behind him, completed Pope's participation in the ceremony.

Or almost so. Utterson sipped his gin, listening for the telltale sounds that would betoken Pope's hasty departure for the evening. During eighteen years in his household,

Pope had never volunteered particulars as to his nightly destination, nor had Mr. Utterson seen fit to question him in that regard. It was, of course, a rather unusual arrangement for a manservant to absent himself in this fashion. But then, Utterson conceded, he was in some ways a rather unusual master.

Such was his wont that he preferred to remain solitary within the precinct of his own premises. Although cook, scullery maid, and housemaid retired to quarters of their own behind and above the kitchen once duties were completed, they were sequestered from Utterson's domain. Following dinner he'd not see them again until after his morning repast, which Pope would serve him in his bedchambers. Precisely at what hour of the night the manservant returned to the house was again a matter of conjecture; he too had a rear room upstairs, and the privilege of carrying a key to the backstairs entryway. Aside from the Popish nature of his name, Utterson could find no fault with the man and respected his privacy, as he did his own.

When, on rare occasions, he found it necessary to entertain friends or business associates, dining out proved a simple solution. Inasmuch as he absented himself from the premises daily in pursuit of his profession, he felt no need to employ a larger staff just to keep up appearances. Pope was charged with full responsibility for maintaining the household and Mr. Utterson had little personal contact with its members. Indeed, there were times when he was hard-pressed to recall the names of those who served him, and he possessed no knowledge of what took place within the confines of the kitchen area or above. It had, he reckoned, been a matter of some several years since he had last ventured to set foot upon a staircase in this rambling old house of his.

And you are a rambling old fool, Utterson told himself. He leaned forward, feeling the heat from the fireplace as he reached for his glass to empty it without further ado. Now the warmth without was matched by warmth within.

Alone, he permitted himself two unaccustomed luxuries—a smile, and another drink. Smiling had never been his habit, nor had overindulgence in spiritous liquors, but despite his austere ways, there were times when Mr. Utterson found himself in need of cheer. And he'd best provide it for himself, for there was little left to be gained from other sources.

Such a thought banished the smile from his lips, but not the glass. This time he gulped his drink, striving to alleviate a sudden chill that the flame from the fireplace could not dispel.

Where did they vanish, those friends in whom he had once found cheer and comfort? Within less than a year all were gone. How he missed those Sunday strolls with his cousin! Richard Enfield, though a distant relative, had probably been his closest companion since school days. And Dr. Hastie Lanyon, who had once shared the secret of yet another departed friend, Harry Jekyll. Now each of them had passed on, leaving him with a burden of knowledge too great to be borne alone.

Was that the real reason he had revealed the truth to Hester Jekyll?

Utterson considered the question as he stared into the firelight. There had been something about the pawky, awkward young woman in straitened circumstances that aroused his sympathies, and of course she was both morally and legally entitled to know the particulars of her uncle's demise.

But were these actual reasons or mere excuses for his conduct? Questions came quickly, answers slowly. He gazed deeper into the fire, deeper into himself.

Yes, upon first reading Harry Jekyll's testament he was tempted by the thought of acquiring the bequest, but conquered his impulse. Not so much out of moral considerations, but because he had no need of such a fortune—and, more importantly, might put himself at risk in appropriating it lest there be other, unexpected claimants. Such had proved to be the case, and in many ways he felt relieved; cleansed of temptation, rid of responsibility, free of guilt. Nor would he necessarily go unrewarded along the path of virtue; doubtless young Hester Jekyll might retain him as solicitor to guide her interests in prudent investment. Granted, that is, if she survived to do so.

Mr. Utterson was not a devoutly religious man, but he prayed that his fears for her were unfounded. If only he had some assurance upon the matter!

In its absence he reached once again for the decanter, but at finger's touch, withdrew his hand. Sorrow was held to drown in drink, but fear could only be inflamed by excessive indulgence. And this was no time to be afraid. The flames cast shadows, and shadows marched across the walls to move silently throughout the house, merging with the murk of the empty, lifeless rooms beyond.

Lifeless. Like Poole. Marching shadows were a matter of foolish fancy, but Poole's death had been a dreadful reality, all the more frightening because it remained unexplained.

Certainly Inspector Newcomen's suspicions seemed both farfetched and unfounded, motivated more by prejudice than pragmatism. Utterson could not conceive of Hester Jekyll committing such a crime in such a manner. Poole had been battered to death, very much the way Sir Danvers Carew had met his fate at the hands of Edward Hyde.

What Newcomen had heard from Poole's widow was unnerving; her description of a fleeing figure evoked memories of Hyde. Or was the fleeing figure merely a figment of her imagination, like his own marching shadows?

Again Utterson's eyes followed the flicker of the flames, as though seeking comfort in their dance and dazzle. At least they were alive while all else around them—shadows, smoke, and ashes—was dead.

Ashes to ashes, dust to dust. Edward Hyde was dead too, dead and buried. Utterson knew that for a fact, and yet the knowledge offered cold comfort. It would appear that one could not rely on "facts" anymore, not after his own experience with Harry Jekyll. What happened to him was contrary to all scientific "facts," but there was no doubting the evidence of his own eyes.

Utterson started at the sudden sound, then caught himself in the realization that the church bells were marking the passage of another hour. It did not seem to him that he had been idling for so long a time. But then time appeared to have lost length of late; hours, days, weeks, and months merged into years. Clocks and chimes had little meaning now. To a man of his age, time was best measured by a mirror.

There had been a cheval glass in Jekyll's cabinet, and now, over the hiss and crackle from the fireplace here in the library, came the echo of Poole's voice. "This glass has seen some strange things, sir." He had spoken in a whisper but Utterson would never forget those words, any more than he could forget the image of the dwarfed body resting face-downward on the carpet below. Resting was hardly the way of it, though. There were those final convulsive shudders, very similar to the one Utterson was experiencing now as he recalled how the figure had been turned on its back to reveal the countenance of Edward Hyde.

Now, over the smell of burning logs, Utterson fancied he could detect the scent of crushed almonds; the odor of poison from the phial that Hyde held crushed in his hand as he expired.

Hyde's suicide was a fact beyond dispute, as was the simultaneous self-destruction of Dr. Henry Jekyll. And there was no doubt regarding the interchange of identities, due to the results of medical experimentation. But if facts proved Jekyll compounded chemicals that changed the body, perhaps he had done more. Jekyll cheated life. Could he also cheat death? Could he rise from the grave again as Mr. Hyde?

"Preposterous." The solicitor murmured the word aloud.

Even if so fantastic a possibility existed, poor Harry would never lend himself to such sacrilege.

Yet Henry Jekyll might. Not his longtime client and friend whom he thought of as Harry, but the man he had never known; the dabbler in the secret and the forbidden. Suppose the fantastic became fact?

If so, Utterson knew what would happen. Should Hyde somehow regain life, or a semblance of life, then inevitably he'd return to the Jekyll house—and find Hester there.

Should any harm befall her, the solicitor's fears, preposterous or no, would be confirmed. Yes, Hyde must find himself drawn to the house; he would move toward it as surely as shadows marched across the walls.

"Preposterous." Again his lips formed the word but closed before allowing its passage, as thought gave way to sudden supposition. If, through any chance and by any means, Hester succumbed to a final fate, then Utterson would remain on record as sole heir to the Jekyll estate. Given the consideration of Hyde's presence, he could still cope with the situation; quickly liquidate a substantial portion of the legacy and flee. Only Inspector Newcomen might suspect his plundering, and once the solicitor placed foot on the soil of the Continent, pursuit would be a fruitless gesture.

So thinking, his mouth moved in a mirthless and soundless chuckle. Who was he to arrogate unto himself the right of passing judgment on poor Harry? In his own thought tonight elements of good and evil had commingled, without the agency of any more chemicals than could be found in two ounces of Bombay gin. How could he presume to probe the soul of another man without first fathoming the depths of his own? He too was both a Jekyll and a Hyde.

Neither aspect of himself occasioned fear. Physically he was confident of the ability to control his actions. But he could not command thought, and knowing this, he was afraid. It was unwise of him to sit alone in this house by night—alone with his thoughts.

But not for long.

Once more Utterson gave a start, prompted by another sudden sound. But this time it was not the clang of bells but a summons sounding from the hall and entryway beyond.

Utterson rose, stiff-kneed after his long attendance before the fire. As he moved toward the door of the library, his shadow joined the others in their silent parade.

Once he reached the hall beyond, the knocking sounded again. The front door was being tapped upon rather than pounded; but to Utterson, unaccustomed as he was to any disturbance at this hour, the noise seemed loud enough to wake the dead. But not those scullery sluggards asleep in their beds backstairs. Now, in Pope's absence, he'd have to do the honors himself. Most irregular. High time to have it out with the servant concerning his nightly meanderings; either that or add a footman to the staff.

A footman would have turned up the gaslight, or at least carried a candle, but Utterson groped his way along the hall aided only by the faint glow issuing from the library entrance behind him.

The tempo of the rapping increased its urgency, ceasing as the solicitor unlocked the door, only to be replaced by the first chime of the church bell.

He opened the front door. There was a shadow-shape on the stoop. Now the shape became a figure as it moved forward into the dim light. The church bell boomed as Utterson stared, incredulous.

"You—?" he gasped.

But the word was lost in the clang of the bell and the crack of the blow that crushed his skull.

chapter 14

A shock. A truly dreadful shock.

Hester put the newspaper down beside the service of a meal she would never finish.

Bertha had brought the paper as Hester seated herself at the table for breakfast. Unaccustomed as she was to such niceties and the convenience of a personal attendant, Hester did her best to appear at ease. Scanning the newspaper was part of the pretense. Actually she had never before enjoyed a late breakfast in all her life, and enjoyment ended before it began, once she read the story.

The item itself was brief, signifying a hasty last-minute insertion, presumably just before the paper went to press, but the shock that followed her reading was prolonged. Now she sat stunned, striving for comprehension.

Utterson dead? The body lying on his own doorstep last night discovered by—Inspector Newcomen?

Hester shook her head, both in refusal of what she had read and reluctance to peruse it again. Nonetheless she steeled herself to lift the paper and examine the item once more.

Utterson . . . Gaunt Street residence . . . The solicitor's person seemingly battered by a blunt instrument . . . discovered shortly after the commission of the deed by Inspector Newcomen of Scotland Yard, who also apprehended a suspect . . . name being withheld pending further investigation . . .

Suspect. She had been too distraught to note this detail at first reading. But it wasn't a detail, not if Inspector Newcomen had the possible murderer in custody. How did the inspector chance to be in the vicinity at the time? And why would anyone wish to do away with Mr. Utterson?

"Begging your pardon, miss—is something wrong?"

Hester glanced up, startled by the sound of her maid's voice. Bertha Tompkins's concern was evident in her glance as well as her voice, and Hester attempted the semblance of a smile.

"It's nothing," she said. "I'm quite all right."

"If breakfast's not to your liking, I'd best tell Mrs. Dorset what you'd prefer—"

"That won't be necessary." Hester shook her head. She was about to say more but the sound of door chimes claimed her attention.

"Excuse me, miss." Bertha wheeled and made her exit, leaving Hester to reflect upon the necessity of finding an immediate replacement for her footman, who had departed despite her request that he remain for a month. It had not occurred to her that Bradshaw's duties would have to be assumed by other members of the staff, thus disrupting the order of the household. But then there was so much she was being forced to learn, forced to accept. And now, the shock of this morning's news—

At the sound of footsteps in the hall, she turned to Bertha

as the maid halted in the doorway. "There's someone wishes to see you, miss. A Mr. Prothore. Shall I show him in?"

"No need." Albert Prothore's voice sounded from the hall as he brushed past Bertha. The action itself was something Hester would not have expected from such a proper gentleman, nor was she prepared for the sight of his haggard features and agitated demeanor.

"Forgive this intrusion." His words came quickly. "I must speak to you at once. Utterson—"

"I know." Hester nodded, then gestured toward the table. "There is an account in the newspaper." She paused, frowning. "Who could have done such a horrible thing—battering that poor man to death? Who is this suspect?"

"I am," Prothore said. "But I didn't kill him."

This was a morning for shocks. Hester heard a strange voice murmuring in a monotone. "Please be seated."

It took a moment for her to realize that the voice was her own. As Albert Prothore responded to her invitation, she managed to regain a measure of control, if not composure. "Might I ask Bertha to fetch you something to eat?"

"Thank you, but that will not be necessary." Prothore shook his head. As he did so Hester noted his loosened cravat, the faintly perceptible stubble of beard, the dislodged strand of hair banding his upper forehead. This was not at all in accordance with the image he was usually at such pains to maintain. Yet seeing him thus she was strangely moved, much as if she would like to take him by the hand to assure him that matters certainly could *not* be as bad as they seemed. What would his Aunt Agatha say if she saw him in such a sorry state?

But this was no time to entertain frivolous conjecture. Hester seated herself in a chair facing her visitor across the table. "You were about to tell me what happened?" she said.

It was mere assumption on her part, but Albert Prothore needed no further prompting. He spoke rapidly, fatigue betrayed only by the slight huskiness of his voice.

It was at Sir John Dermond's injunction, he said, that he ventured into Whitechapel last night. His observations would undoubtedly interest both his employer and Miss Scrimshaw, but that was not a matter of consequence at the moment. His only concern was to establish his whereabouts prior to nine-thirty of yesterday evening. At that time he hailed a cab on Commercial Road for his homeward journey.

It so happened that his home adjoined Mr. Utterson's property on the street directly to the north, and as the cab passed the solicitor's house to go round the square, he noted Utterson's front door was open and something was lying in its shadow.

Ordering the cabby to wait, he left the vehicle, hurried up the walk to the open doorway, and there encountered Utterson's body. The cabby, realizing the nature of his discovery, panicked and sped off. Prothore bent over the victim, seeking a pulse or some sign of life. And it was then that Inspector Newcomen drove up in a hack to find him in this compromising situation and take him in charge on suspicion of murder.

"The time was shortly after ten," Prothore said. There were sharp lines about his mouth. He might be a man on the verge of asking for help against some strong weight of injustice. Gone was the very assured young gentleman Hester had heretofore always seen in control of every and any situation—at least so in his own estimation.

"I know that because I counted the toll of bells just before entering Gaunt Street. And since then there's scarcely been a moment free from the inspector's presence. He badgered me with questions for the greater part of the night. Naturally I denied any involvement in the affair other than that which I have just recounted to you, and which I swear to be the truth. It is my misfortune that there is no one who might serve as witness to my whereabouts during the time I spent in Whitechapel. Apparently this served to encourage Inspector Newcomen's repeated accusations, despite any denial or explanation I could offer. The man's insolence is insufferable."

"Of that I am well aware," Hester responded, then fell silent as her visitor continued.

"He did me only a single service," Prothore said. "Upon learning of my position at the Home Office, he withheld my name from the journalists who presented themselves for an account of the affair early this morning.

"Shortly afterward I was able to repeat my story when brought up before a magistrate. I own it something of a surprise that upon hearing the testimony, he ordered that I be released."

"You came here directly?" Hester said.

Prothore nodded. "It seemed best to inform you of the circumstances as quickly as possible." He paused, frowning. "My only concern was that I might be followed."

"Right you are, sir."

At the sound of the familiar voice Hester rose, turning to face the intruder. If Inspector Newcomen was aware of her indignation at his unannounced entry, he gave no sign of it. In point of fact she was ignored completely as he continued to address Prothore.

"I was curious as to what you might be up to if let out of custody," Newcomen said. "And here you are."

"What business is that of yours?" Now it was Albert Prothore who rose, the set of jaw and shoulders defiant.

"Why, I should think our business is mutual, at least until this case is settled." The big man seemed unmindful of Prothore's posture. "You want Mr. Utterson's murderer brought to justice, the same as myself. Or do you not?"

"I've already answered your questions. I'm no murderer."

"And I'm no fool." The inspector regarded Prothore with a squint-eyed stare. "Inquiries were made among your neighbors. It's been alleged that you and the deceased wasn't on speaking terms. There's that business of the wall you put up behind the garden. The solicitor said it was on his side of the property line and meant to take you to court over the matter."

"True," Prothore said. "But this is hardly a reason to murder a man in cold blood." He paused for a moment, then continued. "And you, of all people, are in the best position to testify regarding my innocence. When you apprehended me you know I didn't have a weapon—nor any means of disposing of one."

Newcomen shrugged. "The cabby, perhaps? Suppose you lied about him taking fright. It may be he was an accomplice and went running off to dispose of the weapon."

"Rubbish," Prothore said. "I have no motive."

"Perhaps you do." The inspector turned to Hester as he spoke. "There's the question of the will. When we had our chat yesterday afternoon, I told you I meant to have a word with your solicitor."

Hester met his gaze. "I seem to recall you saying something of the sort."

"So it's 'seem to,' is it?" Newcomen's feet shifted, but not his gaze. "I put it to you that the thought of what Utterson might tell me was enough to get the wind up. And it was you who sent Mr. Prothore to silence him."

"That's a damnable lie!" Albert Prothore's voice was elevated to a most ungentlemanly level. "There was no communication between us whatsoever. She had nothing to do with this!"

"Am I to take it you acted alone?"

"I didn't say that—"

"There's little enough you did say to put my mind at rest." The inspector sighed gustily. "A heavy cross to bear—just knowing that if I'd called on Mr. Utterson a bit earlier last night, he'd have lived to see this sunshine today." Eyes that Hester thought might have been purposely slitted to a show of sorrow now flashed in sudden determination. "When that lily-livered little beak heard you mention the Home Office this morning, he couldn't wait to turn you loose. But I'm not done with you yet. There are others on the bench as is not so wishy-washy about matters concerning murder, and if I was to procure a warrant for your arrest—"

"You needn't do that!" Hester rose quickly. "I'll tell you what you want to know, everything he told me."

"He?" The inspector frowned.

"Mr. Utterson." Now Hester had the complete attention of both her uninvited visitors. "I gave him my word I'd not speak of this, but now there is no choice." She nodded at Newcomen. "If you would be so good as to close the door before taking a seat . . ."

The inspector complied, and a moment later both he and Albert Prothore sat listening as Hester broke her vow of silence.

It was not an easy matter to disclose, and as she continued she grew increasingly aware of how fantastic the account now seemed. The tale that had been barely believable when told in the dimness of the solicitor's office was utterly incredible in this sunlit setting. But she did her best to convey the gravity and conviction with which the solicitor couched his story. Whatever reservations others might have, there was no doubt that Utterson had told her the truth as he saw it—Dr. Henry Jekyll and Edward Hyde were one and the same.

Engrossed in the telling, Hester took little note of the response invoked. Only upon concluding did she give the auditors her direct attention, and it was to Albert Prothore that she first turned in expectation of support.

His expression alone was enough to signal the burst of words to come. "The man must have been mad! Stark, raving mad. All this business of chemicals and bodily transformations—it's scientifically absurd." Prothore shook his head. "Imagine alchemy and metamorphosis in this day and age. Sheer lunacy, if you ask me."

Newcomen scowled at Hester. "It's easy enough to put words in a dead man's mouth, but you'll not be taking me for a fool. I've a good mind to—"

Whatever the inspector's intentions, his announcement was interrupted by a tap on the door. Now it opened to admit Bertha as Hester rose. "Yes—what is it?" she said.

"Sorry, miss, but I was told it was urgent," the maid murmured.

"Urgent?"

Bertha nodded, displaying the envelope she held in her left hand. "The bobby outside said as to give this to Inspector Newcomer, right off." She glanced with avid interest from one man to the other.

"Right here with you, me gel. And the name is Newcomen." The envelope seemed smaller when transferred to the inspector's huge hand. He nodded at Bertha. "Go outside and ask the officer to wait."

"Do as the inspector says," Hester told the girl. As the maid exited, the big man was already opening the message. It seemed lengthy, as did the scowl that accompanied his reading, and the expulsion of breath that followed.

When at last Newcomen looked up, the scowl had softened to a frown. Folding the paper and restoring it to the envelope, he gestured toward Prothore. "Message dispatched from the Yard," the inspector said. "Bob Snell turned up this morning."

"And who might that be?"

"Your cabby—the one who ran off last night." Newcomen shrugged. "Said it was on his conscience, and when he read the paper he came in to make a clean breast of it."

Albert Prothore nodded. "Then you know I was telling the truth."

"That may be the case. Unless the two of you fixed on the same story beforehand."

Hester could contain herself no longer. "You presume too much, Inspector. I am not knowledgeable in police matters, but I think it unlikely this cabby would come forward with a voluntary statement if he felt it might implicate him in a crime."

"Nobody wishes to be implicated in a crime, miss," Newcomen said, "particularly when it's a hanging offense." Once again he directed his attention to Prothore. "Best to tell the truth."

"As I have," the young man responded.

"Up to a point." The inspector paused for a moment. "But not the whole truth. And it's that I'm after." His left forefinger tapped against the envelope in his right hand. "According to this, your cabby saw someone running suspiciously in the tree-shadows to the left and bounding over a hedge. It was that as frightened him off."

"I saw no one," Prothore said. "But I'm inclined to believe him. That would explain why he fled."

"Too much explaining, if you ask me." Newcomen glanced at Hester as he spoke. "Including that story about Dr. Jekyll. There's a goodish bit more to be learned." Newcomen stuffed the envelope into his pocket. "I'd best be about my business now."

"What are you going to do?" Hester said.

Inspector Newcomen was already moving toward the doorway as he spoke. "Something as will put a stop to all this."

chapter

15

Hester moved across the room to the far window. There was a bar of weak sunshine visible and she gave an impatient pull to the curtains to let that part of the natural world in. This could not truly be happening. She was looking beyond now, across the back garden to that ominous pile of the laboratory where all this horror was supposed to have begun. Supposed? Was she doubting Mr. Utterson's story, too? Prothore's reaction, that of the Inspector—though she would distrust anything from that quarter—had they shaken her so? Her mouth suddenly felt very dry and she quickly repressed a shiver as she swung around to face Prothore.

"What proof can there be—now?"

The other was frowning, but somehow in the disorder of his present appearance, in her memory of his story, he was now a rather different person than the haughty and arrogant man she had so resented. Perhaps his own world had been invaded by a reality that he could not have acknowledged before. She had led a retired life, yes, and her first excursion beyond four safe walls had shaken her. But she had not as far to go as Albert Prothore, secure all his life as a member of a caste designed from birth to give orders and not be challenged save by an equal.

"I don't know," he said. "Possibly Utterson left some account among his papers . . ."

"Possibly—" Hester got no further than that when there came a knock at the door and she started forward, wondering for a moment if the inspector had indeed returned. But at her call it was Hannah who entered, her long face even more set in a sharp cast of disapproval.

"Ma'am, it is Cook, she is all upset." She bit off her words as if she were firing them at some target. "Fish 'as been 'ere and wot 'e said—it 'as 'er all apart as it were."

"Fish?" Hester repeated blankly. It took her a full moment to realize that Hannah was referring to the arrival of the fishmonger's deliveryman.

"Yes, ma'am. And Mrs. Dorset, she's 'ad a turn."

Hannah gave an exaggerated shudder that Hester was certain was a piece of play-acting. "Sam Noggins, 'e says as 'ow when he came around by the back lane there was broken wood all around the door—that door into the court. As if someone was a-trying to get in 'ere—and it must 'ave been in the night, ma'am, 'cause there weren't no such signs when Patty were a-dumpin' the swab water from the scullery."

"The door into the back garden?" Hester looked from the maid to Prothore. "But Bradshaw said that it was securely locked, bolted, has been ever since—" She drew a deep breath.

Prothore was already standing over Hannah. "Show me," he demanded and the sharpness in his voice cut away even more of that languorous tone that Hester found so irritating. There was a new swiftness in his movements, as if he were eager to be in action.

She was not to be left alone, and followed as he headed for the rear of the house, with Hannah now a step or so behind. Mrs. Dorset was sunk into the well-cushioned chair that provided her throne in the kitchen. Her cap was pushed so far to the back of her head that her frizzled gray hair was a wild band over her forehead. She was red-faced and gasping as Patty stood beside her, a glass of some dark liquid in her hand trying to urge it on Cook as a restorative.

Leaning against the table was a young man, a stained apron tied about him, with a very strong odor of fish exuding from his untidy person. He was apparently thoroughly enjoying the scene he had helped to create.

It was Prothore who took command. Sam Noggins was summoned to be a guide. Perhaps Prothore supposed that Hester would remain to help revive the cook. Instead she followed the pair. This was her domain and she would have firsthand knowledge of anything that threatened it.

They surveyed marks that clearly indicated a determined attempt to force the gate into the garden area and behind the courtyard. Prothore shook his head.

"New locks—within this morning certainly. And other reinforcements." He took Hester's arm as if he were her elder brother or had some other kinsman's right to so lead her, and when they returned to the house he said abruptly, "This is no place for you!"

Though she had been shaken by the sight of that scratched door, she was still not prepared to surrender independence.

"This is my home. New locks, yes—"

He did not look as if he had even heard her. "Where is the butler?" he demanded as if she could summon the missing manservant with a snap of her fingers.

"I have not the least idea," Hester replied. The softening that she had sensed in him earlier seemed to have been banished. She told him of the disappearance of the servant after his abrupt resignation from service. Then, because she was indeed at a loss, she added: "Perhaps you, Mr. Prothore, can find someone to take his place."

"You are determined to stay on here?"

"Certainly. If it is indeed as Mr. Utterson declared, this house is mine."

He frowned at the fireplace as if in the dying coals there he could read something as momentous as the horrible story she had learned that very morning.

"You have no friend who is able to come and stay with you?"

"I believe you know something of my circumstances, Mr. Prothore." She was finding it easier now to draw back to her original estimate of him. "I come from overseas and—"

"Overseas! But that is it—of course!"

His eyes were alight and he lost some of that authoritative air. "Miss Jekyll, I would like to make my sister known to you. Margaret, Lady Farlie, has recently returned from India. Her husband's regiment finished its tour of duty, and he may be sending in his papers soon, as he has recently inherited from his uncle. I think"—and for the first time he smiled in a way that changed the image she held of him— "that you and Margaret will get on capitally together. You are of the same type of character. Certainly you can see the advantage of having an acquaintance in somewhat the same situation as yourself. Margaret has been a good many years out of England, with only a few, and curtailed, visits home. She is devoted to Henry and could never be persuaded to leave him for long—so she is finding settling down here something of a puzzle also. I would like very much for you to meet her."

Lady Farlie, Hester thought. Another such as Lady Ames—but maybe not. For some reason she liked what Prothore had to say of his sister. It was plain he admired her, and that there was more than just a family tie between them. To her own faint surprise she found herself agreeing.

"Very good! And I shall see to a locksmith and also look

for a reliable man to live in." All the distress and hesitancy that had been about him when he first arrived had disappeared. He strode briskly and stepped into the cab Hester had called for him with the assurance of a man of affairs with important business waiting.

Cook had been sent to her room for a lie-down. The fumes of brandy she wafted about her suggested that her withdrawal from the scene might be somewhat lengthy. Hester herself, to the openmouthed astonishment of Patty and the consternation of Hannah, set about getting a small lunch. Events had moved so swiftly and it was now well past noon. But Bertha slipped in deftly to aid her and they managed quite well in Hester's opinion.

Suddenly she was more than eager to meet Lady Farlie. But she could not go there dressed as a dowd. When she discussed the matter with Bertha as they worked together, Hannah surprised Hester by speaking up. There was a dressmaking establishment not too far away, she reported, that rented sewing machines. She had a cousin, in business for herself, who rented one from them.

Hannah was dispatched in a cab, money in hand, to get a sewing machine as quickly as possible. The routine of the house had certainly been shattered, but Hester was able to forget for a little while what had made her morning a time of uneasy foreboding.

Bertha next made a suggestion that could provide Hester with a respectable wardrobe in a very short time. The three least shabby of Hester's dresses were hung out on the edge of the wardrobe door, and now, with the assurance of one who knew exactly what she was doing, Bertha selected the one of gray poplin.

"At the sewing room," she said, "we get a lot of clothes— some of them lady's things as you would think could never be used, stained, and torn. But Mrs. Kirby, she can think of things as can be done to make them worth selling. Gets a nice little lot for 'em, sometimes, she does. Now, look 'ere, miss. We takes this and that nice violet stuff as you got at Myers. We drapes it, then we uses that ribbon there, and those buttons of cut steel as you got a card of at Gathers, and finally a rushing of the ribbon here.''

While speaking she was hard at work, pinning and pulling material and dress until Hester could share her vision. By teatime, with the aid of the machine Hannah had brought back in triumph, Bertha, with some help from Hester, had produced a dress that was nothing like the dowdy, out-of-style, limp thing Hester had first shown her.

Inspired by their success, Bertha had gone on to cut out two new gowns. She insisted upon making one that would be suitable for evening wear. It would go well with the chinchilla-trimmed mantle Hester had bought on her whirl-wind shopping trip.

Cook seemed to have recovered far enough to produce tea, though the sandwich slices of bread might not have been as paper-thin as desired. Hester was sitting by the fire in the hall resting her eyes and her cramped fingers when there was a knock at the outer door and Hannah admitted a footman with a note.

Prothore had certainly acted quickly. What she had was a request from Lady Farlie that she excuse the shortness of time and would she come to tea the following day. Hester hesitated only a moment before writing an acceptance. The thought of being able to meet someone who was perhaps as approachable as Mrs. Kirby, and who would certainly not hold her background against her, was refreshing.

But she had had enough of the darkness that seemed to linger even in the well-lighted hall. With no Bradshaw to do his proper duties that night, she made the rounds of the house herself, accompanied by Bertha. Mr. Hobbs, the lock-smith promised by Prothore, had indeed shown up, and was kept very busy. She now had a new collection of keys and tonight, after all doors were locked and window catches in-spected, they would be left beside her bed.

Bertha was still at the machine when Hester entered the disused bedroom they had turned into a sewing room. Hester scolded her gently.

"There is no need to strain your eyes. Off with you to supper or you'll have a bad headache and may not feel like work at all tomorrow."

"I ain't inclined to 'eadache, miss. Seems like I'm blest that way. Poor Missus Kirby, she 'as cruel ones sometimes. They lay 'er sick in bed. Many a time I've seen 'er so. She won't even 've one of us near 'er then. Says any noise make it worse. She takes to 'er room and jus' lies there."

"Can't she get help from a doctor?"

"Says she knows rest is all what 'elps."

"It is too bad she has those attacks," commented Hester. "Now, I mean it, Bertha, put away the sewing."

Two lamps and the candles on the small dressing table were alight, as Hester came into the room that had enchanted her so much on the day she had first seen it. She went to the small desk and opened her journal. But even as she picked up her pen, she found it suddenly difficult to order her thoughts. Order her thoughts, that was an expression of her father's that had often rung in her ears as a command. He had had no time for an emotional response to anything.

Her father, with his quest for complete good, complete evil—had, in his way, walked a path close to Dr. Jekyll's. It was the first time that comparison had occurred to her. Her father's research had been undertaken through the printed page; he had struggled to draw wisdom from earlier ages. Dr. Jekyll had sought another path. Because he was a man of science and not a philosopher, he had taken the riskier and more dangerous way of physical experimentation, which had ended in foul defeat. Her father's way had also warped him—had robbed him of emotion—while the doctor's research had transformed him into a creature of emotions which could not be controlled. Had her father ever, during his life of austere scholarship, been aware that he had also stepped beyond certain limits?

Both of them had sought, both of them had found—but in the doctor's case the taint lived on. She sat staring straight into the lamplight. During the day she had been able to avoid thinking about the horror of Utterson's death, but now memory broke through and could not be dismissed. Resolutely she opened the journal, determined not to give way to what she realized was fear. She was a Jekyll; could this strange obsession touch her? She did not believe it, she dared not! As carefully as if she were transcribing some passage for her father, Hester set down the events of the day.

Prothore's part in the action—she remembered how distraught he had been earlier when he had told his story—that was such folly that she had to believe that Newcomen was also a man under an obsession. Such were clearly dangerous.

There were marks on the back gate. Well, London was certainly not devoid of thieves. A large house might well attract their attention. But with the newly changed locks there was no chance of a lost key giving a stranger entrance. Bradshaw! For the first time she wondered about the abrupt flight of the new butler. He had been for some years in this house, keys could well have come into his hands—but if he were on good terms with any questionable person there would have been no need for that attempt at forcing the back gate. She hoped that Prothore would be as good as his word and see that she had a reliable manservant soon.

Hester made herself write on. The only thing that gave her spirits a lift was the note that had come from Lady Farlie. She made herself concentrate on the morrow and turn her back on today.

But once she was ready for bed she could not settle down. Something to read? She remembered those well-filled bookcases in the library. Hester had had no time to explore their contents but surely they could not be all medical books or scientific material. There would be no harm in finding out—

several times in the past when her nerves had been over-wrought she had been able to forget worries and irritations and woo slumber with what lay on a printed page.

Lamp in hand she resolutely went out into the hall, down the stairs. It was like venturing into some cavern, and she pulled her wrapper closer together at the throat, shivering, but refusing to surrender to what could only be illogical uneasiness.

In the library she lit two more candles, leaving a pool of light around the desk while she held her lamp high and went to the edge of the bookshelves. As she had expected, there were mainly treatises of a scientific nature, but she persevered and at length the name of Dickens shone out in tarnished gold. She pulled the nearest such volume from the shelves and went back with it under her arm. *Our Mutual Friend.* She frowned a little. Not too cheerful a tale in itself but certainly interesting enough to hold back thoughts she had no desire to welcome this night.

Hester blew out the candles and hastened along the big hall and up the stairs. She was eager to leave the chill dark of the lower part of the house as speedily as she could.

Once back in her room she settled the lamp on the bed-side table and went to the window. The only thing she disliked about the room was that its windows looked out on that ominous courtyard. Now she could not help herself, drawing aside both drape and curtain to look out into the night. The moon was full and for once no clouds obscured it. But there were shadows along the wall. From this height she could see a little of the back street, and though there were lights glowing in the higher windows of the buildings, it seemed unnaturally quiet and deserted.

Shadows—

Hester clutched the window curtain in a very tight grip. Had she seen a queer flutter of a . . . shadow coming toward the newly enforced gate? Nonsense—

She came away from the window highly annoyed at her-

self. Next she would be hearing housebreakers creeping up
the stairs! A very small covered jug sat on her table. As her
hands touched it she felt warmth, and then she saw a cup set
out beside it.

Bertha—the girl must have brought it up when she returned from her own belated meal. This was a thoughtfulness
that Hester had not expected. She uncovered the jug and
sniffed tea with an herb scent. Pouring herself a cup, she
drank and then retired to bed with Dickens firmly open to the
first page, fully intending to escape into the world drawn by
that master storyteller until drowsiness overtook her.

Hester's perception worked better than she had thought.
She had read less than five pages before the book actually
fell out of her hand. She laid it aside, put out the reading
lamp, and settled into her pillows, sure that she would have
a full night's sleep before her now.

chapter

16

Hester awoke with an odd sense of having been else-where—in some dream, but without memory of it except that it was vaguely distressing. Bertha had opened the drapes and there was a cup of tea waiting for her.

Sunlight streamed into the room as Hester pulled herself up and Bertha turned smilingly to look at her.

"'Tis a rare fine mornin', miss. Sun does change the look of things, don't it now?"

Hester took her watch from the pocket on the bed drapery. Nine o'clock! She had never before dawdled beneath covers as long as this that she could remember.

She drank her tea while Bertha fussed about the wash-stand, putting out a large fresh towel and moving a tall can of hot water. The sunlight had once more turned the room into the fairy-tale place she had first seen and Hester felt a surge of well-being and pleasure. This was not yesterday but to-day, and she had before her the meeting with Lady Farlie.

"There's this as came for you, miss. Brought around a half hour ago."

Bertha freed a square envelope from her pocket and laid it down on the bed.

Hester recognized Lady Farlie's handwriting.

"Dear Miss Jekyll," she read, "I know that this is extremely short notice, but there has been a change of plans and now I offer you a slightly different invitation. Our son, Robert, has returned home unexpectedly and suggested that we attend tonight the production of that amusing play, *Pinafore*, at the Savoy. Albert has not only produced tickets—which at such short notice is very commendable—but will accompany us. I hope you will consider my invitation to join us for dinner and go on to the theater. Perhaps this is an intrusion when we have not yet met. But we would very much like you to be our guest. We dine at seven, so that we may be on time for the play. If you do wish to accept this rather informal invitation, we would be most pleased."

Hester reread the note. It did seem strange that she would be asked to join what must clearly be a family outing, when she had never even met her hostess. Yet the tone of the note, judging by Lady Ames's world, was very cordial. Perhaps a refusal might even offer offense, and that she certainly did not want to do. She thought about it while she dressed and then ate a leisurely breakfast. At last she decided to accept. She had heard about the Savoy and its reputation as one of the "sights" of London. The *Pinafore* musical production had been many times mentioned. A real ship's deck was supposed to be laid on the stage. And Hester had never seen a real play. Any new experience that led to the widening of one's knowledge was to be cultivated.

Bertha had made a good choice in cutting out the dinner gown, and if they hurried and got it finished she would make a respectable appearance. She found Bertha already in the sewing room at work on the dusty rose taffeta. Hester smoothed one of the pieces with her hand; she had never before owned anything as gay in color. Yet judging by what she had seen in the shops this one was very subdued.

"It will be just right, miss," Bertha said, industriously sewing seams on the machine, "and that is truly your color. You ought to have pearls—"

"Pearls." Hester laughed. "No, there will be no pearls." It was impossible for her to imagine owning any jewelry except the cameo pin she believed had been her mother's. But Bertha was frowning.

"You must have something! Oh, I know." She jumped up from her chair, laid the material on the bed, and went rummaging among the fashion magazines and papers in which Hester had so recklessly invested. Flipping hurriedly through one of the magazines, Bertha came to a page and pointed out the fashion plate thereon. The lady, dressed in a gown similar to Hester's, wore about her throat not pearls but a ribbon holding an artificial flower for a charming touch.

"The very thing," Bertha said.

They spent a most labored day. Cook seemed to have recovered from the attack of nerves brought on by the report of "Fish" and was back in good form with the luncheon she served Hester. Hannah had taken her acceptance of the evening's entertainment to the Farlie house. Hester had almost thought to snatch it back at the last moment. Though she might be properly dressed, she did not know what a dinner might entail.

At Lady Ames's she had never been served anywhere except in her own room, and she could guess that the Farlie establishment would differ greatly from Mrs. Carruthers's boarding house. Life in Canada had not prepared her for such an occasion. Even as she stood at the fatal hour in her new gown, with Bertha giving a twitch of the overdrapery of the skirt, and looked into the wardrobe mirror to see herself fashionably clad for the first time in her life, Hester felt uneasy.

She knew that she would feel out of place, but she also

worried that the Farlies knew of the story she had told Prothore. How long had they been back in England? Had they read of the Hyde case at all? Jekyll was not a common name. To hear it might awaken memories of something sensational, and that would certainly shadow any friendship she might wish to pursue.

There came a pounding at the door, which made Hester a little flustered as she caught up her evening purse and fan. Bertha smoothed the mantle across her shoulders, and she descended the stairs to see Prothore waiting in evening dress and looking more at ease than she had ever seen him before.

"Good evening," he greeted her and she replied with the same innocuous words. He was watching her so intently that Hester was disturbed. Had she chosen the wrong dress? Or was it that he could only see in her the worn respectable dowdiness of her earlier state.

When they were seated together in a carriage she felt that she must say something even though he was so silent.

"It was most kind and thoughtful of your sister to ask me."

"Margaret was pleased you would come on such short notice." But he did not even look at her, staring straight ahead.

"I am sure she is a very pleasant and kind person," Hester said, struggling to keep the conversation going.

He seemed to arouse then from his meandering thoughts, but it was not comments concerning his sister that he voiced now.

"Did you truly believe Utterson's story?" That came with the force of a demand.

"Yes. And I think you also would have believed it if you had heard Mr. Utterson when he told it." She clutched her fan tighter. Hester hoped that she would be allowed to forget for a little while all horrors the doctor's confession had aroused in her.

Prothore was frowning now. "It is too impossible, it can't be!"

"Mr. Utterson believed in it. He told me that he had a letter from Dr. Jekyll explaining it all. Perhaps the letter—"

"I shall start inquiries concerning that. But Miss Jekyll, do you wish to continue to stay in that house? I do not think that can be to your good. Sell the place and buy something more to your taste."

"Mr. Utterson told me it would be some time before my inheritance is legally recognized. Thus I must stay there." She smoothed one gloved hand over the other.

"At any rate," he was continuing, "I shall see that you have a new butler. Bradshaw's disappearance I cannot account for."

"He gave notice and I told him if he wanted a reference he must stay through the month. Then I heard that he was gone and had not even asked for the portion of his pay due him."

"What explanation did he give for wanting to leave?"

"That he was not used to service where the police came. I think that I was not respectable as he saw it." She laughed.

"Utter and complete nonsense." Prothore's voice was sharp.

"I was told that ambitious servants who wish to work themselves up in the world have a dislike for being part of an establishment where the police are apt to come." She hesitated and then asked the question that had lingered at the back of her mind ever since her conversation with Inspector Newcomen. "This Newcomen, will he continue to pay visits?"

"He is a determined man. I have made some inquiries concerning him and they were all agreed on one point, that the inspector, once onto a case, never lets go until he is satisfied."

Hester felt a sudden chill, and pulled her cloak closer about her shoulders. To have her house haunted by Newcomen was not a prospect she faced with any pleasure.

The cab had stopped before a house with brilliantly

lighted first-story windows. "Ah, here we are," Prothore announced. He offered her his arm as they went up steps to the door.

Before he had a chance to use the knocker a boy, perhaps just in his teens, threw the door wide open.

"Uncle Albert! You are the tops for getting the tickets. Mamie and Mother are all primped up and it's going to be really great!"

"Robert, you have a guest," Prothore said in a voice that dashed the other's enthusiasm.

The boy colored and gave a small bow in Hester's direction. "I'm sorry, Miss Jekyll."

"But you need not be," answered Hester. "The treat we have been offered tonight is something to be very excited about."

"This is Robert, my nephew," Prothore said. And the boy gave another stiff little bow.

"Mother's in the drawing room." He was quite subdued and Hester made a guess that Robert greatly desired his uncle's good opinion.

Hester straightened as Prothore took her mantle and gave it to a footman. Placing the required tips of fingers on Prothore's arm, she allowed him to escort her to meet Lady Farlie. Was she about to face another Lady Ames? But to her relief the lady who arose to meet them halfway across the room was certainly quite unlike that plump and arrogant female.

She was tall and her complexion dark. Her hair, of which she had an abundance, had been braided and then wound around her head to form a crown into which had been inserted a pin in the form of an exotic bird, a peacock whose eyes and tail glittered in the lamplight.

Her earrings were also of glittering stones and matched a necklace made of drops, with pearls in each. The gown was dark blue but patterned on the bodice and in her overdress were golden flowers and leaves.

She looked regal, Hester thought. But the smile on her hostess's face was far too welcoming to make one uneasy. She took Hester's hand in hers with a grip nearly as firm as a man's.

"Miss Jekyll, it is very good that you have consented to share our outing. I have been away from home too long. You will forgive me if I do not quite know the rules anymore."

"I never did know them," Hester blurted out. "I am from Canada."

Lady Farlie laughed. "I see that this may be a case of blind leading the blind. But doubtless we can assure each other."

Hester felt warm and she also felt more at ease than she had with anyone but Mrs. Kirby.

The four Farlies met at the dining table. Colonel Sir Henry Farlie was a silent man but could smile at the talk about him, and sometimes interpose a shrewd remark or two. He was obviously somewhat older than his wife for there were gray streaks in his hair and his clipped mustache. The children were Robert, who had opened the door, and Mamie, who was wearing a white dress that did not become her dark complexion. She seemed shy and did not look at Hester except when they were introduced.

Most of the talk around the table was of the coming treat. "They say," Robert declaimed, "that a whole ship's deck sits on the stage and the theater has the new electric lights and—"

"A number of wonders, eh?" commented Prothore. "The lights are worth seeing."

"And we won't be seeing them unless we hurry," said Lady Farlie.

Lady Farlie, the children, and Hester had the family carriage, and Prothore and the colonel would come by cab. Though they arrived in good time they had to take a place among the cabs and carriages discharging passengers.

They waited for the rest of the party in the circular foyer

where the famed lights made the white, yellow, and gold of the walls glitter and the decorations gave Hester the feeling she had entered a palace. Surrounded by bejeweled ladies in their fashionable gowns, for a moment she felt awkward and ill at ease, then dismissed her concerns. She was here to see a show, not *be* one. They were at last ushered into a box, where the chairs were covered with blue velvet facing, and when the gold satin curtain finally rose Hester pushed all her worries away and allowed herself to enjoy the show.

She was still a little bedazzled when the end came. Lady Farlie smiled at her. "There now, that is an excellent feast for someone who has been away from it all. Henry," she said, turning her head toward the colonel, "I believe I shall favor going to theatrical performances."

The colonel smiled. "Right enough, Margaret. And you, Miss Jekyll, will you too become a theater-goer?"

"Perhaps I shall be tempted," she said. "But right at present I thank you for the invitation to see this performance and providing a memory that will linger a long time. You are most kind and generous."

"We all have to thank Albert, it was his idea—and an excellent one to be sure," said Lady Farlie. She held out her hand to rest on Mr. Prothore's arm. "I think my little brother has turned out very well!"

Prothore laughed. He seemed more at ease than usual and was nearly another person this evening. Among his family he dropped some of that arrogant attitude Hester disliked so much.

This time she took a cab with Prothore, who was humming one of the tunes from the show. "Thank you again for a wonderful evening, even more for introducing me to your sister and family. She has asked me to go shopping with her tomorrow, and also to Mundies. She wishes to take out a subscription. I shall do the same."

"You have a preferred author, Miss Jekyll? Rhoda Broughton, or Marie Corelli?"

"I have heard of the writers you mention," she said, "but I prefer books on travel."

"You do?" Then he mentioned a volume that had been one of her father's discards, and she was able to make a serious comment or two. "Egypt can be a fascinating place," he agreed. "It might be an excellent thing for you to investigate the chances of a Cook's Tour to such a country."

"If Dr. Jekyll's estate is settled in my favor, I might indeed do that!" Hester was excited at the thought.

They had swung around into the square where she lived and she was glad to see that the lantern affixed directly above her door shone very clearly. Another cab was pulled up not too far away, as if waiting for a fare to come out.

Hester drew out her key, ready to use it, when the door of the cab opened and she saw a strange figure standing there. It was not until he spoke that she knew him to be Newcomen; she heard Prothore draw a deep breath.

"Inspector!" Hester snapped. This man frightened her a little. She also experienced a flash of irritation that he should end her pleasant evening by appearing like a carrier of bad news. "Inspector, what is the meaning of this intrusion?"

"Why, I hunt a murderer, as everyone in the house knows. I am after Hyde."

"But Hyde is dead." She was bewildered. "I told you—"

"You told us a wild story—something out of the dreadfuls. You may not have had a hand at the beginning of this affair but you are taking a part in it. I want Jekyll and I want Hyde—both of them!"

"But they are *dead*," she returned, still unable to understand what the inspector was saying.

"Are they now? Well, I can give you proof that Hyde still walks this earth. We opened his coffin today, you see. And, miss—it was empty!"

chapter 17

"Naught to worry, miss."

Hester shook her head. "I'm all right, Bertha. And it's high time you were off to bed." She placed her cup on the tray as she spoke. "Please take this with you."

"Yes, miss." But Bertha made no move to withdraw. "Would you want for me to stay until you falls asleep?"

"Thank you, but that won't be necessary." Hester masked her true feelings with a smile. "Good night, Bertha."

"Good night, miss."

This time the girl picked up the tea tray and carried it with her to the door, which closed behind her noiselessly. Lying propped up against the pillows, Hester strained to hear the sound of footsteps in the hall and on the stairs beyond.

Nothing was audible, nothing at all. By this time the hall

and stairway were empty. She was alone here on the upper floor of the house. There was a lock on her door, but using it meant Bertha would have to pound for admittance in the morning, for there were no duplicates of the keys that rested beside Hester's pillow.

She stared at the silvery symbols of security. That's what they were, of course—mere symbols. Doors that were locked could be opened by other means. She remembered Utterson's account of how Poole had battered down the red baize door to Dr. Jekyll's cabinet and discovered the body of Mr. Hyde.

With the memory came disturbing realization. They were dead now, all of them dead. Poole and Utterson, victims of violence. Dr. Jekyll a suicide, by his own hand. Or could it be called his own hand, once transformed into that of Edward Hyde's? And was Hyde actually dead after all?

Hester thought of Newcomen's sudden, unexpected revelation tonight. Unexpected, unwelcome, and unnerving. What could it mean?

The question, like the grave itself, was an empty one. Open graves, open doors; neither truly revealed their secrets. And unopened, they afforded no real protection.

How difficult it had been for her to reject Bertha's suggestion of staying until she slept! Partially it was out of consideration for the girl after so long and arduous a day. Then there was the matter of her own pride; a stubborn unwillingness to admit the extent of the trepidation that assailed her. Beyond which, the kernel of the difficulty; there would be no sleep for her this night, not after what Inspector Newcomen had so abruptly announced.

Afraid? Hester lowered herself on the pillow atop the bolster. Of course she was afraid, but the worst of it was that she did not know what she feared.

Was it Hyde dead, or Hyde alive? *Or dead-alive?*

There had been a time when all of these considerations would have seemed impossible. That Hyde existed or had ever existed was in itself a defiance of what she had hitherto accepted as natural law.

"And what of you, Father?" she murmured. "Would you accept such evidence in your quest for absolute Good and absolute Evil? And would you conceive that the living proof resided in a member of your own family?"

Despite herself, for a fleeting moment this notion brought a genuine smile to her lips. She frowned it away quickly as she recalled Albert Prothore's advice. Upon hearing about the opening of the grave, he had urged Hester to leave the house immediately and take residence in a hotel. "If not, I am certain my sister would be happy to afford you temporary accommodations," he told her.

Only her insistence and the knowledge that she still had a partial staff in residence prevailed over his strongly voiced concerns. He then suggested that Inspector Newcomen post an officer on duty to guard the premises.

To this Newcomen demurred, and rightly so. Nothing had occurred here to indicate a threat of possible danger; under such circumstances the best he could do was to alert the regular patrolman assigned to the area around the square. "But mind the locks," he said.

The admonition was unnecessary. Hester had indeed minded the locks, each and every one, after the two men took their departure. Now there was nothing more until morning. Though sleep was beyond her grasp, she could at least close her eyes and attempt whatever measure of rest attainable.

Turning out the lamp, she snuggled into the warmth of the quilt. There was still a faint glow from the embers in the fireplace that did little more than add a reddish cast to the darkness. Beyond the window the night wind whispered promises of autumnal chill to come.

For a moment Hester's thoughts strayed to those mean streets she had traversed with Captain Ellison, and the forlorn denizens who huddled there. What would be their fate when winter came?

Once again she renewed her vow. Whatever the extent of the estate, a portion of it would be devoted to aid the plight of those less favored by fortune. It was not pity alone that moved her, but gratitude, upon reflecting how close she had come to sharing a similar lot.

Now she had been spared. And tonight had in many ways proved a revelation; an assurance that she could accustom herself to the standards of polite society, and that not all of its members were boorish ogres. The Farlies had accepted her without question, and Albert Prothore was once again appearing in quite another guise. It was as if all the stiffness and starch that had irritated her at the first could be put off like a coat. In fact with his family his friendliness and small signs of concern for her had been oddly warming in a way.

It was almost as if she met him for the first time, but then this had been a night filled with new experiences. Her meal was one of them; Hester had known hospitality before, but this was a revelation of what it meant to really dine out. And of course the theater was pure enchantment.

Hester sighed. Why couldn't that enchantment have continued? Why did the evening have to end with the ominous news delivered by Inspector Newcomen?

No answer, save for the whisper of the wind.

And here in her room the reddish glow dwindled and died. The darkness deepened like that which yawned from an open grave—the open, empty grave of Edward Hyde. She was fleeing that grave now, running through the tangle of windswept streets where shadows slumped in mute misery.

Shadows that can rise out of the grave can come into your house, into your life, come to take it over. All she could do was flee as she did now, running upstairs through the crooked corridors of the house, clutching the keys of salvation.

Hester blinked, awakening with a start to find herself actually holding keys in her hand. She must have dozed off without realizing it, and it was then that the dream came.

Presently it was fading as swiftly as it had come, and while she grasped the keys, the other elements eluded her. Something about trying to escape from Hyde, something to do with seeking salvation. The Salvation Army? That hadn't been a part of her dream, though in it she recognized some of the streets she'd traveled with Captain Ellison.

No, salvation lay somewhere else. That's why she had taken a tight grip on the keys. And now she must take a tight grip on herself until she remembered. It was important to remember.

Time ticked away. There were moments when she dropped beneath the surface of slumber but not into the deeper depths of dream. Hester had only a vague awareness of the coming of dawn and none whatsoever of Bertha's arrival until silence was broken as the girl set down the tea tray.

"Good morning, miss."

Her words were muffled, almost inaudible. Hester glanced toward the girl quickly and found herself staring at a tearstained face. "Why, Bertha!" she exclaimed. "You've been crying! What's the matter?"

"They've gone," the girl said. "Cook, 'Annah, Patty, and Ratsby, too—packed up and took off, th' lot o' 'em. Must of cleared out afore dawn, 'cause when I comes down to the kitchen at sunup there weren't a soul to be seen."

Hester was sitting upright now. "You mean they left without notice? Surely Mrs. Dorset could have waited on some sort of explanation for such conduct."

Bertha shook her head. "It was she as stirred up the others. Right tiddly, nipping at that bottle regular an' making out she'd been took with the vapors. Scared, that's the truth of it."

"I know she was upset because the courtyard door might have been tampered with," Hester said, nodding. "But she seemed recovered by the time I went to dinner last evening."

"'Yde," Bertha said. "She kept on about a Mr. 'Yde as used to come 'ere in the olden days. Mostly it was 'Annah she spoke to, but Ratsby and I 'eard our share." A quaver crept into the girl's voice. "Is it true, miss? Did this Mr. 'Yde shut himself away in that place across the courtyard an' take his own life there?"

"It seems so, Bertha." Hester firmed both face and voice into a counterfeit of composure. "But there's nothing to be afraid of."

"Dorset said different. She said as 'ow this Edward 'Yde's ghost comes 'an goes in the night."

Hester swung around the side of the bed and fitted her feet into the slippers waiting there on the floor. "I'm surprised at her." She strove to keep her tone light. "And even more surprised that Hannah, at least, would believe such nonsense."

"Per'aps they didn't at first," Bertha said. "But after Dorset told what that inspector 'ad to say last night about the empty grave—"

"Eavesdropping!" Composure failed Hester for a moment. "I didn't realize she overheard us."

"She 'eard, all right. Said as 'ow it proved 'is ghost was rised and on the prowl. A evil spirit, come 'ere to make mischief."

"So that's what frightened them off into the night." Hester nodded as she slid her arms into the robe that Bertha now held outstretched. "I appreciate your loyalty in not joining them. You're a brave girl."

"Thank you, miss." The accompanying smile brightened her tearstained countenance. "Someone needs to stay 'an look after you. An' now as we've new locks on all the doors—"

With the words came the recollection Hester had been searching for at the time of awakening. Now, as the girl opened the drapes, she called to her.

"Bertha—do you remark what I did with that card Mr. Hobbs gave me?"

"The locksmith, miss?" The girl nodded. "I do believe you set it in the tray on the 'all table. You wants it now?"

"Please to stay with me while I dress. Then we'll go down together. Between us we should be able to manage something for breakfast."

Hester dressed, grateful as much for Bertha's presence as for her assistance. The sky beyond the window cast a gray gloom over the garden and courtyard below. Even after Bertha brought the gas log to a blaze, it could not totally dispel damp chill and dim shadow from the sunless world without.

Further fires were kindled for comfort when they descended the stairs together, to which Hester added the cheer of candles. Assured that locksmith Hobbs's card was resting where Bertha had recalled, Hester pocketed it and led the way to the kitchen.

Mrs. Dorset's departure had indeed been precipitate, to judge from the state in which they found the cook's domain. A good thing she and the others, like Bradshaw, had not waited departure to demand wages; none would be forthcoming under these sorry circumstances.

Hester checked the thought with a rueful smile. How quickly one who had spent a lifetime of near poverty could slip into the imperious attitudes of the upper classes! All it took was a few days and a few pounds to transform the country mouse into a tyrannical tigress. Given their lifetimes in such a situation, it was a bit easier to understand Lady Ames and Miss Scrimshaw. On the other hand, Captain Ellison and Mrs. Kirby were not of that mind; they had chosen the right course, and she must follow it, too.

But now there was another course to follow, once she and Bertha concluded breakfasting. Reaching into her skirt pocket, Hester pulled out Mr. Hobbs's card and handed it to the girl.

"Do you know this address?" she asked.

Bertha nodded without looking at the lines of print. "Yes, miss. The shop's around the bystreet an' two squares down."

"Good. I would like you to go there now and see if you can fetch the locksmith for me."

Once Bertha was dispatched on her errand, Hester set about gathering up the breakfast dishes. Midway through the task she paused, setting them down again with a smile of rueful realization. Hands such as hers were not destined to be immersed in dishwater. What would Lady Ames remark upon seeing her thus engaged? More to the point, what would Bertha say?

Here, servants seemed more snobbish than their masters. It was the one trait that both cut across all classes of society and at the same time bound them together.

Hester forced herself to be seated. From this vantage the kitchen appeared vast, indeed; she would not wish to spend much time in it alone, nor condemn herself to solitary confinement in any of the rooms of this formidable house. She wondered that Bertha was not afraid to stay; perhaps she judged it preferable to the prospect of life in the streets.

Whatever the reason, Hester was grateful for her presence, and regretted even this temporary absence.

More quickly than she would have thought, the absence ended as Bertha signaled her arrival at the front door.

Hurrying down the hall to admit her, Hester was pleasantly surprised to see that the girl was not alone. Standing beside her, a portly, ginger-mustached man bobbed his head in greeting.

"'Obbs, m'um, at your service."

Hester smiled. "Thank you for responding so quickly."

The locksmith squinted toward Bertha through rimless spectacles as he spoke. "Caught me at the proper time, she did. I 'ad me a commission to fit winder-catches for a greengrocer's shop clear off on Oxford Street, but word come not to 'urry, seeing as 'ow the place burned down last night."

His bespectacled stare was fixed on the hall beyond the point where Hester stood in the open doorway. "Your gel here says it's a matter of some emergency. If you'd oblige me with a look . . ."

"By all means." Hester stepped back. "Do please to come in."

Hobbs entered, then followed her along the hall. Behind them Bertha closed and locked the front door, then hastened to catch up to them as they neared the kitchen.

"Problems 'ere, m'um?" the locksmith asked. "I 'ope nothing went amiss with our work yesterday. It's only I've young Sethers to reckon with. A likely lad, but still a new 'pprentice—"

"There are no complaints." Hester cut him off quickly. "You did an excellent job. It's just that there is probably more that must be done."

"Probably, m'um?"

"See for yourself and tell me what you think." Hester started toward the hall door that bisected the servants' quarters beyond, glancing toward Bertha as she passed. "If we have visitors at the front door while I'm gone, call out to them to wait. Then come directly to me."

Bertha's eyes widened. "Yer means to go inside over there?"

"Do not concern yourself, Bertha. Mr. Hobbs will be with me. Just stay here and do up the dishes."

Without waiting for a reply, Hester took a candlestick from the table, opened the door, and moved down the narrow unlighted corridor with Mr. Hobbs following directly behind. Pausing before the exit at the far end of the hallway, she reached for her keys and peered down at them in semi-darkness.

The locksmith moved up beside her. "Let me give you a hand, m'um," he said, and did just that, extending a pudgy palm.

The eyes behind the spectacles were keen, the fleshy fingers adroit. In a matter of moments the door was open and they moved into drab daylight beyond.

The back garden stood untended, a wilted wilderness overgrown with weeds. Hester reminded herself it would be needful to employ the services of a gardener in addition to other requirements for a household staff.

Now they were crossing the courtyard, footfalls crunching dead leaves, scattered victims of autumn winds. By the time they reached the entryway to the building on the far side, Hester was grateful for its shelter.

There was only the single door here on this side of the gabled two-story structure, but no lock had been affixed to it, and both the metal knob and the keyhole plate beneath were rusted.

Mr. Hobbs stubbed a finger outward. "Where paint 'as peeled, you can see rot in the wood. A lock won't 'elp; what's needed is a new door."

Hester nodded. "There are other things." She started reaching toward the doorknob but Mr. Hobbs intercepted her.

"Allow me, m'um."

His efforts resulted in a grating of rusty hinges and a surge of damp issuing from the open doorway. Darkness lay beyond.

Hester gripped the base of her candlestick; the taper it held was fresh, the wick still white. She turned to address the locksmith but he had already anticipated her request. A moment later the candle put forth a blossom of flame.

Mr. Hobbs reached forward. "Let me take that for you, m'um," he said. "Best I go first."

They started forward into the musty murk of a hall entryway, flanked by a wide door. Again it was the locksmith who anticipated Hester's movements by opening the door, giving access to a large room cluttered with boxes and dusty tables.

Mr. Hobbs glanced at his companion. "Do you wish a lock for this?"

"I doubt there is a need," Hester replied. The locksmith went over to two doors at the right. The first proved to be a closet, but the second revealed a steeply slanted stairwell descending into darkness that defied the candlelight.

Hobbs's hesitation was broken by Hester's nod. Slowly he set foot upon the uppermost treads. "Take care," he murmured.

His words were punctuated by the creak of stairs protesting the weight they bore. The air was more damp below and the darkness deeper, but the light of the flame was sufficient to disclose the contents of the cellar.

The locksmith frowned. "What need d'ye suppose he 'ad for all that lumber?"

"I haven't the faintest idea. Dr. Jekyll purchased this property from the heirs of a surgeon named Donner. Perhaps the original owner stored materials here against a time when he might enlarge the building."

Mr. Hobbs shrugged. "I take it Dr. Jekyll 'ad no such plans."

Hester allowed her nod to serve as a reply. She had no desire to discuss Henry Jekyll's plans, or even to speculate what they might have been.

Upon turning, it was she who led the way back up the stairs, into the tiny hall, and up to the door at its end. Here again the knob turned easily, and once more there was a telltale rasp of hinges as the door swung open.

This time the grating sound echoed, rising and resounding with an eery pitch through the recesses of the chamber beyond.

Like a scream, Hester told herself. This room must be the one described as Dr. Jekyll's surgical theater. How many times had real screams risen here? How much pain had poured forth, how much blood had been shed? This scene of suffering—had it also been the scene of death?

Very likely so, for she remembered hearing about Mr. Hyde having entered from the bystreet by "the old dissecting room door." Which meant that either Dr. Donner or Dr. Jekyll, perhaps both, had brought cadavers here. If so, for what purposes?

Since this was a surgical theater, its first proprietor may have performed autopsies for the benefit of medical students. But Dr. Jekyll had no students, at least not to her knowledge. Any dissections he conducted here must have been part of the process he described only as his "experiments"—a vague term used deliberately, and undoubtedly with good reason.

Hester did not care to dwell upon that reason. Mr. Hobbs's words came as a welcome interruption to her thoughts.

"I warrant you'll want a stout lock 'ere," he commented. "And a bit of oil on those 'inges while we're at it." His squint was directed through the open doorway and into the recesses of the room they were entering.

To her relief there was no hint of horror in what the wavering candlelight dimly disclosed. If a table still stood in this room, it was completely obscured by the array of crates and boxes stacked and rising to obstruct a view of the glass-guarded cupboards on the far wall.

The locksmith glanced at her. "Shall I move some of this so's to get through, m'um?"

"Don't bother. I think we can find a way around it." Hester noted that the jumble of crates and cartons did not extend to the near side of the room, where a path seemed to have been cleared along the wall. "Let us try here," she said.

As Mr. Hobbs raised the candle to peer forward across the narrow open area, its flicker revealed the outline of a stairway rising at the end. He advanced toward it and Hester followed reluctantly.

Hardly the word, Hester corrected herself. It was not mere reluctance but a much stronger feeling. Fear was a part of it of course, though only a part; the dread she recognized mingled with another emotion that could only be identified as a kind of horrid anticipation.

She knew what was upstairs—Dr. Jekyll's cabinet, his combined private office and laboratory, his sanctum sanctorum where deeds that were hardly saintly had been performed.

The path along the side of the wall, though unobstructed by heavy objects, was littered with dust and a scattering of straw from opened packing crates.

"Easy now, m'um," Hobbs murmured.

His warning was unnecessary. As she moved behind him up the staircase, the fingers of Hester's right hand curled to grip the balustrade. Glancing forward she saw the locksmith halt upon the landing and stand as though transfixed. When she reached his side the candlelight revealed the reason.

He was staring at the open entrance to Dr. Jekyll's cabinet. Hester remembered Utterson's account of how Poole battered down the red baize door with five blows from an axe, and the proof of his story lay just across the threshold. Broken panels and smaller bits of wood were heaped upon the faded carpeting beyond; all that remained within the frame of the doorway were a few splinters of metal hinging.

"Tut-tut!" Mr. Hobbs sounded almost reproachful. "No lock needed here, either." Now his voice held a questioning note. "Bit of trouble, I take it."

"Apparently."

Hester's reply was perfunctory, and deliberately so, for she had no intention of confiding in the locksmith.

Mr. Hobbs stepped over the shatterings of boards and panels inside the doorway. Halting beyond, he turned to elevate the candle for her benefit.

"Careful, m'um," he said.

Now Hester surveyed the cabinet she had just entered. Oddly enough, what she observed seemed almost so familiar as to lessen her fear.

Here, much as Utterson had described, was a somewhat commonplace room, dimly illuminated by the light from three barred windows and Mr. Hobbs's candle. There was a fireplace, a tea table, a business table, several comfortable chairs, bookshelves, and a tall cheval glass. Only the presence of the glazed presses full of chemicals and a third table beside them distinguished this quiet, carpeted room from the ordinary.

Carpeted.

Hester stared down and fear returned. In her mind's eye she could see what Utterson had so vividly described—the dwarfed and stunted body of Edward Hyde sprawled lifeless there on the carpet.

But it was not the thought that this room had contained a suicide's corpse that moved her now; it was the fantastic explanation of its true identity that lent ghastly color to the mental vision.

To banish it she quickly redirected her gaze to Mr. Hobbs. The locksmith was already on the other side of the room, examining the windows with something almost akin to admiration. "Stout bars, these," he said. "No need to 'ave replacements."

Hester nodded, and moved toward the bookshelves. "Would you be good enough to bring the candle closer?" she murmured. The locksmith obliged and for a moment she stood there satisfying a natural curiosity. At least she presumed this to be so, although it was difficult to determine just why people gravitate to observe the contents of bookshelves when entering a strange room. Would the interest lie in the books themselves or in the character of their owner? A man is known by the company he keeps; is it also possible to discern his nature through the books he reads?

Certainly Dr. Jekyll's library seemed to offer few surprises. At first glance the shelves appeared to contain nothing except medical works, plus a few that dealt with religion and philosophy. She reached toward one of the latter.

"Watch out!"

Hester felt the sudden grip of Mr. Hobbs's pudgy fingers tug her wrist back.

Staring down, she saw the great black spider emerging from behind the volume and scuttle across the shelf.

She could still see its huge and hateful image long after their hasty departure from the building and welcome return to the comparative security of the kitchen in the lock-guarded house.

Hester did her best to dismiss the memory during her discussion with Mr. Hobbs. A carpenter must be summoned to measure, construct, and install the necessary door replacements. The man he had in mind would be available within a day or two, though it would probably take another few days before the doors would be finished and ready for the locks that Mr. Hobbs would then furnish for them.

The idea of waiting that long was an uncomfortable one, but Hester accepted the necessity, and she comforted herself with the promise of future security.

It was only after Mr. Hobbs's departure that the vagrant thought emerged. *Love laughs at locksmiths.*

But what of hate?

What of the hateful, hate-filled Edward Hyde who had come to horrid life and met a horrible death in that shadowy domain where his memory still lingered like a palpable presence?

Hester's mouth firmed in resolution.

Locks were a temporary safeguard at best, but she must limit her major expenditures at the moment. When she came completely into her inheritance that building would come down at once.

She only hoped it would be soon.

chapter
18

Hester reconsidered her options at the breakfast table. There was no sun today, only gloom and a suggestion of fog. Even when she did not draw aside a curtain to face the courtyard, she was continually aware of the dark and noisome building. That must be changed, she thought, her fingertips clawing the tablecloth.

There was no way of obliterating the looming bulk that now, against all rules of perspective, appeared to throw a menacing shadow over the house itself. No, but it could be emptied—that was entirely possible. Swept bare of everything that might remind one of its former master and the evil he had brought into the world therein.

It would be a formidable task, rightly enough. One that she and Bertha could certainly not hope to tackle. No, she would need men to bring all the chests, furnishings, stacked boxes, and the like into the open. And where was she going to find those men? More to the point, for the immediate future, where was she going to find a new cook, housemaid, kitchen maid, footman, and all the rest of the help needed to run this house?

The door opened softly and Bertha came in with a fresh pot of coffee.

"Bertha, where do I go to hire another staff?" Hester asked impulsively. She knew that there were hiring offices in London, but she had no experience with them. Of course, she might appeal to Lady Farlie, but she felt it would be an imposition. And she also preferred to conceal from Prothore's sister the reason for her household staff's hasty departure.

Bertha set the coffeepot carefully on its tray.

"Miss, there's Mrs. Kirby. She 'as others 'sides just us girls as needs work. There's some as 'as been left with no places 'cause their people died, or went off to foreign parts. There's them too as 'as bin turned off without no characters 'cause somebody in the family took a dislike to 'em unfairly. Mrs. Kirby, she knows 'bout such, an' if she speaks up for them you can be sure they is truly 'onest an' good workers."

Mrs. Kirby, but of course! Hester could understand that warmhearted woman's struggle to help out just such servants as Bertha mentioned. Look at Bertha—why, what would she do without Bertha now? As for the men needed to clear the laboratory and that unholy chamber above—why, perhaps Captain Ellison could help her with that.

"I am going to take your advice, Bertha. Summon a cab in an hour. I shall be off to Mrs. Kirby." She glanced to the clock on the mantel. "Or is this too early to visit her?"

"Laws, no, miss. Mrs. Kirby usually be at her desk by noon, busy with accounts an' such."

Hester dressed in one of her old plain dresses and put aside her new mantle for her waterproof. The air, when she stepped up to Mrs. Kirby's door, was both moist and clammy, the nasty odors that clung to pavement and ancient buildings in this part of the city seemingly more pungent today.

It was not one of the girls who opened the door this time, but a thin woman whose flushed face was covered with many tiny bluish veins. Her nose was bent to one side as if it had once been broken and never treated. And the few wisps of hair that escaped from under the edge of a cap well pulled down on her head were of that brassy red so trying to anyone sentenced to grow it. She was wiping coarse, reddened hands on a dingy apron as she looked at Hester in open surprise. So blank was the stare that Hester was somewhat daunted.

"Mrs. Kirby, is she in?" she asked. "I am Miss Jekyll—"

Was it only her imagination or had there been a flash of something like life in that blotched face when she mentioned her name?

"Yus, miss." The woman spoke with so thick an accent Hester could hardly understand her. "Th' missus be in th' parlor. I tell 'er."

Leaving the door open she padded off, her misshapen feet showing clearly beneath a too-short skirt, shrouded in what looked like very old soft slippers. Hester waited a moment and then stepped inside, closing the door behind her. As that clicked into place the woman was back.

"Missus says come in." Having delivered that speech, she turned her back on Hester and shuffled off down the hall, leaving the visitor to make an unheralded entrance into the parlor.

Mrs. Kirby was not at her desk, but rather in a chair near the fireplace, thick shawl about her shoulders. She had none of her usual vigor, her face was pale and strained.

"But you are ill!" Hester burst out the first words that came to mind. "I should not be disturbing you!"

Mrs. Kirby smiled and sat up a little straighter. "Nonsense, my dear. I do feel a little poorly, yes, but having a visitor will banish what my dear mother used to call the gloomies. I am sorry that Murch had to answer the door but this is class time for the girls. Dear Miss Camely, the daughter of the vicar at St. Giles, comes one morning a week and

teaches reading and writing. It is very kind of her. Poor
Murch has not had too good a life and she is a hard worker
but not what one would call a proper parlor maid. Now, what
have you been doing, and how is Bertha working out?"

"Bertha," declared Hester, "is a treasure. I do not know
what I would do without her, especially now. It was Bertha
who suggested that I come to you for advice." Quickly she
expressed her need for a new household staff as soon as possible, but she did not explain more than that the servants
who had been with Dr. Jekyll were no longer with her.

"I see." Mrs. Kirby nodded. "And what do you need in
the way of a household?"

"A cook, of course, and a kitchen maid, also a parlor
maid. The house is large but many of the rooms are closed
up and I do not use them. Then a butler, or if that is not
possible at least a dependable footman." She repeated what
Bertha had said about the needs of servants who had lost
their chance for future employment through no fault of their
own.

Mrs. Kirby had slipped a little farther down in her chair
again, and to Hester she seemed paler than when the girl
had first entered the room.

"Bertha is very right. And I do know of several who have
been having a very difficult time of it."

"There is one other thing." Hester did not know what
impulse made her speak, but she voiced her desire to clear
the laboratory building completely as soon as she could, and
asked Mrs. Kirby if she thought she might gain the aid of
laborers from the Salvation Army.

"There are surely some who will be very glad for a few
days' work," her hostess agreed. "Now I shall just look at
my ledger and find—" But she was never to finish that sentence. She had struggled free of her shawl and was standing
up when suddenly she caught desperately at the back of the
chair to support herself. Hester moved quickly to her side, at
the same time calling out for help as she steadied Mrs. Kirby

against her. But the weight of the other woman was more than she could handle and she was afraid both of them would fall.

The door opened so quickly it slammed back against the wall, as Murch came in with a long stride far different from her earlier shuffle. She frowned blackly at Hester and almost dragged Mrs. Kirby from the girl's hold.

"Now, dearie," she said in her husky voice, "up t' bed with you it 'tis! You 'ad no cause to come out of it noways this day."

Hester moved to offer help again but a second, very angry scowl warned her off. Slight as Murch seemed she was fully equal to the task of maneuvering her mistress out of the room, though it was plain that Mrs. Kirby was no longer fully conscious. Hester watched her raise Mrs. Kirby from one step to another as she led her aloft. The girl hesitated, unwilling to leave until she was sure just how the older woman fared.

At length Murch came down the stairs. She still frowned and burst forth as she went to throw open the front door.

"Don't you come worryin' 'er agin, you 'ear. She 'as been 'aving one of them 'eadaches of 'ern. Tear 'er near to pieces they do. She is better in 'er bed and there she's goin' to stay." She left Hester no time for any comment or question but slammed the door firmly and decisively behind her.

Then, before Hester could go down the step to the walk, she was nearly whirled off her feet by a slight form that flung herself at her and clung, her body shaking with tearing sobs.

Instinctively Hester held her, or the girl would have fallen to the ground. It was as if upon reaching Hester she had exhausted the last of her already overtaxed strength. Her head fell back and Hester saw, to her horror, Sallie's face, now disfigured by bruises, a trickle of dried blood from a split lip dried across her chin.

"'Ere now, wot's all this?" The cabman who had been

told to wait for Hester looped his reins about the stock of his whip and climbed stiffly down from his perch.

"Oh, miss, please . . ." Sallie's hands kept a tight hold on Hester's skirt. "They'll be comin', they will! Oh, please—"

She gasped and went limp. Had not Hester already taken a good hold on her, she would have collapsed on the pavement.

Hester made a quick decision. She doubted if Murch would even open the door now should she knock again. And Mrs. Kirby was in no shape to take on what seemed to be a major problem. She spoke quickly to the cabman.

"Help me get her inside and then drive back as quickly as you can to my home."

For a second or two the man looked dubious and then, after Hester had gotten in, he lifted Sallie so that she could hold the half-conscious girl against her.

She begrudged every moment they spent snarled in the heavy traffic of the main streets it was necessary to cross. However, before they reached their destination, Sallie roused, and she raised her head from Hester's shoulder, looking about her with a dull lack of understanding until some fresh terror seemed to strike her and she pulled away.

Hester caught both the girl's hands in hers. "Sallie!"

"Oh, miss—I was tryin' to get to Mrs. Kirby. She let me out and told me to run—she didn't 'old with such doings. Oh, miss, what will I do, what will I do?" Her words became the wail of a heartbroken child.

"Sallie, you are coming home with me. Mrs. Kirby is ill and I do not think she can care for you at present. There is nothing to be afraid of, truly."

Sallie shook her head. "You don't know, miss." Her bruised face twisted. "You don't know as to what they did!"

"You will tell me, Sallie. But do not try to talk now, child. It will all come right, I promise you it will!"

Sallie's head still shook but she settled back against the seat, and when Hester again put her arm about her, she sighed and relaxed.

Hester again commandeered the aid of the cabman to get Sallie up to the door of the Jekyll house. The door opened before Hester knocked and Bertha swept forward to help the half-fainting girl. It took a while before Sallie was settled in the morning room, sipping at a cup of tea loaded with honey, which Hester held for her since the girl's hands shook so she could not control them.

A loud knock on the outer door resounded through the hallway outside the half-open door and Sallie screamed, striking out so that the hot tea spattered across Hester's gown.

"They's come! They'll take me! Oh, miss." She clutched at Hester in a grip that carried the pressure of her fingers through the material of Hester's sleeve to cut into the flesh beneath.

For a moment or so Sallie's fear was so contagious that Hester wondered if the girl was speaking the truth. Could whoever had so mishandled the child followed her across the city to threaten her here? She bitterly regretted the loss of Bradshaw.

Bertha had disappeared and now she came back. "I looked through the window, miss. It's Mr. Prothore," she reported.

"Let him in at once."

"Miss?" Sallie's hold grew even more desperate. Gently Hester pried the girl's fingers loose.

"It is all right, Sallie. This gentleman is a friend. I will stay with you until Bertha comes back, and then I shall have to leave you for just a little while. But you must not worry. You are truly safe here."

When she first saw Albert Prothore she knew for a single instant a silly desire to throw herself at him much as Sallie had done to her on Mrs. Kirby's doorstep. There was something about this rather stiff-appearing young man in his very correct morning coat that suggested the safety of normal life. She had confidence in what he might offer for Sallie's case.

However, it would seem that he had come full of news himself.

"I have heard from the inspector," he said so swiftly after he had spoken a formal greeting that she had no time for her own story. Instead she knew a sudden thrust of fear. What new trouble was going to descend upon her as thick as a fog?

"He believes now that the body was taken from Hyde's coffin by Resurrection men—"

"Resurrection men?" she repeated without understanding.

"A nasty business," Prothore said quickly. "One that should not be mentioned to a lady, but I knew that it might in some manner relieve your mind to know. Bodies have many times in the past been taken secretly from newly interred coffins and sold to unethical medical persons for the purpose of dissection. It was once a very prevalent practice. So much so that families were obliged to provide guards for graves to prevent it. Now it only happens occasionally, but two bodies have been taken during the past three years from graves not too far from Hyde's. So that could logically explain his own vacant coffin."

"I see—" Hester began, when, without a knock, Bertha came into the hall from the morning room.

"Please, miss," she said breathlessly. "It's Sallie, she's gone all to pieces."

"Sallie! Oh—" Without realizing that she was doing so, Hester reached out and laid her hand on Prothore's arm. "Please, you will think that I bring nothing but difficulties to you but this is something . . . I think something horrible! Can you find time to listen to—"

He did not allow her to complete the sentence. Instead his other hand closed warmly over hers where it lay upon his arm and he came at once with them.

Within the morning room Sallie was sunk far down in the chair to which Hester had earlier guided her. She no longer cried, made no sound at all. Hester swiftly disengaged herself from Prothore and crossed to the girl's side. She slipped her hand under Sallie's chin and brought her bruised face up into the light.

Sallie stared straight before her, giving no indication that she was even aware of Hester's touch.

Hester went down on her knees and drew the girl close.

"Sallie, dear—Sallie!"

The girl's head turned slowly and this time her eyes did focus on Hester. She tried to twist out of Hester's hold.

"You don't want to hold me, miss." Her voice was steady but she spoke in an emotionless monotone. "I did fight, miss, I did. But they was too much—so they made me bad, real bad."

"Sallie, dear." Hester spoke with all the warmth she could summon. "You are not bad—remember that! You are not bad. Can—can you tell me what happened to you?"

Sallie's eyes were still on Hester's face and she spoke as might a young child reciting a lesson.

"I—I felt poorly, miss, 'cause I fell in the kitchen, slipped on some spilled grease. Mrs. Kirby, she was upset— told me to go and lie down. Mrs. Kirby, she is always kind to us, always!" There was some emotion in that assertion, as if Sallie held to the thought desperately.

"So I laid down for a little; that Murch, she came up with a cup of something she said would help the pain. I didn't drink it all—it tasted nasty—though I knows as 'ow things that are good for you usually do. But after I drank that I got sleepy. Then—" She swallowed as if she were having difficulty saying the words.

"And then . . ." Hester prompted.

"It was queer, like—like a dream, only it was real. There was two of 'em—men. They talked a little in whispers but it weren't any such words as I ever heard before. They had a big baglike thing an' they put me in it. I couldn't move then, miss, I couldn't. It was like all my bones 'ad melted like. An' I could make no noise, either. They carried me out of the room but I couldn't see nothin'. There was someone else there—a woman. She talked kind of muffled an' she used those other words, too.

"I think they took me up to the roof, miss. Though that part is all muzzy. An' when we come down to the street again they must have 'ad a cab waitin'. We rode in that for a while an' they didn't take any more notice of me then, as if I were a bundle of wash or the like.

"The cab stopped an' when they lifted me out the edge of the bag thing they had over my face fell off. I saw a street lamp an' there was a sign, too. It said Cadogan Square. They carried me around the back of a big house. There was a place there for carriages, I think.

"Somebody 'ad a door open an' they took me in an' dropped me on the floor, 'ard. T'was then that I found I could move a little, but when I tried to get out of the bag, somebody gave me a clout 'cross my ear as made my 'ead ring an' I can't remember right after that.

"When I knew things ag'in I was on a bed. An' *he* was there lookin' at me!"

The glassy stare came back into her eyes.

"'E was a gentlemen so 'e was. But 'e—'e was worse than m'dad, 'cause when I tried to fight 'im 'e 'it me. 'E—went to a table an' got a little whip, miss. An' then 'e used it. 'E used it till I couldn't fight 'im anymore an' 'e did it, 'e used me, miss. An' all the time 'e was talkin' 'bout what 'he was goin' to do to me—awful things, miss. I knowed badness all my life but not such badness as that! Please, miss, it's true— I fought 'im as long as I could. An' 'e kept sayin' as 'ow 'e liked 'em as 'ad spirit. An' 'e laughed, an' laughed! It is all true, miss, I swear it is so!"

"I believe you, Sallie." Hester felt sick. She had heard of such things, even though no lady was supposed to know that this filth existed. But to have it happen to someone like Sallie—

"Cadogan Square!" For the first time Prothore spoke.

"You do not know which house, Sallie?" His tone when he addressed the shivering girl was gentle.

"No, sir. But 'e—'e was dressed like a gentlman, 'e was. 'E 'ad a red silk wrap 'bout 'im an' a fine shirt an' 'e talked grand like a real nob. 'E 'ad gray hair an' long wide whiskers alongside his jaws. An' there was a scar under 'is one eye. I do remember true, sir. Seems like I'll never forget 'im—'e was a devil, so 'e was."

Suddenly Sallie's taut form relaxed in Hester's hold. It was as if the telling of her slavery had released her from some bondage.

"How did you get free, Sallie?" Hester asked quietly.

"Oh—that. I was so 'urted I could only think as 'ow I must get away before that one came back again with 'is whip an' all. I was sure 'e locked the door, but all of a sudden it opened an' a woman came in— Miss, this be truth—she was a lady an' she 'ad been crying, 'er 'air was loose, it was gray an' atangle, but 'er robe was all ruffles an' lace.

"She said I must come quick an' she was near as afraid as I were, miss. But she 'elped me get on my clothes an' then she took me down the stairs an' through a place near a kitchen, I think. Then she opened a back door as was bolted an' gave me a push out.

"Told me, she did, to go as quick as I could 'cause she could not 'elp me anymore. I—walked an' I walked an' sometimes I just fell down an' 'ad to wait till I was a bit rested. I knew if I could get back to Mrs. Kirby she would 'elp. I don't know 'ow long I was walking so . . ."

"How can it be possible!" Prothore was standing, staring at the wall as if he saw pictured there all Sallie had told them.

Hester was quick to answer. "I propose to believe Sallie, sir."

"Faulkner!" Prothore exclaimed. "I had heard rumors, yes. But to believe any gentleman could sink that low! Listen," he said now, directly to Hester. "Can you keep Sallie here overnight? I am going to Newcomen. This certainly is of greater importance than a plundered coffin. And I have been led to believe that if anyone can do something, it will be the inspector. You know"—he looked at Hester now as if he were seeking to offer apology—"I had heard that such things happen, but I also believed that nine tenths of such stories were merely infamous gossip. Gossip in certain circles can be extremely lurid and have little or no foundation in fact. But this is one time when perhaps we can make sure that such a crime will be answered for. As soon as I can I shall see you again, Hester."

And he was gone before she had a chance to answer him.

chapter

19

Hester's hands were shaking while she helped Sallie take a warm bath and used what remedies Bertha could find to spread across the welts that had broken the skin of that thin young body. Having wrapped the girl in one of her own nightgowns, she put her to bed, but left a lamp turned low on the near table.

Once back in her own chamber she rang the bell for Bertha and prepared to once more inspect the fastening of the house. Though good sense told her it was hardly likely that Sallie's assailants would have traced the girl here, she could not put aside an apprehension that seemed to grow by the moment. The house was so very large and there were only the three of them. Hester did not believe that Inspector Newcomen would appear at this hour; he would be far more likely to come in the morning.

When Bertha arrived she gave her one of the lamps that

had been placed on the desk, and she herself took up the larger one. They started down the stairs.

"Sallie, she said as 'ow them men took her out of 'er bed. But that be very queer. Missus Kirby, in 'er 'ouse things don't 'appen."

"Mrs. Kirby has been ill, Bertha." But even as she spoke, Hester struggled with an unvoiced question. Sallie's bruised and torn flesh bore witness that she had indeed undergone the ordeal she described, but how had she been taken out of a house of refuge, and carried away? On the other hand, why should Sallie have made up such a story? There was a real mystery here.

Prothore's comment, which she remembered more vividly now, would suggest that he actually knew Sallie's attacker. And if Sallie told the same story to Inspector Newcomen, would he believe it? The word of a battered child might not be enough to hold against a denial from a so-called respectable member of the upper ranks of society.

"Murch." Bertha's voice cut through her worried thoughts. "She's been with the missus for a time. 'Most two years now. She was a nurse once, they say, only she gave the wrong pills to a lady as she was takin' care of. They didn't prove nothin' against 'er. Only no doctor would send 'er on a case again. T'was 'ard luck until the missus took 'er on. She'd do anythin' for the missus, she would. But she ain't no fool, neither. If any man came trampin' in the 'ouse to carry someone out, she'd 'ave known it. Miss, I ain't a-sayin' as 'ow Sallie didn't 'ave any bad time, but what she said 'bout bein' carried out—that don't sound true." Bertha's voice held an indignant note. "There's somethin' wrong!"

"We shall go over the whole matter in the morning. Sallie is in no state to be closely questioned again tonight." Hester tried the front door. It was indeed firmly locked and Bertha had also remembered to shoot the bolt after she let Prothore out.

But when Hester gave Bertha the second lamp to hold and

pulled aside the drapes to inspect the window fastenings, she noted not only that the twilight faded very quickly indeed, but that there was a storm already in progress. She could hardly see the nearest street lamp, so thick was the curtain of falling rain. And she was suddenly aware of the blasts of wind that lashed the heavy downpour against the wall and windows. Hester shivered. The fire she had ordered kept going in the hall fireplace had near smoldered away, and she told Bertha to put down her lamp and build up the flames.

Even though the flames came to life again, Hester looked uneasily around her. The light from the revived fire and the two lamps they had brought with them did very little to banish the shadows creeping out from corners and walls.

She drew a deep breath and suddenly felt ashamed. Was she to be daunted by wild fancies? The house was like any other, and she was a reasonable human being with a mind that had been trained not to give room to fancies.

They continued their checking of the locks. The whistle of the wind outside became louder as they eventually reached the serving quarters of the house. There were live coals in the cookstove and Hester, putting her lamp on the table, raised the teakettle from the hob. It was full enough to give them each a cup of tea. She had not eaten since lunch and realized she was very hungry.

With no thought this time of demeaning herself in the position of mistress, she helped Bertha bring out of the stores enough for a meal, which they shared seated at the kitchen table. The bread was more than a day old but not too dry, and there was some cold sliced beef and butter, even part of a slightly stale cake. Hester took note that they must replenish their stores on the morrow.

They had finished stacking their dishes when Bertha gave a sigh.

"It do be 'ard on the missus, these bad 'eads. She 'as such

pain with 'em. She 'asn't got no one as seems to take note 'cept Murch and she's no doctor.''

"We must find out in the morning how she is," Hester agreed. "I do not think that she will feel able to tell me about any staff. I think I shall have to ask Lady Farlie for aid. We cannot continue without help."

The rain still beat fitfully against the windows, which were dark squares on the shadowed walls. This house of gloom was not where she wished to make her home. It seemed somehow to reject anyone or anything that disturbed its dusty silence. If her claim to Jekyll's estate proved legitimate, she would sell it.

This city was not all of England, and what she had seen of it certainly had not been to her liking. London itself had a dual nature—the smiling Dr. Jekylls of polite society masking the presence of the malevolent Mr. Hydes lurking in the lower depths. No, this was not for her. There must be some other town, where she could find days of real sunshine and gentle breezes, a garden, a small house. For a moment she allowed herself to dream of living in a small house where she and perhaps both Sallie and Bertha could be in peace, away from the grime and horror of this city. Why, they might even be able to establish a refuge such as Mrs. Kirby had done, taking children out of the dark into the light and seeing that they had a chance for a good life!

"Bertha, do not worry about washing up," she said, getting up a little stiffly from the hard kitchen chair. "I shall be—"

She was not to finish that sentence. A scream tore through the house, clearly audible above the moaning wind. Hester snatched at the nearest of the lamps. There was no need to return to the hall in order to reach Sallie. The servants' backstairs were close to hand. Gathering up her trailing skirt in one hand and holding the lamp in the other, Hester hurried up the steep stairs.

She could hear Bertha behind her, but another throat-racking cry of fear led her to nearly drop the lamp. Then she was out on the carpeted hall above. A figure clung to the wall there, edging toward her, and a breath later the light of her lamp showed her Sallie, her hair in wild locks about her shoulders, the nightgown so entangled about her feet that the girl fell forward even as Hester set down the lamp on the floor and hurried to her.

Sallie's eyes held that blank stare, as if she looked beyond into a place filled with such terror that she could not abide with it and was wit-blasted by what she had seen.

"Sallie!" Hester caught the girl in her arms. They were both on the floor now as Sallie fought to free herself from Hester's hold.

"No! Please . . . please—"

"Sallie—" Hester raised her voice, tried to reach the girl's wandering mind. "You are safe, child!"

Sallie whimpered and then a shadow of intelligence was back in those blank eyes. She gazed up at Hester.

"'*E* was comin'—" she stammered.

"No, Sallie, there is no one here but Bertha and me. You are entirely safe."

Sallie's shaking hands closed over her arm in a tight grip. "'*E* can't come?"

"No one is coming to hurt you again, Sallie. You have had a bad dream. And you are chilled." The girl was shivering so hard she also shook Hester. "Bertha will bring some hot gruel." She glanced to the other girl. "Help me get her back to bed, Bertha."

Sallie was close to a limp weight but they once more got her against the pillows and well covered. Hester moved a chair to where she could sit and hold Sallie's hand in hers as she spoke to Bertha.

"Do you mind going down again, Bertha?"

"I got the lamp, miss. An' I'll put the other at the top of the stairs, since you got that one 'ere." She nodded toward the lamp on the table, which Hester had not turned up to its highest gleam.

Both lamps in hand, she left and Hester continued to watch Sallie. That small bruised face turned on the pillow so once more her eyes met Hester's fully.

"They can't get me now, can they, miss?"

"Of course they can't!" Hester reassured her.

The wind howled loud enough to be heard through window and muffling drapery. There was a slight swaying that Hester did not like, some draft must have found its way in. But she did not try to break Sallie's hold to see what caused it. Nor was this any time to ask more questions of Sallie. How had Sallie really gotten into the hands of her assailant? That story of being carried from Mrs. Kirby's—

Sallie's eyes had slowly closed but her hold on Hester had not relaxed. Hester shifted a little in her chair and Sallie's eyes opened instantly, her grip tightening even more.

"Miss—!"

"I'm not going to leave you, Sallie," Hester promised as the door opened and Bertha came in, a bowl and spoon on a small tray. "Now, Sallie." Hester got up, freed her hand, and lifted the girl a little on the pillows. "Bertha has made you some gruel. I am sure you will feel better when you have finished it."

But when Sallie tried to spoon some of the mixture into her mouth, her hands shook so that Hester had to feed her. Her swollen lips made it a painful business and Hester took it very slowly.

Bertha had gone, but, before the bowl was emptied, she was back, this time with a small teapot and a single cup and saucer, which she set down on the bedside table.

"For you, miss." With efficiency she built up the fire, and then, passing through the connecting door, she brought a shawl she draped about Hester's shoulders.

"That is kind, Bertha," Hester told her gratefully. "You get some rest now. Take the room where we have been sewing and sleep there." She did not like to think of Bertha alone in one of the small servant rooms at the top of this gloomy house.

"Thank you, miss. Drink your tea 'fore it gets cold now. Good night."

"Good night," Hester returned, but she was more aware of the fact that though her portion of gruel was not yet finished, Sallie seemed to be lapsing into slumber again.

As Hester set the bowl aside, the girl gave a little sigh and settled back amongst the pillows as though at last ready for rest.

Hester poured herself a cup of the waiting tea after she had drawn her shawl closer about her. She took a small sip. It was sweet, as if loaded down with honey, the same type of restorative they had pressed on Sallie earlier. Only Hester found it far too sweet to her taste, much as she did not want to hurt Bertha's feelings.

Sallie was well asleep again. Hester went softly to her own chamber, teacup in hand, and emptied its contents into the slop jar. Then, gathering a second shawl and a throw from her own bed, she was back with the child. Selecting the most comfortable chair in the room, she drew it close to the bed.

Now that the house was silent within, she became aware the storm seemed to have died down. Yet she found herself listening as if she expected some happening that had not yet come. Finally she went to the hall door of the room and, for no good reason she could give, stood with her ear against it. There was no sound.

Back once more in her chair, her feet at rest on a small footstool, yet close enough to the bed to be aware of any move from Sallie, Hester rested her head against the tall back of the chair, and, in spite of all her best intentions, her eyes closed. How long she dozed so she did not know but she came awake and sat upright.

Her first attention was for Sallie but the girl had not moved.

Hester pressed her lips together tightly, her hands curled into fists. She was certain that she had awakened because of some sound. The fire had burned quite low again. She made herself move to the hearth, put some lumps of coal on. But she did not lay aside the brass-handled poker, keeping it still in hand as she went toward the hall door.

This time she opened it a crack to hear the better.

There!

As well carpeted as the stairs might be, the old wood creaked under weight.

Someone was coming.

Now she could see light, a wavering glow that could only be that of candle flame. Without thought Hester opened the door wide.

Bertha stood at the top of the stairs. She uttered a startled gasp and looked at Hester as if her mistress were an apparition.

In one hand she held a candle, which now tipped perilously to one side so the wax dripped to the carpet. In the other hand there was a gleam of metal. Bertha had armed herself with one of the large carving knives.

"Bertha, what are you doing?"

"Oh, miss." The girl's voice was low-pitched but there was truly fear in it. "Oh, miss, I be comin' to fetch you. There was a noise—"

"What sort of noise?"

Bertha hesitated, frowning. "Summat like a door closin' wiv the 'inges gone to rust—"

"Here, inside the house?"

Bertha's frown deepened. "It could be."

For a moment Hester felt the tingling of sudden fear, then dismissed it with a shake of the head. "But that's quite impossible. We checked the doors together. And all the hinges were oiled when the new locks were installed."

But even as she spoke, her banished fear returned. New locks had been installed throughout the house, but not the laboratory across the way, where the outer door was yet to be replaced.

Hester started forward. "Come with me." She gestured with her poker. "And put that thing away before you cut yourself with it."

The girl thrust the knife through the belt of her apron and moved up beside her mistress, holding the candle high.

Together they entered the sewing room and crossed to the window. Hester halted and looked outward. The rain had ceased but the sky was clouded and the night was dark. Staring down at the black bulk of the building across the courtyard, she scanned the entrance. To her relief the outer door *was* closed.

It was not until she started to turn away that she saw the momentary glimmer through one of the upstairs windows. A light, flickering in that ill-omened cabinet above the far end of the laboratory! And then, literally in the blink of an eye, it was gone.

"Bertha, did you see it?"

"See what, miss?"

"The light across the way."

Bertha shook her head. "No, miss." She glanced down at the candle flame. "Per'aps it be a reflect'un on the glass from this 'ere."

The answer made sense—at least the sense Hester wanted to believe in now. Still, she must be sure.

"Please lift the candle," she said, then looked out as Bertha complied. But there was no sign of a reflection in any of the upstairs windows.

"Move it about, Bertha. The light may have been cast on the pane from a different angle."

Again the girl complied and for a long moment they both fixed their gaze on the darkened windows. Then, as the candle sputtered, Bertha glanced away, poking to clear the wick. It wasn't until Hester started to turn once more that she caught the flickering flare from the corner of her eye. An instant later it vanished, but now she knew there had been no mistake. And what she had seen was not a reflection.

Bertha looked up at her mistress. "Miss—?"

Involuntarily Hester's grip tightened around the handle of the poker. "Come!" she ordered, crossing to the doorway, then gesturing Bertha to precede her along the hall and down the stairs to the landing below. There she halted.

"What is it, miss?" Bertha's voice seemed to come from a long distance away. Hester shaped words with a mouth that was suddenly dry.

"Let me have the candle," she said. Bertha complied, and in its closer light Hester consulted her watch. The time was nine-thirty. And though the rain had ceased, the heaviness in the air hinted that this was but a temporary lull. She must take advantage of it now; there was no other choice.

"Bertha." Hester had to force herself to speak calmly. "Do you know how to reach Pembroke Square?"

"Yes, miss. Three squares south an' one east."

Hester nodded. "I recall Inspector Newcomen saying a police station is located at the corner crossing. You will please to go there immediately."

"But, miss—"

Hester ignored the interruption. "Inform them we are in need of a constable and ask if he might accompany you here at once."

The girl frowned, bewildered. "They'll want a reason—"

"Tell them there appears to have been a break-in out back. And that it would be best to notify Inspector Newcomen as quickly as possible, since he is concerned in this matter. I think mention of his name could be helpful."

"Ooh, miss, then there be some mischief what you've not told me—"

"Bring a constable and we'll see." This was the time for firmness, not faltering. "Now take your shawl and be off."

Before Bertha could utter further protest Hester was guiding her on a candlelit journey ending at the front door. Here she thrust the keys into the girl's hand. "I shall be upstairs with Sallie, so use these when you return." For the first time her voice betrayed the urgency seething within her, but not the fear.

And it was the fear that mounted with her as she climbed the stairs. Once Bertha had departed on her errand, with the front door closed and locked behind her, fear remained Hester's sole companion. When she reached the room to find Sallie soundly sleeping, there was momentary relief, but it was not until she made another visit to the sewing room that a further inspection dispelled her dread. The building below and beyond the window was dark once more.

Perhaps it had always been so, and the lights had indeed been no more than reflections. In such a case the police would take her for a fool. Still, better to risk their ridicule than the possibility of perils seen or unseen. In any case, she hoped Bertha would not be long.

Returning to her post, Hester dropped into a chair at the bedside. Thank heavens the child was safe! Safe, and so deep in slumber after such an ordeal. In this, at least, she could be envied; as Hester leaned back she wished it were possible for her to close her own eyes, if only for a moment. And, in a moment, she had. It had been a trying evening.

chapter
20

It had been a trying evening for Albert Prothore.

Getting about in the storm was the least of it; a stroke of luck provided him with transportation just around the corner from the Jekyll house. Nonetheless his journey was hardly pleasant; storm or no, the Strand was jammed with cabs and carriages at this hour. The discomfort of wet garments only served to intensify his impatience as the hansom's pace frequently slowed to a crawl.

Meantime his thoughts were racing. What Sallie had told them must have come as a shock to Hester, but his own immediate response was one of sheer outrage. That low and debased creatures like Sallie's father might perpetrate such infamies he could at least understand, though not excuse. Even the little he had learned thus far while investigating in Sir John's behalf was enough to explain deeds born of degradation and desperation. But Faulkner's role in this affair was another matter. It was he, and others like him, who made it possible for the panderers and procurers to ply their filthy trade here and abroad, for poverty-stricken parents to sell their children, for children to sell themselves.

Upon approaching Trafalgar Square the cab, impeded by traffic ahead, came to a jarring halt, and this time the pace of Prothore's thought followed suit.

Hold on now, he told himself. Not so fast; no point jumping to conclusions. Club gossip about Faulkner was scarcely a substitute for hard evidence. There were other residences flanking the four sides of Cadogan Square, and any of these might well harbor elderly gentlemen with perverse inclinations. There would be no reason to mention his suspicions to Inspector Newcomen unless he could substantiate them. If Mrs. Kirby or any of her household staff furnished anything by way of proof, it would be time enough to speak up. Until such a juncture, what he meant to tell the inspector concerning Sallie should be sufficient.

Admiral Nelson stood steadfast against thunder, lightning, and driving rain, but Albert Prothore was grateful for the protection of the cabman's brolly as he was escorted to the shelter of Scotland Yard.

Once inside he was on his own in the crisscross of damp hallways flickering in the fitful flare of gaslight. Rain or shine, the corridors here remained crowded, the cubicular offices occupied, twenty-four hours a day. It was all very well to speak of law and order, but there seemed precious little of the latter here. Law and disorder would be a more appropriate description. Prothore was forced to make no less than three inquiries before finally finding his way to Inspector Newcomen's diminutive domain.

Newcomen was properly surprised by his visit and even more taken aback by the account of Sallie's ordeal. It required nothing more on Prothore's part for the inspector to take action.

"No sense sending constabulary around until we know

what we're after," he said. "What's wanted is prompt investigation. I'd best deal with the matter directly. D'ye have the street address?"

"I do." Prothore nodded. "Better still, I'll go with you."

"That won't be necessary, sir."

"By your leave, I should like to accompany you. Miss Jekyll is greatly concerned—"

"As you please." Newcomen busied himself donning a greatcoat preparatory to braving the storm. "But meaning no offense, sir, since this is by way of being official business, it's understood that I'm to ask the questions."

"Agreed."

The rain was still pelting down as the inspector led Prothore by a circuitous route to the square. Here, much to the young man's surprise, a cab stood at the curbing, then rolled forward immediately as they appeared.

"Jerry," the inspector murmured. "Reckon I'm his best customer."

And so he seemed to be, judging from the alacrity with which the cabby produced a brolly and ushered them across the walk and into the waiting vehicle. Prothore noted that Jerry had a second umbrella for his own use already opened and mounted above the driver's seat. The horse, less fortunate, had to be content with a battered specimen of straw headgear with a brim wide enough to protect both eyes from the onslaught of rain.

Once settled and rolling Prothore took confidence in the realization that the first stage of his mission had been accomplished. This confidence, he acknowledged, was increased by the presence of his companion. Inspector Newcomen was by no means the sort of chap one would seek out as a dinner guest or partner for a game of whist, but in a situation like this he was an ideal repository of trust.

During the drive he asked many questions. Mainly he seemed concerned with Sallie's veracity, though the lack of details in her story didn't trouble him overmuch.

"Drugged, I venture," he said. "Small wonder she couldn't tell more. Unless, of course, it's all twaddle."

"But there'd be no reason. And we both know she was in harm's way before." Prothore glanced at his companion. "Would you think it likely her father might have been behind this attack also?"

"Possible." Newcomen shifted in his seat as the cab lurched. "Bears looking into."

Prothore frowned. "It would appear you have a great deal to look into. This business of the grave robbery, as well as murder. And have you yet discovered the whereabouts of Mr. Utterson's manservant?"

"Pope?" The inspector shook his head. "No telling where that one disappeared to. Sunk without a trace."

"Do you surmise he might be responsible for his master's death?"

Newcomen sighed. "That's a hard nut to crack. What's lacking here is motive. Nothing in the house seems to have been disturbed, and the victim's wallet hadn't been emptied, so it wasn't robbery. I had a word with Utterson's clerk and the charwoman on hire for weekly cleaning, and they know nothing about Pope, or if there was bad blood between him and the deceased."

Prothore glanced sharply at his companion. "Would Pope have known the truth about Dr. Jekyll?"

"Not likely. Utterson was a closemouthed man."

"But his chief clerk, Robert Guest, must have had some inkling."

"That may be. But I still hold murder springs from motives, not inklings."

The inspector's tone was brusque but Prothore ignored it. Peering through the window at his right, he observed that the downpour had slackened; gas lamps kindled radiant reflections from rain-soaked cobblestones, transforming gutters into glitter. Yet lightning was far from plentiful here and the intervals between held only darkness in their depths. A cold wind slithered through the streets, and even inside the cab, with the added though somewhat dubious protection of his damp inverness, he felt sudden chill.

Could it be occasioned by fear? Such emotions were, of course, foreign to English gentlemen; if indeed he was afraid, it was not for his own safety.

Hester was his concern, she and the two girls unarmed and unsecured in the night. Even if no danger threatened from without, the very house that held them had been the scene of tragedy before; perhaps it harbored other perils still. He determined to return there without a moment's delay once the meeting with Mrs. Kirby concluded.

The rain had ceased entirely by the time Jerry brought cab to curb before the residence that Albert Prothore recognized from the other evening. It was hard to realize how much had happened during the short span since the night he had rescued Hester from Sallie's father and his companions.

Prothore tempered the thought with a rueful smile. "Rescued" was hardly the proper term; "forcibly removed" was closer to the mark. What a senseless little fool he thought her to be, coming to a place like this on that occasion! And yet here he was tonight, himself returning to the scene of— what? A crime, the suspicion of a crime, or merely the focal point of a hysteric child's flight of fancy?

Whatever the answer, he hoped it would be forthcoming shortly. The thought of Hester's plight could not be banished, but he did his best to concentrate on the mission at hand while accompanying Newcomen from the cab. Jerry had dismounted from his perch; he was feeding something by hand to the wet and weary horse as a reward for services rendered.

The wind seemed to swirl more swiftly even in the brief time required for the two men to proceed along the walk and up the steps to the front door. Prothore tugged at his hat brim to tighten it against rising gusts. The rain would be returning soon.

Once within the shelter of the doorway he stood waiting as the detective knocked. It was a matter of some moments before the energetic summons was answered. When the door inched open, the face that peered cautiously outward and upward bore no resemblance to Hester's description of the lady residing here.

"Yus?" The utterance was midway between a query and a croak.

The big man nodded. "We wish to see Mrs. Kirby," he said.

"'Oo 'ud I say is callin'?"

"Inspector Newcomen."

The croak took on a guarded tone. "Yuh wiv th' p'leece?"

"Scotland Yard."

"Missus don't be 'ere."

The door started to close far more quickly than it had opened, but Newcomen's right boot wedged in the crack. "Not so fast," he retorted. "I'd like a word with you."

"Th' missus be aout." Again the thin sloven attempted to push the door shut but the inspector's foot remained firmly lodged. His hand tugged the edge of the door, pulling it forward to widen the opening.

There was a murmur of protest. "'Ere, whatcher abaout?"

"Mind if we step inside to talk?" Newcomen said.

The woman shook her head. "The chil'ern is asleep. I'll not 'ave yuh makin' a disturbance."

The inspector made no reply, but retained his hold on the door to keep it open at this angle.

Now Prothore obtained a better view of the woman who confronted them across the threshold. From beneath a cloth cap reddish curls framed a blotched forehead and a crook-nosed face mottled by broken veins. He recalled Hester's description of the domestic she had encountered here, and tried to remember the name she'd mentioned.

Then it came to him and he smiled quickly. "Murch, isn't it?" he said.

"Yus." The eyes blinked assent.

"I am a friend of Miss Jekyll's, who came here to visit Mrs. Kirby this afternoon. It is important that we speak with her at once."

The woman frowned. "Th' missus 'as gone out."

"When?" It was Newcomen's interjection.

Murch shrugged. "Some'ut nigh a hour ago, per'aps a bit more—"

"The rain was coming down in buckets then." The inspector spoke sharply. "Why would she go out in the middle of a storm?"

Murch hesitated; when she replied she directed both her gaze and her answer to Prothore. "The lady 'oo was here— Miss Jekyll—did she say as 'ow the missus took sick?"

"I believe she did mention something about Mrs. Kirby suffering from headache."

"She got wuss wiv the storm. Come on somethin' fierce, it did. There be naught I could do to ease 'er, so I sent word round to Captain Ellison, 'oping mayhaps she might be of 'elp." Murch drew breath with a wheeze. "An' Gor bless the good lady if she don't drive up straightaway in a cab to fetch the missus to her very own doctor."

"She's there now?" The inspector's query was lost amidst the growl of thunder, but his next words were audible. "Do you know the doctor's name?"

Again the frown and the shake of the head, broken abruptly by the sudden pause. "'Old on—I b'lieve Captain Ellison did make mention to the cabby when I 'elped bring the missus aout. A Dr. Warren, she said. At Number Seven, Oxhall Lane. Yus, that be it—"

"Thank you, Murch." Prothore made the acknowledgment quickly, conscious that Inspector Newcomen had already turned and was descending the steps. There was a flicker of lightning, and again thunder sounded over the sudden patter of rain.

Prothore turned and followed Newcomen back to the

waiting hack. By the time he entered, the gentle patter grew into a downpour drumming against the cab's roof.

Was this a new storm or a continuation of the old? Even as it came, he dismissed the question as unimportant. What mattered now, as lightning flared and thunder boomed, was the knowledge of Hester's situation. When he left her, long hours ago, he had given his promise to return; what must be her apprehensions now? Would she realize that his absence was due to circumstances beyond his control? And even if she did, what comfort would that assure in the face of possible hazard at present?

These questions too must be dismissed, as he gave voice to others that rose after Newcomen had instructed Jerry of their destination.

"I'm curious, Inspector. Considering the girl's story about being carried off over the roof, mightn't we have had a look upstairs? We were already on the premises—"

"On, but not in." Newcomen jabbed a fat finger forward to emphasize the distinction. "Only one way to enter without permission, and that's with a warrant in your hand. Seeing as how this location is City, not Metropolitan, I'd get no help from the bench here, and no mercy if I forced my way in. Mrs. Kirby can answer questions about what's upstairs."

The rain hammered down and the cab swayed in its course as Jerry swerved to avoid the deeper pools in the pavement. Lightning split the sky, and the thunder responded with a roar of pain. Its echo was lost in the rain, the clop of hooves, the clatter of wheels, the creak of carriage springs.

Turning to the window at his right, Prothore faced the fury beyond.

"Hester—"

He wasn't aware the word had escaped his lips until Newcomen nudged him. "Don't trouble yourself about Miss

Jekyll, sir. We'll look in on her directly once we've spoken with Mrs. Kirby."

Prothore nodded. "It's just that I gave my word to return, without realizing how long this matter would take. By now she must be quite concerned, what with the child to care for and the storm—"

The hand that had nudged him now rose to gesture interruption. "Understood. Perhaps you'd ease your mind by going to the house directly."

"Then we'll not see Mrs. Kirby?"

"I can do so alone. No reason for you to delay further."

"In that case we shall need another cab." Once more Prothore's gaze went to the carriage window and the slash of rain beyond. "How can we find—"

Again it was the inspector's hand that interrupted as he banged to signal the cabby's attention. The conversation that followed was brief, terminated by a grin from Jerry as he squinted down from the opening above.

"Right." His voice rapsed over the sounds of the storm. "Right as rain."

Fortune favored Prothore in his travels for a second time this evening. Within the space of a few minutes Jerry managed to hail and halt a cab that had just discharged its passenger at a residence on Fratney Place.

The seat was still warm when Prothore took the previous occupant's place. After giving the cabman instructions he could relax, secure in the knowledge that he was on his way.

"Oxhall Street's just ahead here," Newcomen had told him. "Once I've had a chat with the lady, I'll join you at the house. It shouldn't be long."

But time stretches in the clutch of impatience, and Prothore's journey seemed to him interminable. Thunder ruled the darkened, rain-drenched streets, and in its wake was the rattle of wheels, the thud of hurrying hooves, the crack of the cabman's whip.

All this he heard but did not heed, once premonition possessed him. Something was amiss; something he could not surmise but merely sense with an intensity that grew by the moment. Nerves, of course. Prothore tended to regard himself as one not given to agitation, but that had changed now. So much had changed within so short a span. How little he had known of the real world, or the miseries and mysteries it contained! In his own fashion he had been as guileless and naïve as Hester herself.

Hester. It was she who unnerved him now, the thought of her in that huge and lonely house, huddling against the storm and—what? *Something else.* Something lurking, something looming.

He peered through the window, past rivulets of rain, and noted a hack curbed on the bystreet directly around the corner from his destination.

As the cab pulled up before the front door Prothore had already extracted a note from his wallet. Refusing both change and the offer of umbrella-escort, he hurried up the walk and the sound of his knocking rivaled the rumble of the thunder.

The door swung open, revealing reassurance. Bertha stood in the hall, lamp held high.

"It's you, sir!" She too seemed reassured now. "Please to come in 'afore you catch yer death! Such weather as we be 'aving—"

Prothore crossed the threshold and the maid closed the door behind him, sliding the bolt into place. He glanced at her quickly. "Miss Jekyll—is she all right?"

Bertha nodded. "I just looked in on 'er. She's upstairs with Sallie. 'Ere, let me take them wet things."

Removing his hat, he handed it to the maid for placement on a peg projecting from the rack in the corner beyond the door. He turned and loosed the fastening so that she could remove his inverness. The girl lifted the wet garment from his shoulders and he breathed a sigh of momentary relief. Momentary and premature.

For it was then that pain stabbed between his shoulder blades and Albert Prothore fell forward as the knife drove deep.

chapter 21

Hester awoke to thunder, startled not only by its roar but by the realization that she had dozed off in spite of her determination to remain alert.

The crash was still echoing as Sallie stirred in response, eyes open and oval in alarm. Hester's hand moved quickly to the girl's shoulder, arresting both her movement and her outcry.

"Don't be alarmed, Sallie. It's only thunder."

"I know, miss."

Hester's fingers stroked the bare flesh of her charge's arm, then halted. "Your skin is like ice, child! You need an extra blanket. And you might do with a nice hot cup of tea." Hester rose. "I'll go put the kettle on."

"Please, miss, let me come with you."

"I'd rather you stayed here. It will only take a moment."

"Please—"

The entreaty echoed in her eyes could not be denied. She rose quickly as Hester nodded.

"Are you sure you'll not find it too chill?"

"No, miss." Sallie's bruised lips parted in the semblance of a smile.

"Come along, then." Hester took the girl by the hand and led her to the door of the morning room.

She strained to hear above the rush of rain. Surely Bertha must have reached Pembroke Place before the storm broke. By now she should be returning, unless something unforeseen had occurred.

Resolutely Hester put the thought aside when, hand in hand with Sallie, she started into the hall. And stopped, in sudden alarm, at sight of the figure rising from the shadows of the staircase and moving toward them.

Alarm gave way to reassurance as she recognized Bertha. "Thank goodness you're back!" Hester exclaimed. "And the police—"

"There aren't any police," Bertha said. "You'd best come with me."

"With you? Where?"

"No questions." The girl's voice was flat.

"I don't understand." Hester frowned. "Look here—"

She broke off suddenly as Bertha stepped forward. Both hands moved swiftly, the left grasping Sallie's shoulder, the right rising to hold the knife blade against her throat.

The blade was bloody.

"Bertha—!"

"Shut your mouth." The girl's grip tightened as Sallie gasped. "You, too! One sound an' yer done for." She nodded at Hester. "Back stairs now. You first."

It was a nightmare, Hester told herself. That's what it was, that's what it had to be. At any moment the thunder would rise again and she would awaken in her chair at Sallie's bedside.

But the thunder *was* rising and she was *here*, descending

those steeply slanting stairs with Sallie behind her. Sallie, Bertha, and the knife. The bloodstained knife.

Now, the kitchen, and Bertha thrusting the keys into her hand. "Unlock the door," she said.

The voice came clearly, not in the drone of dreams; the metal key was cold and solid to the touch. Outside the surge of rain swirled across the courtyard as they hastened to the shelter of the bulk, which was no longer totally black. In nightmare or reality, light flickered from the windows of the upper level at the rear, and smoke billowed from the chimney that rose on the roof above.

Then they were inside and for a moment Hester halted. Sallie cried out as the tip of the knife blade grazed her throat. Bertha ordered them on and they moved forward into the dark laboratory, along the narrow path bordering the wall, then up the sagging stairs at the far end, the stairs that led to Dr. Jekyll's cabinet.

That's where the light issued from; the light of flames dancing in the fireplace, the light of the tall candles on either end of the desk.

Crouched behind the desk, but turned so as to gaze into the flare of the fire, was the cloaked figure casting its sable shadow against the weathered wall. Hester stood staring while Bertha moved forward, holding threat to throat as her captive trembled.

The figure nodded. "Good work, girl! And now we shall conclude it."

At the sound of the words, Sallie cried out. "That's the 'un! The 'un what 'ad me took by them slavers!"

Hester didn't recognize the voice but now, as the figure rose and turned, she recognized something all too familiar. Despite the stunted body and the distorted face, there could be no mistake. The creature was Mrs. Kirby.

chapter

22

"You know me, eh?"

The voice issuing from the twisted lips was deeper and more resonant than Hester remembered it to be. The bulging brows, slanting cheekbones, and jutting jaw rendered the face feral. Now the woman nodded, splayed hands busy on the desk before her.

"Here." One hand pushed papers forward, the other dipped a pen in the inkstand and extended it. "I require your signature."

Hester peered down at an unfamiliar sight that was nonetheless recognizable; a document prepared by means of a typewriter. As she reached toward it, Mrs. Kirby's broad hand covered the surface, then peeled the topmost sheet back to reveal a second, which displayed a blank space at the bottom of the page.

"No need to read it." The pen jabbed down. "Your name goes here."

"What am I signing?"

"Call it a stay of execution if you like." The woman's chuckle rose above the hiss and crackle of the flames on the open hearth. "Sign and the child will be spared. If not—"

The pen rose in a slashing gesture.

The eyes of Hester's companions told the story; Sallie's wide with terror, Bertha's slitted and intent upon the blade pressed against her captive's throat.

The creature behind the desk was gazing at them too, and in a moment she nodded, her voice knife-sharp. "As you wish. Now, Bertha, now—"

"No!" Hester reached for the pen, reversing it quickly to scrawl her name at the bottom of the second page. As she flung the quill onto the desktop, Mrs. Kirby's mouth slitted to a vulpine grin.

Blotting the signature, the woman laid the document on the desk to her right, then glanced past Hester as she spoke.

"What kept you?" she said. The grin had disappeared. "What kept you? I told you to give her the draught."

"She didn' drink 'er tea."

"No matter. You had the knife."

"I'd not go up against 'er poker." Bertha spoke rapidly. "She spied lights over 'ere and sent me orff to fetch the rozzers."

"But you didn't go?"

The girl shook her head. "She give me the keys when I went out. I waited a bit to be sure she'd gone upstairs again. Then I let meself back in."

The woman nodded, smiling. "What happened?"

Bertha glanced at Hester. Pushing Sallie forward at knife-point to the side of the desk, she bent forward and whispered her reply.

As the seated figure listened, the grin broadened. "Excellent, my dear. Excellent!"

"Thank you, m'am."

"Take the girl downstairs, Bertha. Go by way of the other

door, the one Monsieur Philippe pried open when we came in tonight. He's waiting with a cab on the bystreet. Victor and I will meet you later at the appointed place."

Listening, Hester arrived at fresh perception. The side door gave access to the laboratory below from the bystreet. It was the one that both Poole and Mr. Utterson had referred to when describing the comings and goings of Mr. Hyde.

As for the names Mrs. Kirby mentioned just now, they were doubtless accomplices, the men Sallie had spoken of in her account of abduction. That much seemed evident.

But not to the child. There was no hint of comprehension in her vacant stare as Bertha guided her past the shattered, scattered fragments of paneling from the smashed-in door. Sallie seemed in a state of shock, completely unaware of her surroundings, and realizing this caused Hester to remain silent. Under the circumstances unawareness could be a blessing, but it was one that Hester herself was denied.

Once Bertha and Sallie departed she was only too mindful of the situation in which she found herself; alone with this woman she knew but did not know, this being that should not be.

The storm raged outside, the blaze within. Logs must have been brought to feed the fireplace, for the flames leapt high and Hester fought giddiness in the mounting heat, conscious of the scrutiny from across the desktop.

She forced herself to confront that stare, found voice with which to challenge it. "How could you bring yourself to this? Have you taken leave of your senses?"

"Quite the contrary." The deep voice held a hint of mockery. "My senses have come to me, after a lifetime of suppressing them." The speaker shook her head. "The years I wasted mending the woes of the unfortunate, tormenting myself over the misery of others! Small wonder I endured the agonies of constant megrims until remedying my own suffering eased and opened my mind. Then I knew."

"Mrs. Kirby—please, listen to me—"

Hester faltered, for the woman took no heed, continuing without pause as she stared into the feeding flames. "That which we call 'evil' is only our natural state. The truth is we're animals with animal instincts that cry out for gratification."

"Is this how you justify what you have done to Sallie?" Hester formed and firmed her accusation. "It was you who sold her, wasn't it?"

Cloaked shoulders shrugged. "What if I did? She's not the first, nor will she be the last. There's no shortage of waifs in the world, nor any lack of demand on the part of those who desire to possess them."

"I don't understand," Hester murmured. "Surely you must have some compassion, some feeling of remorse—"

Again a chuckle sounded. "Those so-called pangs of conscience vanished with the megrims, thanks to Dr. Jekyll's medicine."

"Dr. Jekyll!"

Mrs. Kirby nodded. "In the past he had attended to the ailments of my young charges. When my own affliction became unbearable I sought his help. He compounded a simple elixir that relieved me of distress."

Hester's frown was framed in firelight. "There can be nothing simple about medication that brings about results such as these." Then realization came. "That was no headache remedy—it had to be the potion Dr. Jekyll was administering to himself."

"Not in the beginning. On several occasions I sent one of my charges round for a fresh bottle of the compound, but it was only after the last time that the changes began. On this occasion I entrusted Murch with the errand, and it was she who made the mistake.

"In light of what happened, I questioned her later. Dr. Jekyll concocted the mixture and poured it into a bottle. Upon doing so he was called away by his manservant. Murch tired of waiting, took the bottle and departed. There were, she admitted, several similar bottles resting side by side atop the desk, none bearing labels. It is not difficult to realize which one she brought me."

Hester's frown deepened. "You weren't aware of the difference at the time?"

"Indeed I was, but since it promptly rid me of my affliction, I thought Dr. Jekyll had merely substituted a stronger preparation. As you can see, I soon had reason to learn its strength when the changes began." Again the rasping chuckle.

To Hester, its import was more eloquent than words. Dr. Jekyll had been terrified by his transformation; Mrs. Kirby seemed exultant. When the supply of ingredients ran out the doctor gave way to despair. But under similar circumstances this woman appeared to embrace her altered state.

As if divining her thought, Mrs. Kirby shook her head. "The changes came, but I knew no fear, once I realized their source. I soon surmised the concoction was for Dr. Jekyll's private use, in which case he must also have prepared something to reverse its consequences."

"Yet you made no effort to inquire," Hester murmured.

"Do you take me for a fool? If Jekyll discovered I'd learned his secret, how long do you think it would be before I had a visit from Mr. Hyde?" The woman shrugged. "Nor was I in need of antidotes at first. The drug's effects lasted for but a few hours, disappearing completely once I had slept. By the time I'd consumed the contents of the bottle, it was a different story. I take it Dr. Jekyll found himself in the same predicament; the effects were now involuntary and there was no further means of obtaining an antidote.

"I can only wonder if he too endured the megrims that now returned to herald such transitions. I only know that for a time I suffered the tortures of the damned. It is only of late that such symptoms have finally given way. And unlike

Jekyll, my changes are more transitory, and when they come, I welcome them."

"Do you no longer have headaches?" Hester's query was born of confusion. "But both Captain Ellison and Murch told me—"

"Exactly what I told them." The sly smile spread. "Once I retire, no one presumes to disturb me, or take note of my movements."

"By way of the rooftop." Hester nodded. "Just as Sallie said." She paused. "How many other children have you used so?"

"That is none of your concern. The shelter has proved valuable in satisfying demands both here and abroad."

Her meaning was plain, but Hester demurred. "One need not stoop that low to obtain income."

"Don't take that holier-than-thou tone with me!" The woman's smile vanished. "At first I had other plans. Once I realized the truth about Dr. Jekyll's disappearance, I meant to seek out his solicitor and exact a suitable sum from the estate in return for keeping silent. But before I could act, you came out of nowhere to spoil it all."

"Please, Mrs. Kirby—if you'll only listen—"

"Have no fear, I've always listened to you most attentively, my dear." There was a hint of sardonic amusement in the reply. "Your unwitting revelations prompted me to take action lest my own involvement come to light."

Take action? Mrs. Kirby had killed to protect her secret. Poole died because he knew about Dr. Jekyll's potion; Utterson, because he knew that much more. And now—

Hester voiced the thought as she shook her head. "It will do you no good to dispose of me. Bertha and Sallie share knowledge of your dealings."

"Bertha is my creature. She will never betray me!"

"How can you be certain of that?"

A clawlike hand dipped beneath the level of the desktop, then rose quickly. "This is my assurance."

Hester stared at the muzzle of the weapon. "And the child—?"

"Do not waste your sympathies on her. It is your own fate that must concern you now."

"You wouldn't dare risk killing me!"

"No one will know. When they find you with this in your hand, the verdict will be one of suicide."

Hester frowned. "But they'll investigate. They'll realize I had no reason—"

A taloned forefinger tapped the typed document on the desk. "This is your reason. What you signed is a full confession of your perfidy—how you discovered Utterson's knowledge of Jekyll's identity as Hyde, forced him to assign the estate to you, then did away with him. And lest there be an autopsy performed on Hyde that might reveal he was Jekyll, you stole the body from the grave and destroyed it." The vulpine grin returned. "That is what I did, of course, but they'll never know. This account merely states you have undergone a last-minute change of heart and intend to destroy yourself instead."

Again Hester frowned. "But the money—"

"—will be mine." The forefinger stabbed down. "This is also a last testament. You direct that as partial atonement for your crimes, your estate shall pass to charity—namely to me and my good works among the needy."

"Are you mad?" Hester's outburst could not be contained. "They'll never believe you!"

"*They?* Who are these people you refer to? Who in London knows you well enough to judge your nature?"

"Albert." Hester spoke quickly. "Albert Prothore. He'll be here soon—"

Again the raucous laughter sounded. "Will he, indeed? The woman leaned forward. "What do you suppose Bertha was whispering about, eh? She told me that while you tended the child your precious Albert did appear. It was Bertha who dispatched him."

"She sent him away?"

"Once and for all." The woman stirred, cloak rustling as she rose, trigger cocking as she aimed her weapon. "Don't move." The murmur was faint against the seethe and crackle of the flames. "Close range. As if by your own hand."

Hester tried to edge back without seeming to do so. She could control the movement of her body but her thoughts trembled.

He was dead. Albert was dead. Now she knew the meaning of the blood on Bertha's knife. She was indeed the older woman's creature, the wretched, evil creature of her mistress's madness.

And Mrs. Kirby was mad, just as Dr. Jekyll had been, when the power of the potion possessed him. Hester inched away, feeling the heat of the fireplace fanning her back.

The muzzle was leveling. A talon tightened against the trigger.

"No—!" Hester screamed.

And screamed again, as a bullet tore through Mrs. Kirby's cheek, shattering bone. The second shot sounded from the doorway and the cloaked figure reeled back, stumbling against the projecting base of the hearthstone. One of the flailing arms caught fire and in a moment the cloak was ablaze.

It seemed to Hester that the rest happened very quickly; the turn to the doorway, her recognition of Inspector Newcomen moving into the room accompanied by the constables, their attempts to smother the flames. But however swift, the effort came too late.

When at last the burning cloak ceased smoldering, it held only the charred corpse of what might once have been a human being. Perhaps something less than human.

Or more . . .

chapter 23

The dreary, everlasting rain that had meant London to Hester since her arrival had apparently done its worst, ending in the heavy storm on that night now two weeks past, as if the last of its flood had been sent to wash away more than the grime that plastered walls and streets. Hester sat at the small desk, her journal in her hands. Maybe someday she would be able to read it again. She had made herself set down the details she had known of the adventure—her part in it—and what she had been told by others.

She looked slowly around the room, from the cheerful fire on the hearth to the silken draperies at the windows, the bed with its coverlet of delicate flowers embroidered by skillful fingers perhaps two generations ago. Never, she knew, could she successfully express to dear Lady Farlie, Margaret as her hostess had insisted upon being called, or to Sir Henry what their instantly offered assistance had meant in the days just past.

It had been Margaret, when Hester was still dazed and distraught, who had appeared in a carriage, carried her off from that sinister house to this nest in the Farlie's own home.

While both Margaret and the Colonel had been with her in full support at her last interview with Newcomen, even now she gave a small shiver remembering that.

Quickly she glanced at her watch. A quarter hour yet before it would be time to go. She put aside her pen and wondered how long she would continue to feel that small stab of fear. It was all over, yes. She was welcomed into this fortress protected by friendship and the warmth of family she had never known before.

But—

Albert, as she had seen him last, braced against the pillows on that narrow bed in Dr. Hammond's nursing home. Albert who could have so easily have been lost had Bertha not aimed an inch or so too high with that murderous blade of hers. Bertha whom she had liked so well, had accepted so eagerly—Bertha whose outer form might not have been twisted, but who, inside, was as blackened and shrunken as—

Hester put her hands over her eyes. Much of the comfort of the room had vanished—as if it had been a blown-out candle. Bertha—and that—that *other*.

The girl thought she could even begin to believe that there was absolute evil in this world. The more of the story she had learned from Inspector Newcomen, the darker and stronger seemed to be the webs wickedness could spin.

Bertha and her prisoner, Sallie, had been taken by the inspector's men even as the older girl was forcing her captive into a waiting cab. There were others whose part in the crime had not been known until she whose will held them fast to serve her purposes was gone. The cabman, two other ruffians Sallie could identify—the ill-favored Murch—

Only the one who had been the center of the web had

escaped; if indeed her terrible fate might be called an escape.

Even as Dr. Jekyll, Mrs. Kirby had lived two lives. Unlike
the doctor she had not regretted her metamorphosis from the
gentle, ministering widow, whose actions had aroused admiration and respect, to her role as a notorious procurer.

Sometimes Hester thought now she could never again be
quite sure of anyone. What did lie behind the respectable
mask-faces of many of those she saw passing in the street?

Bertha and the men were in prison awaiting trial but even
that would not be what justice demanded—only what men
thought to be justice. Newcomen admitted that he had had
orders "from above." Scandal, that unforgivable sin that
must ever be avoided, dictated that the true story be locked
in the minds of a few. Bertha, murderous though she had
planned to be, would be charged under a lesser crime.

And Sallie. The second shock of Bertha's attack on top of
her own frightful experience had changed the once bright
and happy child into a white-faced, shivering creature who
cringed from any touch and seemed to have lost all the lively
intelligence she had once shown.

Captain Ellison had taken her—she would be protected,
treated gently, sheltered from anything that would hold evil
memories. She had been moved already down to a cottage in
Cornwall belonging to Captain Ellison's sister and there she
would be given a quiet life, treated with kindness, which
might someday break through the barrier evil had set around
her. Hester was told she could not see her, that it was best
for Sallie to be in no way reminded of the past.

But even if she might not see Sallie, she could provide for
her future and she already had, working through Sir Henry's
solicitor, who had taken over her affairs at the Colonel's request.

Thus she had learned about the will. Mr. Utterson had
moved to make very sure that she would be provided for.
Since the will of Dr. Jekyll had given him the property, he

had, in turn, drawn up papers passing it along to her, binding the gift as tight as any man learned for nearly fifty years
in the law could. But she would never enter that house
again. Sir Henry had assured her it would be sold.

She might not be any great heiress but she would be provided for in a comfortable fashion—and perhaps her own
wishes that some of the small fortune be given to the Army
and used for such as Sallie would take the taint from it.

There was a knock at the door.

"Hester, dear—?"

She was out of her chair in a moment, already reaching for
her hat.

"Coming, Margaret!"

There was her mantle, her gloves, and, last of all, what
had been waiting since this morning in a vase on the win-
dowsill, a bouquet of fragrant roses—not red, but a pale
cream that had caught her eyes at once when she and Mamie
had been on an errand to match thread for Margaret.

The stems were wrapped in damp cotton and then in the
silver paper to make a festive gift and she smelled them as
she took them from the vase.

"Why, Hester, what beautiful flowers!" Margaret was
waiting in the hall for her. "They are so fragrant. Gentlemen
often make the pretense that such things as fine scents do
not mean much, but I have seen Albert pick a rose such as
these for his buttonhole at times. And—oh, Hester, such
marvelous news!" Lady Farlie laid a hand on the girl's arm.
"Henry had a word with Dr. Hammond this morning—they
will let us bring Albert home tomorrow!"

Hester felt the warmth of color in her cheeks. She had
gone every day to the nursing home with Margaret—first
tense with guilt for it was because of her and her concerns
that he had been nearly killed. He had been found, after
great loss of blood, by Newcomen. But somehow Prothore
had not allowed that guilt to linger. Even on that first day
when he had been so weak and white, and Dr. Hammond

seemed to her to radiate a false cheerfulness, Albert had looked to her and smiled a little.

Through the other days they had talked generalities, with Margaret to start cheerful topics of conversation. Then once, when his sister had left the room to confer with the head nurse, Albert had spoken hurriedly and urgently to her.

"You must not in any way blame yourself—"

How had he guessed that this heavy guilt was her hourly burden, never to be forgotten?

"I was—I believed—" She tried to marshal her words properly but they would not come, and Albert's face was blurred by tears she hoped she would not shed. She had always been so sure—

"People with far more knowledge of the world than you have were equally deceived," he had continued quickly, hitching forward on his pillows. "Newcomen himself—and who could know more of the dark part of the city than he— had not the least thought of such imposture until the very last."

"Bertha—she—" Even after knowing the truth for so many days, Hester could not associate the Bertha who had been so cheerful and companionable in the sewing room with that stranger holding a knife, already bloodstained, to Sallie's throat. The Bertha she had believed in and trusted had never really existed.

"You are not to blame yourself!" His voice was an order, sharp, with that in it which once would have stirred her anger. "Look at me, Hester!"

Nor could she deny that demand. She blinked and blinked again and raised her eyes to his.

"You have been blind but with better cause than I can offer. This devilish affair started long before you came to London. Me, I was content never to look below the comfortable surface of the life I lived since birth. I did not want to know—you learned and were ready to strive to help. No one

could have foreseen the hidden poison that Jekyll had released and left behind him.

"In the end, Hester, it was your part in the affair that
brought that evil into the open. If you had not come to
London, taken a part in this, what would that woman have
continued to do? How many more Sallies would have fallen
prey to her? In her own words you heard that she delighted
in what she had done, in what that which was evil within her
had been released to accomplish. Jekyll came to realize his
sins, she gloried in hers. This is the truth, Hester, you must
believe it."

Margaret had returned then and from that visit they had
never had a chance to talk so intimately again.

Jekyll—the name now seemed like a brand to her. Some
earlier trouble must have driven her father away from the
company of his cousin, led him to change *his* name. What
further horrors might lie hidden in the past?

Now as she was seated in the carriage and the scent of the
roses strong, she longed to be away from here. Margaret had
bustled in beside her, a lidded basket handed in by the footman, to be most carefully balanced on her knees.

"Mrs. Brodie's cream pudding," she informed Hester.
"She was kitchen maid at our old home and she always had a
soft heart for Albert—treats for his sweet tooth whenever
Nannie wasn't around. We were lucky to get her again. Next
week when we go to Marsden she will be so prepared to
bully all the tradesmen that we shall be served the very best
at every meal.

"Marsden . . ." Lady Farlie smiled. "That used to mean
paradise to us when we were small! Oh, Hester, it will be
such a delight to show it all to you. The old pony cart—yes,
that must be furbished again so we can go berrying in the
brambles. They grow so thick along some of the lanes. And
Albert will be his old self in no time.

"You know that report that he was so determined to do for
Sir John? Henry tells me that it has caused a sensation at the

committee and there is a chance that Albert will be given a post if Sir John can prevail, which of course he will."

She nodded vigorously as she paused for breath. Hester had been nerving herself during that flow of words to say what must be said. She wet her dry lips with tongue tip.

"Margaret, I—I cannot possibly come with you to Marsden. You have been more than kind, you have allowed me to be one of you for a little while. But there is rumor and there is gossip. I bear a name that is whispered about. The police have taken a deep interest in me and my affairs. Surely you know that I understand what all this must mean. Your brother was drawn into my troubles because he was a gentleman of courage. I shall not allow any shadow from what has happened to gather against him or any of you.

"There is work I can do. Since I have means on which I can now live, I will also have time to give to some cause—"

"Hester!" There was something so peremptory in Lady Farlie's voice that it silenced her for a moment. "You are not one to hold to self-pity! Do not turn to that now. We are not of social London, nor do we have ambitions in that direction. Those we wish for friends will be our friends. Yes, there is always gossip. Too many so-called ladies lead such dull lives that gossip is their one main contact with their fellows.

"You are well served in that you have come from the colonies, you have not been known, and you need only be yourself to halt all gossip—or at least ride it out.

"Hester"—again her voice changed—"what is Albert to you?"

Hester colored. She had asked herself that question so often during the past few days.

"You have spoken of a career for your brother in politics," she answered slowly, trying to straighten her thoughts out in her own mind. "There gossip can be indeed deadly. I am not suitable to attract a man who undoubtedly has a distinguished career before him."

"I asked," Lady Farlie repeated in a voice that approached sternness, "what is Albert to you?"

Hester tried to turn away her eyes from those blue ones that laid a demand for the truth upon her.

"I—I would be his friend."

"Hester, I know my brother. Though we are some years apart in age, still we were close until I left home. I said that my mother did not write me, but Albert did—very faithfully. Each mail brought at least two letters from him, sometimes more. He cultivated as he grew older the shell that made of him the proper young man of society, but underneath there was still the Albert I knew. He has never been interested in any girl before. You have been very good to him, that shell was growing far too hard. Albert wants more than friendship—are you prepared to grant him that?"

Hester swallowed. She had the feeling that she was in some train carriage being rushed along far too fast, to a destination that was so strange she might not be able to ever understand it. Albert—what did she want, truly?

"Give me a little time . . ."

Lady Farlie was smiling again; her firm, plump hand closed over Hester's and the roses moved in their wrapping, loosing again some of their perfume.

"Time? You will have plenty of that with Albert coming home tomorrow. Sometimes one thinks too much—rather one must feel. Trust to that now, my dear."

THE DRAGON REBORN

Sequel to *The Great Hunt*

Book Three
~of~
*The Wheel
of Time*

by

Robert Jordan

Praise for *Eye of the World*

"A powerful vision of good and evil...fascinating people moving through a rich and interesting world." —Orson Scott Card

"Richly detailed...fully realized, complex adventure."
—*Library Journal*

"A combination of Robin Hood and Stephen King that is hard to resist...Jordan makes the reader care about these characters as though they were old friends." —*Milwaukee Sentinel*

Praise for *The Great Hunt*

"Jordan can spin as rich a world and as event-filled a tale as [Tolkien]...will not be easy to put down." —*ALA Booklist*

"Worth re-reading a time or two." —*Locus*

"This is good stuff...Splendidly characterized and cleverly plotted...The Great Hunt is a good book which will always be a good book. I shall certainly [line up] for the third volume."
—*Interzone*

The Dragon Reborn
coming in hardcover in August, 1991

BESTSELLERS
FROM TOR

☐	50570-0	ALL ABOUT WOMEN	$4.95
☐		Andrew M. Greeley	Canada $5.95
☐	58341-8	ANGEL FIRE	$4.95
☐	58342-6	Andrew M. Greeley	Canada $5.95
☐	52725-9	BLACK WIND	$4.95
☐	52726-7	F. Paul Wilson	Canada $5.95
☐	51392-4	LONG RIDE HOME	$4.95
☐		W. Michael Gear	Canada $5.95
☐	50350-3	OKTOBER	$4.95
☐		Stephen Gallagher	Canada $5.95
☐	50857-2	THE RANSOM OF BLACK STEALTH One	$5.95
☐		Dean Ing	Canada $6.95
☐	50088-1	SAND IN THE WIND	$4.50
☐		Kathleen O'Neal Gear	Canada $5.50
☐	51878-0	SANDMAN	$4.95
☐		Linda Crockett	Canada $5.95
☐	50214-0	THE SCHOLARS OF NIGHT	$4.95
☐	50215-9	John M. Ford	Canada $5.95
☐	51826-8	TENDER PREY	$4.95
☐		Julia Grice	Canada $5.95
☐	52188-4	TIME AND CHANCE	$4.95
☐		Alan Brennert	Canada $5.95

Buy them at your local bookstore or use this handy coupon:
Clip and mail this page with your order.

Publishers Book and Audio Mailing Service
P.O. Box 120159, Staten Island, NY 10312-0004

Please send me the book(s) I have checked above. I am enclosing $ _____
(please add $1.25 for the first book, and $.25 for each additional book to cover postage and handling.
Send check or money order only—no CODs).

Name _____

Address _____

City _____ State/Zip _____

Please allow six weeks for delivery. Prices subject to change without notice.